More Critical Praise for *Anna In-Between*

"A psychologically and emotionally astute family portrait, with dark themes like racism, cancer, and the bittersweet longing of the immigrant."

—*New York Times Book Review* (Editors' Choice)

"Nunez has created a moving and insightful character study while delving into the complexities of identity politics. Highly recommended."

—*Library Journal* (*starred review*)

"Nunez deftly explores family strife and immigrant identity in her vivid latest ... with expressive prose and convincing characters that immediately hook the reader."

—*Publishers Weekly* (*starred review*)

"Nunez offers an intimate portrait of the unknowable secrets and indelible ties that bind husbands and wives, mothers and daughters."

—*Booklist*

"The award-winning author of *Prospero's Daughter* has written a novel more intimate than her usual big-picture work; this moving exploration of immigrant identity has a protagonist caught between race, class and a mother's love."

—*Ms. Magazine*

"A new book by Elizabeth Nunez is always excellent news. Probing and lyrical, this fantastic novel is one of her best yet. Fall into her prose. Immerse yourself in her world. You will not be disappointed."

—Edwidge Danticat, author of *Brother, I'm Dying*

"*Anna In-Between* is Elizabeth Nunez's best novel. Nunez proves that a great writer, armed with intellect, talent, and very little equipment, can challenge a multibillion-dollar media operation. As long as she writes her magnificent books, characters like the Sinclairs, characters with depth and integrity, will not be hidden from us."

—Ishmael Reed, author of *Mumbo Jumbo*

"In crisp, clear, and beautifully turned prose, Elizabeth Nunez has written a fascinating novel that will profoundly affect the way in which many readers now view the Caribbean. We welcome the voice of the infinitely wise narrator, Anna, who is an expert witness to the seismic changes that take place within and without. A wonderful read."

—Lorna Goodison, author of *From Harvey River*

"Elizabeth Nunez has written a contemplative, lush, and measured examination of how a family history can reflect the social history of an island, and how twined together, like fragrant vines, the two can remain."

—Susan Straight, author of *A Million Nightingales*

"Nunez's fiction, with its lush, lyric cadences and whirlwind narrative, casts a seductive spell."

—*O, the Oprah Magazine*

Anna In-Between

BY ELIZABETH NUNEZ

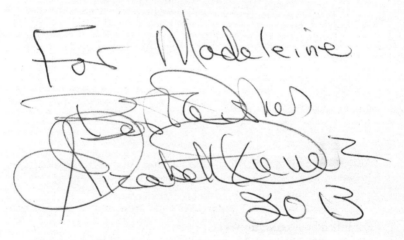

For Madeleine

AKASHIC BOOKS
NEW YORK

Published by Akashic Books
©2009, 2010 Elizabeth Nunez

ISBN-13: 978-1-933354-69-5
Library of Congress Control Number: 2010922711

First paperback printing
Printed in Canada

Akashic Books
PO Box 1456
New York, NY 10009
info@akashicbooks.com
www.akashicbooks.com

For Jordan and Savannah Nunez Harrell

CHAPTER 1

Morning. Seven twenty-seven. The bell rings, calling the family to breakfast. Anna makes a quick, final check in the mirror. Three more minutes. Everything is in place. Her hair is brushed back smoothly across her head and gathered at the nape of her neck with a brown tortoise shell clasp. No need for makeup. After a cold winter in New York, the heat from the Caribbean sun has stirred her blood to the surface and left her face flushed, her brown skin glowing, her lips fiery bronze. One year short of forty she still attracts attention, a second look, though not necessarily an admiring glance. Her facial features set her apart from most of the native-born blacks in New York who trace ancestors to West Africa. With her long nose, deep-set eyes, high cheekbones, and red-tinged toffee brown coloring, she is often mistaken for an Ethiopian, sometimes an Indian. A visible immigrant.

The bell again. Another number drops on the minute column on the digital clock. Seven twenty-nine. She runs her fingers around the waistband of her white shorts, tucks in the light pink–collared knit shirt she has chosen carefully, twirls, adjusts, checks herself in the mirror again, bends down, tightens the straps on her brown sandals. She is ready. Prepared.

Another bell. The last. Seven thirty. She leaves the bedroom and walks down the corridor toward the family dining room. Her parents are already seated, her father at the head of the table, her mother at his right.

At the right hand of the Father. The lines of a remembered childhood prayer flit across her brain. A little girl, too young to understand place, she had climbed into her father's chair. "Sit down, Daddy. Sit down." She pointed to a vacant chair. But her father kept moving, pacing back and forth behind her, scratching his chin, his forehead furrowed. Her mother came to his rescue and lifted her out of the chair. "That's Daddy's place," she said.

"Anna!" Her mother has heard her footsteps. "How lovely you look!"

As if the spoken word were a tangible thing, Anna feels *lovely* spread across her face and pull her lips back into a broad smile.

Her mother is impeccably dressed—as she always is. This morning she is wearing one of the American dresses Anna bought for her, a beige linen shift with large white buttons that run from the neck to the hem. On her mother the dress looks elegant, much more than had ever seemed possible to Anna when she picked it out from the sales rack at Bloomingdale's.

"Your complexion was sallow when you arrived," her mother says. "But look at you now!"

At seventy-one, Beatrice Sinclair is still as beautiful as the picture Anna has carried in her head from the first time she left home more than twenty years ago. In that uncanny way that husbands and wives grow to resemble each other, her mother resembles her father. The color of their skin is butterscotch brown, their features an amalgam of the aboriginal, the conquerors, the enslaved, the enslavers: the Amerindian people who first lived on the island, the Europeans who for centuries claimed it, the Africans brought there on slave ships, Indians and Chinese who exchanged indentured labor for the hope of land ownership; others, like the impoverished Portuguese, who came seeking their fortune. But in the nineteenth century the island was not yet El Dorado, though there was money to be made in cocoa and sugarcane. One century later the Spanish explorers would be proven right. Not yellow gold, but black gold— oil—lay in abundance in swollen pockets under the island's coastal waters and across its southern lands.

Objectively, the resemblance between Beatrice and John Sinclair ends there, with this combination of Amerindian, European, and African blood that runs in their veins. But husbands and wives who have lived together this long often unconsciously mimic each other's expressions, softening objective differences, molding distinctive features so that one barely notices that the shapes of the faces are different, that the noses, eyes, and mouths are not the same. Beatrice's face is rounder than John's, her eyes deeper and darker, her cheekbones raised high like those of her Amerindian aboriginal ancestors. The shape of their lips is inverted, Beatrice's top lip fuller than her bottom lip, John's top lip thinner. Indeed, both of John's lips, the top and the bottom, are quite thin. When he clamps his mouth shut in anger, his lips disappear. His nose is long, bent at the tip; hers flares slightly at the end of her nose bridge. Yet the impression they give is that of relatives who share a similar lineage.

"The bell was for us," Beatrice Sinclair says, a sort of apology directed to her daughter. "You needn't have come out."

But Anna is in her mother's house and she knows that as long as one's parents are alive, one is still a child, *their* child. If one returns to the house where they raised you, where you were a child, a dependent, you show respect, you obey their rules, no matter if you are nearing forty, no matter if you have a big job, with big responsibilities, as she has, as a senior editor at the Windsor publishing company in New York City, head of the company's imprint, Equiano Books, with the power to say yes or no, to fulfill or dash the hopes of writers. So she holds her tongue. She does not say, *How did you expect me to sleep through three bells?* She does not say, *You wanted me up. The bell was to make sure I would be here on time for breakfast.* She has not forgotten the rules: breakfast at seven thirty; lunch at twelve thirty; tea at four; dinner at six.

"I was already awake," she says. She greets her parents formally. "Good morning, Mummy. Good morning, Daddy."

In her parents' house, in the home of Caribbean parents, the child says, Good morning, Mummy. Good morning, Daddy. At night before she goes to bed she says good night to her parents. This is the custom, the respect that is expected even of grownup children, even of adults nearing forty.

"I heard you when you got up, Daddy," she says to her father.

He was wearing pajamas when she saw him through her bedroom window at dawn, the fabric at the top of the pants bunched together in his hands like a bouquet of flowers, the two ends of the string drawn through the loop of waistband dangling loose at the opening. She had given him the pajama set and the bedroom slippers he was wearing, both she had bought in winter, conscious even then that the sleeves and pants of the pajamas were too long, the slippers made of velvet, too thick for this tropical climate. Her chest tightened when he bent down, releasing one hand to pick up the rolled up newspaper the paperboy threw over the gate. So much dignity. An old man in his pajamas, wearing velvet slippers to please her, holding the top of his pants in one hand to keep them from falling. He is not in pajamas now, but he has on the same shirt and shorts he wore the day before, a sea blue cotton shirt that is wrinkled, khaki shorts that are stained. Her mother has long given up her battle to change this habit he has of wearing the same clothes day after day. The logic of his defense has left her frustrated. "Wasting water in a drought," he says in the dry season when she tells him that Lydia, their helper, would happily wash his clothes. In the wet season he takes the offensive, challenging her to criticize him. "Do I look untidy?" And in truth John Sinclair never looks untidy. Even in a wrinkled shirt and stained pants, he is stately, a gentleman in retirement.

"Oh, yes, Singh," her mother says drily and glances at her husband.

Singh is their gardener. He has worked for them for more than forty years. Singh will be seventy-eight this year.

"I let him in," John Sinclair says. "He's waiting in the garden for you, Beatrice. Something about the orchids."

It was the insistent ringing of Singh's bicycle bell that woke her that morning and drew her roughly out of a deep sleep, leaving her in a daze until the scent of oranges and dew-soaked grass cleared her head and brought her to the present, here, the place of her birth, the Caribbean, once her home. And after the bicycle bell, there were the familiar sounds she had memorized: the key turning in the lock of her parents' bedroom door, the soft patter of her father's slippered feet along the corridor, the jangle of the house keys as he searched for the right one to unlock the wrought iron gate that closes off the sleeping quarters. Then the loud thud, metal hitting the stone pillars, when he pressed the button on the kitchen wall that opened the electric iron gate. The gate is there to protect them from thieves, from the rash of criminals spawned overnight by huge profits to be made from illegal drugs. All, to Anna's mind, useless, for a schoolboy can scale the iron railings with ease.

"I don't know why you keep having Singh come," her father says to her mother. "I can't see what he has to do. We hired two boys to cut the lawn and trim the hedges. What's left for Singh to do?"

"He weeds." Beatrice plucks invisible threads from the skirt of her dress.

"The boys we hired can weed," her father says tersely.

"He weeds my flowerbeds. I don't want those boys to weed my flowerbeds. They don't seem to be able to tell the difference between a weed and a seedling for one of my flowering plants."

"Then train them, Beatrice."

"Singh is already trained. He knows what to do."

"I just don't see the need for Singh, that's all." Her father mumbles these words; he does not say them with conviction.

Her mother shakes her head. Her expression is one of pained forbearance.

Anna wants to distract them. She asks her father to pass the bread to her.

"Lydia made it," her mother says. "Your father and I are really lucky to have her as a helper." Her tongue lingers on the last word. Ever since the island became a nation, helper, not maid, is the term she must use when she refers to Lydia. She smiles coyly as if waiting to be commended for complying. Her husband looks up at her approvingly.

The loaf of bread is a perfect brick shape, the crust a warm honey brown, the sides golden. Lydia bakes the bread the day before but under orders from Beatrice Sinclair she does not slice it. She has placed the bread and a serrated knife on the breadboard, next to Mr. Sinclair, on his left side. It is Mr. Sinclair's duty to slice the bread at breakfast. He does so now, cutting off four pieces, and passes the breadboard first to his wife, who takes one, and then to his daughter, who takes another.

"Have two slices, Anna," her father says, still holding the breadboard in front of her.

"The two left are for you," Anna replies.

"I can cut more."

Her mother pushes his hand away. "Anna is watching her waistline," she says.

"She doesn't need to watch her waistline," her father says. "She looks just perfect to me."

Anna smiles at him gratefully and he takes advantage of her gratitude. "So what do you think, Anna? Do you think we still need Singh?"

She will not fall into her father's trap. Her parents may argue, but they always end up on the same side. "Mummy must still need him," she says, hoping she has found a middle ground that will please them both.

"Yes. Singh takes care of my orchids," Beatrice Sinclair says.

"Hmm." Her husband raises his chin and brings his lips together.

"Besides," Beatrice says, "we can't just let him go. He's been with us too long. If we let him go, we'll have to give him a pension."

"I'd rather give him a pension than have him walking up and down the lawn doing nothing," John Sinclair says.

"He's not doing *nothing*," her mother responds adamantly.

John Sinclair reaches for the serving dish in front of him. Lydia has prepared sardines with onions. She has aligned the silvery fish in rows in the middle of the oval platter. On the top, she has put glistening circles of sliced raw onions and surrounded them with red tomatoes on green lettuce leaves. The arrangement is beautiful, almost too good to eat.

John Sinclair offers the platter to his wife. She is still simmering from his response. Her lips are pursed. "In any case," she says emphatically, spooning two sardines and some of the garnish on her plate, "I need Singh."

That is the end of that, Anna thinks, but her father gets in one last stab. "You know, Anna, your mother does not need Singh to weed her flowerbeds or to help her with her orchids."

He is looking across the table directly at her, deliberately bypassing her mother. It is a strategy he sometimes uses, one that unnerves her mother. Anna wants to say, *Speak to her, not to me, she's your wife*, but her father has rescued her from her mother's criticism. Her mother's comment about her waistline was not benign. Anna has lost all the weight she gained when her husband left her, but her mother has not ceased to intimate with her constant reminders, wrapped deceptively under the guise of the solicitous urgings of a concerned parent, that if not for her ballooning waistline her husband might have returned to her, or, at the very least, another man would be attracted to her.

It bothers Anna that at her age she should allow her mother to have this power over her, that her mother's one remark about her waistline should have her harboring desires for vengeance. It irritates her more to admit she has dressed for her, that she has carefully chosen the outfit she is wearing because she knew it would please her. That she felt a warm flush in her chest when her mother said, *How lovely you look.*

She will not come to her rescue. Her mother wants an ally, but she will keep her head averted, her eyes focused on her father.

"Your mother needs Singh," her father says, "so she can have someone to boss around. Singh does what she tells him to do."

For five long minutes they eat in silence—an eternity it seems to Anna. Neither says a word to the other. Her mother lowers her head and concentrates on the food on her plate, carefully placing pieces of sardines on the back of her fork. Anna feels embarrassed for her. She cannot deny her mother enjoys her role as mistress, as boss of the domestic affairs of her home, but her husband has exposed her in the presence of her daughter.

She is about to say something flattering to her mother when her father reaches for his wife's hand. "Which man would mind doing some little thing for the most beautiful woman in the world?" he says to her.

To Anna's surprise, her mother's eyes light up.

After breakfast they go their separate ways, Anna to her room to fetch a novel she plans to read in the veranda. It's a luxury she will permit herself today. Tomorrow will be time enough to begin the work she has brought with her from Equiano Books. Tomorrow, with her blue pencil she will tackle the manuscript from a new writer she has recently discovered. Today, she will read a polished work that does not need her critical eye.

The veranda is the coolest part of the Sinclairs' sprawling one-story ranch-style house. The home was designed for them by an architect, a local man trained in America, in the '50s when ranch-style houses were *de rigueur*, and is unquestionably the most fashionable in their neighborhood. The problem, though, is the ceilings are low and trap the heat inside. Fortunately, Anna's mother had insisted on a covered veranda with cool terrazzo floors. It is a large veranda, with high ceilings made of polished dark wood, and extends along almost the entire length of the house, enough space to allow Mrs. Sinclair to entertain large parties outside of the living room. There are three sets of wicker furniture in the veranda, which Mrs. Sinclair has made comfortable with plump, colorful cushions, a bar with six stools for Mr. Sinclair, as well as a powder room for the ladies. To provide privacy for his client on the side of the veranda that faces the street, the architect built a low wall punctuated with five enormous U-shaped dips above which hang huge baskets of green fern. Right angled to this wall are glass sliding doors which open to the living and dining rooms. Mrs. Sinclair has arranged a rock garden around a tall red-trunked palm tree in an un-covered section of the veranda, and in another uncovered part she has allowed Mr. Sinclair to build a pond for his fish. Anna guesses that her father is at the pond, feeding his fish. She will chat with him awhile before settling down with her novel.

As she approaches the corridor that leads to the kitchen, she overhears her mother giving instructions to Lydia for their lunch. "Use plenty of garlic and thyme. Mr. Sinclair likes his food seasoned well."

They are both facing the sink, their backs toward her. They cannot see her and they do not hear her when she slips into the breakfast room and waits, partially hidden by the wall bordering the open-arched entranceway to the kitchen. Her mother is standing close to Lydia, her body bent toward her, her head and shoulders just inches away. Next to her mother's butterscotch brown complexion, Lydia's plum-colored skin seems darker than it is, almost purple. A light film of sweat that has spread across the back of Lydia's neck and along her bare arms glistens in the sun-light streaming through the kitchen window. Under a gray apron, she is wearing old, faded clothes: a brown skirt and a blue jersey. The apron is rumpled and stained, but the skirt and jersey are clean and pressed. These are not the clothes Lydia wears to work. She wears fashionable clothes to work, bought for her in America by a son who, like many immigrants, sends her, three times a year, a barrel packed with clothes and food and things for her house. He's a good son, she says, though she wishes he had not emigrated. She misses him; he is her only child, but America is the land of opportunity, she tells Anna. Look at you. You leave too. My son come back when he save enough money to buy a house here.

Lydia is Anna's age, but it is difficult to tell. Her breasts sag, her stomach rises like leavened bread, her waistline has long expanded. Lines crease her forehead, gray hair sprouts around her hairline. Her dark brown eyes have long lost their sparkle; the skin under them is purple. Her mouth spreads quickly and easily into a smile, but when it settles again, her thick lips gather tightly together, a defense against the world. For years, she lived with a man who beat. It has only been seven years, the length of time she has worked for the Sinclairs, since she had the courage to leave him.

Anna's mother is pointing to a bowl of frozen raw chicken on the counter next to the sink. "Use lime to clean it," she says to Lydia, "but not too much. I don't want to taste lime in the stew."

Lydia's back is rigid, her shoulders and head stiff. She does not move. She says nothing in response to Mrs. Sinclair's instructions. She just stands there. Silent.

Anna can barely hear her mother, but she can tell she is continuing to issue more instructions to Lydia. Then she raises her voice: "You understand what I want you to do, Lydia?"

Lydia draws damp hands down her apron. "Miss Sinclair, I understand a long time now what you want me to do."

Lydia's tone is carefully calibrated. It suggests neither insolence nor slavish acquiescence. There is almost a childishly innocent ring to her words, but Anna is certain that her mother cannot fail to realize that she has been rebuked, reprimanded. Of course Lydia knows what she has to do. There is no question: Lydia is a much better cook than her mother is now.

"You're a good worker," Mrs. Sinclair says.

Lydia tosses her head and laughs.

If Lydia is appeased, Anna is not. She is bristling, burning up with indignation. Her mother spoke to Lydia as if she were a headmistress, Lydia a schoolgirl; as if she were an overseer, a boss on a plantation. Lydia well knows her parents' taste. Her father is right. But it is not only Singh her mother needs to boss around; she needs to boss Lydia too. How important she must feel to have two workers in her service whom she can control.

This is the legacy of colonial rule on the island, the manner of the colonizer toward the colonized mimicked now by the island's middle class.

Even as she thinks this, Anna knows she is being unfair. Her mother may consider Singh and Lydia her social inferiors but she does not question their humanity. If by chance one of them were to dive in a pool where she is swimming, she would not order the management to drain the water. The English were famous for doing things like that on the island. In England they posted signs that read: NO DOGS, NO COLORED.

Lydia is nodding her head now. She is saying agreeably, "Yes, Mrs. Sinclair. You're right, Mrs. Sinclair." Anna is offended for her sake, but Lydia does not seem bothered. "I don't use so much salt the next time like you say, Miss Sinclair."

Anna walks away. She has her hand on the sliding glass door in the dining room and is about to go to the veranda with her book when her mother calls her. "Anna." Her mother's voice is subdued, soft for a woman who only moments ago seemed to be demanding that her authority be acknowledged. Anna has no choice but to turn around. She is just steps away, within hearing distance. It would be rude to pretend she has not heard her mother.

"Will you take a message to Singh for me?" Her mother brushes her hand across her face. The movement is slow, limp. "Tell him to work on the seedlings in the nursery today. If he has time, he should clean up the anthurium beds." Her mother's hand drops to her side as if a weight is attached to it. She seems tired, her energy suddenly drained. The circles under her eyes are darker than they were at breakfast.

Guilt rises in Anna's chest. Has her father's unkind comment about her mother's bossiness taken its toll in spite of the compliment he gave her afterward? Was that scene with Lydia just her mother's way of restoring her dignity? Shouldn't she have been more sympathetic? Lydia seemed very capable of defending herself. Lydia does not need her sympathy.

"Singh is expecting you," Anna says. "He told Daddy he's waiting for you in the garden. Something about the orchids."

Her mother sighs. "I have to do everything," she grumbles. "Take care of the cooking *and* the gardening."

Anna feels her anger rising again, but she restrains herself. In the mildest tone she can muster, she says, "Lydia can do the cooking, Mummy. You don't have to do it. And if you tell Singh what to do, you don't have to stay in the garden."

"You don't understand," her mother says.

"What don't I understand, Mummy?"

"In this country," her mother says slowly, measuring out each word, "you can't just leave people to do what you tell them to. They have to be supervised."

She means the working class, she means people like Lydia and Singh. But Anna knows that if it seems people in the working class need to be supervised, it is because they see no future for themselves in the work they are consigned to do.

"You are wrong, Mummy."

"You don't live here," her mother responds. "You don't know."

Her mother's words sting her to the core. She may not live here, but her roots are here. She was born here; she spent the first eighteen years of her life here; this is her country too. She wants to say all this, but her mother does not look well. Her skin is dull and her eyes lack luster. She has taken one verbal assault from her husband, she does not need another. "I'll give Singh your message," Anna says quietly.

"Good." Her mother draws her hands across her lips. "I think I'll rest awhile in my room."

Anna hesitates by the door. For a moment she thinks of following her mother to her bedroom, of asking if she needs her help, but she changes her mind. It is hot in the house; she wants to be outside. She wants to sit in the shade of the veranda. She wants to take off her sandals and rest her feet on the cool terrazzo tiles. And she is here for a month. There will be time enough for talks with her mother.

CHAPTER 2

Singh is in the nursery. He is sitting on a tiny wood bench, a child's bench, brushing something from his lips, crumbs from the dhalpourie he has just eaten for breakfast. At his feet are a thermos and a paper bag crumpled into a ball. His bicycle is leaning against the sapodilla tree. He has tied it to the tree trunk with brown rope. It is an ancient bicycle. A black Raleigh, made in England. The letters *Raleigh*, scrawled across the crossbar, are painted green and bordered in white. For the barest second, Anna catches her breath, her windpipe contracting with the flash of remembrance: the smell of bicycle oil heating up in the sun, staining the edge of her dress when she gets on. She is ten. "The spokes will get rusty if you don't oil them down," her father says. It is her first bicycle, a gift for coming first in exams in her class.

The spokes on Singh's bicycle are rusted in spots. It pains her to look at them.

"Miss Anna!" Singh has seen her. "You here!" He bolts up from the bench.

"Sit, sit, Singh." Anna waves him away. "Sit and finish your breakfast."

This is the first time she has seen him since she arrived on the island four days ago. Lydia works for her parents every day except Sundays. She comes at seven each morning. On weekdays, she leaves at five o'clock sharp. On Saturdays she works a half-day. But Singh works only three days a week for her parents. He arrives at dawn, at five thirty, and leaves at three.

"How long you stay dis time, miss?" Singh settles back down on his bench.

"A month."

"A whole month? Your mother and father must be glad to have you for a whole month."

In spite of his age, Singh's hair is thick and jet black. He has slicked it down with coconut oil. It shines in the sunlight and the sweet scent of the oil tickles Anna's nose.

He does not dye his hair, Singh says. His people do not gray. When his father died at ninety-eight, he had a full head of hair, jet black as his own.

Anna's father is practically bald. At fifty, his head was already marked with a monk's tonsure. Now, except for a gray semicircle that starts at his ears and dips low at the base of his head, the surface of his head is smooth, not a strand of hair in sight.

They are both old men with longevity in their genes, but on the matter of hair, Singh has the upper hand. It is a triumph over her father he rarely exercises. Once, many years ago, Anna heard him say to her father: "Bossman, like soon you go have no hair at all on your head." It was an expression of compassion, not a boast.

"So you're still here, Singh," Anna says.

"Who go garden for de madam better den me?" Singh grins. He has all his teeth. Her father has lost half of his and wears dentures. "I doe use tootbrush like rich people," Singh had once explained. "I does use cane stalk to clean between my teet."

She does not know Singh by any other name. Singh, he has been to her and to the rest of her family. They do not know his first name.

It is a Hindu name, yet Singh says he is Christian. His mother and father, seeking a better life for their children from the poverty they knew in India, had indentured themselves to the British colonial powers. They arrived on the island with the second wave of immigrants, sometime in the late 1800s. His parents converted. "It easier for dem," he said. "Dey get work if dey say dey Christian. But we does still fly de flags and make puja."

"You're looking good," Anna says.

Singh's skin is the color of dark brown chocolate. His mustache, like the hair on his head, is jet black. His face is unlined. The bones are pronounced, his skin taut. His muscles bulge on the calves of his legs and on his forearms. Only his eyes betray his age. They are old man's eyes, fixed in sinkholes above his cheekbones. Like her father's eyes, they are beady, the fire in them extinguished, replaced by a glare that is embarrassing to her: the old man asking for answers to questions he is afraid to articulate. Where has the time gone? How much time do I have left? What will happen to me when I die?

"Is de wife," he says. "She keep me young."

He remarried for the third time the year before. The new wife is thirty, almost ten years Anna's junior.

"I hope *you* are keeping her young, Singh," Anna says.

He throws his head back and laughs. He is wearing black clogs. Not clogs really; he has cut down his tall black rubber boots so they cover the upper part of his feet and leave his heels exposed. On him, the look is unconventional, fashionable even. Youthful.

"De wife not complaining," Singh says.

Anna avoids his eyes. "And your daughters?"

"De big one gone to Canada. She husband take she and de children. De middle one still here. She give me five grandchildren. I still have de littlest one with me. She going to university."

The littlest one is twenty-two, the daughter he had with his second wife who died two years ago. She is the same age as his first granddaughter. He is proud of her, the first in his family to go to university.

"Good for you, Singh."

"I tell de wife I know how to make children," he says.

"You're not planning to have more, are you, Singh?" Anna asks, aghast.

He pats his head. "De wife want one."

"Not at your age, Singh!"

"I still strong, you know, miss."

She knows what he means and she does not want to encourage him in dialogue about his sexual prowess. Not that he would be explicit. He has too much respect for her. And he knows his place.

How casually she accepts that. *He knows his place.* Her friends in America would be shocked to hear she thinks this way, her African American friends especially. Not that she believes one should be consigned permanently to his place. One should aspire to, and be given the opportunity to attain, the highest rung on the ladder to success, but having a place and knowing where others are in relation to one's place is to have the comfort that order brings, the reassurance of stability. Now that she is here, in the Caribbean, no longer in America, she finds there is something very civil about such notions. There are no surprises, no rude intrusions. One can depend on certain courtesies, respect and deference granted and assumed. Singh will say no more than he has already said. *I still strong.* He giggles childishly when he says it.

"Your grandchildren will keep her occupied," Anna says.

"I tell she dat. But she say all woman want child of dey own." His eyes crinkle and his mustache spreads over his top lip. "So you come to see me, Miss Anna, or you come to take my bench? Don't think I forget. I remember how you use to like to sit in de garden on dis bench."

"That was a long time ago, Singh. I was a little child in those days. You can keep the bench."

"So if you don't come for de bench, what you come to tell me, miss?"

"My mother says she won't be coming out today."

The contours of Singh's face change abruptly. His eyes darken, his lips tighten. "Anyting wrong with she?"

"No. Not at all. No," Anna says quickly.

"She does always come out in de morning time."

"Well, not today. She told me to tell you to work on the seedlings, and if you have time, you should weed the anthuriums."

"Someting wrong." Singh does not frame these words in a question. He states them as an indisputable fact.

"No," Anna says. "Mummy is fine."

Singh gets up and scratches his head. "Madam does always come out in de morning time. Someting wrong with she. She say to me Monday dat today we work on de orchids. She does always do what she say."

"There's nothing wrong with Mummy."

"I don't know, miss." Singh shakes his head.

"She's probably tired this morning. And it's hot."

"Is hot every morning, Miss Anna, and she does still come out."

"Mummy's getting up in age. You can't expect her to do the things she used to do."

"So she start today?" There is both accusation and worry in Singh's voice.

Anna brushes him off. "*Today* Mummy is tired."

Singh keeps his lips closed.

"Do you want me to call my father?"

"What for?"

"He may know what my mother wanted you to do with the orchids."

"De bossman have nothing to do with de garden," Singh says irritably.

"Shall I go ask Mummy what she wants you to do?"

Singh wipes his hands on the sides of his pants. Flecks of the split peas from the dhalpourie flutter to the ground. "No," he says. "Don't bother she. I already know what she want me to do. I go work here in de nursery. You tell madam I weed de anthurium bed too for she."

Anna leaves the nursery. She does not look back. She senses that in spite of his declaration to begin working, Singh has remained where she has left him, standing next to her child's bench, still puzzling out the reason for her mother's absence.

Her answers have not satisfied him, but she will not allow him to transfer his anxiety to her. Her mother looked fine at breakfast. After breakfast, she was her usual self, giving orders to Lydia. And if her mother's stern exchange with Lydia has left her exhausted, that is to be expected. She is not young anymore. She is way past middle-age. She cannot be expected to be spry every morning. On hot days, she cannot be expected to stand in the brutal sun that blazes down on the garden.

She finds her father squatting at the edge of his fishpond. His feet are firmly planted on the narrow pebbled border, his knees spread apart to the height of his chest, his backside hovering inches away from the ground. In one hand, he is holding a thin, black pole. At the end of the pole is a small green net. He scoops the net down into the water and up again. He repeats this movement several times, peering into the net when he brings it up, once disentangling a tiny fish squirming inside. Next to him are a tin watering can, a large gray stone, and a block of wood. He scoops the net down in the water again. "Ah hah!" he shouts. "Got you!" He pulls up the net. From where she is, Anna can see two legs wriggling out of the holes in the bottom of the net. Frog's legs.

"What's that you have, Daddy?" Anna approaches him.

"Frog. They eat my fish." He lowers the net to the watering can. The frog wriggles and squirms, trying to escape, but her father sinks two fingers into the sides of its neck, pulls it out of the net, and deposits it into the watering can.

"I catch one at least once a week," he says. "Now we're at the end of the dry season, I find more in the pond. They come out looking for water."

"What are you going to do with him?" Anna stands next to her father.

"Oh, take him to the river," her father answers, straightening up.

He will not kill any living thing. It wasn't always so. When Anna was a child, he hunted and fished. Twice a month, on Fridays after work, he was gone. Her mother fought him over both, for both were dangerous. The island was still home to fauna left stranded from the great Amazon jungle on the chunk of land broken off in a continental drift. Hunting in the rain forest her father could be attacked by ferocious wild cats or bitten by the poisonous snakes that slithered silently through the matted ground, and if not snakes, he could find himself lost in the thick entangling trees and vines. On a fishing trip, he could be caught in a storm in the open sea. His boat could capsize. The latter had indeed happened and he almost drowned. Still, given a choice, Beatrice Sinclair preferred her husband to fish rather than hunt. She preferred this because his fishing partner was a lawyer, a man from a prominent family. His hunting partners—there were four of them in all—were villagers from the countryside. When they came to meet him in their battered open truck, one could hear their pothounds howling from blocks around.

Beatrice's point was that John was no longer a young man without responsibilities. He had a wife and a daughter. His hunting friends were fine when he had no one else but himself to feed. Now he had to think of his future. A man is judged by the friends he keeps, she said to him. To his bosses, he would appear to be a man without ambition. That was the way he would be viewed by the colonial government if he continued to be seen by the entire neighborhood in ragtag clothes, drunk, surrounded by men who could barely read and write, and with a pack of howling pothounds. Not that she objected to dogs in general, but these were dogs that bred with any other dogs and ate from any pot.

And indeed John Sinclair was often drunk when he came home from hunting, stinking of stale rum, sweat, and animal entrails, his arms around the shoulders of his hunting partners, they too stinking of stale rum, sweat, and animal entrails, the dogs straining against their leashes inside the truck, scratching the wooden barrier with their sharp nails, yapping and barking, joyous from the hunt.

John wore his most ragged clothes when he went hunting, torn shirts under torn shirts, pants he hid from his wife before she could pack them away for charity. In these clothes there was no way to distinguish him as a man who not only could read and write, but who, except for an injustice done to him (his mother insisted) would have won an island scholarship to Oxford University. That injustice, according to Mrs. Sinclair, John's mother, was the doubt cast on the results of his Cambridge A-level chemistry exam that was graded in England. His score was perfect, or near perfect. He had to have cheated, the colonial government declared. But John had a photographic memory and had spent months memorizing the pages of his chemistry textbook.

Justified though Mrs. Sinclair was, and Beatrice's advice

not unfounded, John nevertheless rose up the ranks in the Ministry of Labor. When he ultimately left the colonial government it was for a better paying job at the island's top oil company for a boss who did not care if he fished and hunted, or with whom he fished and hunted. So his weekends continued as before, even after he retired from the company at the early age of fifty-two. Then one day it ended. His fishing partner, the lawyer, suffered a heart attack while they were out at sea. John did all he could to save him. He pumped his chest, he breathed into his mouth, he pleaded with him to recover. There were no boats in sight, no one to help them. For one hour, under a ferocious sun, John held his friend in his arms and watched him die.

Shock and grief left John stunned. He lost weight, he hardly smiled, he moped around the house or paced the garden restlessly, seeing nothing around him except for the pictures in his mind.

Beatrice became frightened. The dark mood that had settled over her husband scared her. To pull him out of his stupor, she bought him a fish tank, a large one mounted on a metal frame with long legs. Inside the tank she put artificial sea reeds, sand, chunks of white coral, and a dozen fish of various colors. John was not unappreciative, but it bothered him to see fish so confined. "It's like putting them in a prison," he said. A pond was what he wanted for the fish. He pointed to the place that would be perfect for this. It was the spot in the garden at the edge of the veranda where Beatrice had planted her orchids.

Beatrice was proud of this orchid garden, particularly of its location, for it faced the glass sliding doors to the living and dining rooms, providing a spectacular view for her guests. But she wanted back the husband she had married, so she asked Singh to dig up the orchid beds and replant the flowers.

It is at the edge of this pond that Anna is standing, watching her father put the frog he has fished out of the water into a watering can.

"Do you always take them to the river?"

"That's where they belong," he says. He picks up the block of wood near his feet and places it over the opening in the watering can. He secures the wood with the large stone that he puts on top of it. "They'll try to scramble out of the can if I don't stop them. And this frog is a big one."

"You're kinder to them than they are to your fish," Anna says.

"Don't know about that. I don't think this frog appreciates me taking him away from his breakfast. Hear him?"

Anna can hear the frog scratching the sides of the can. It is desperate to get out. "But you're going to set it free," she says.

"Yep. That's what I'm going to do now."

"Why?"

"Why?" Her father wrinkles his forehead. "That's a silly question."

"I mean, isn't this a lot of trouble for you? You pull him out and now you have the trouble of taking him to the river."

He has his hand on the watering can. "No trouble at all," he says. "You don't want me to kill it, do you?"

"Oh, no. But perhaps you can get something, some sort of thing that they don't like and put it in the pond. That way they won't return."

"Poison?" He is standing erect now.

"Not something to kill them," she says, flustered. "Some kind of organic something. Not a chemical."

"If the frogs won't like it, the fish won't like it."

"But can't you find something that only the frogs won't like?"

"Oh, Anna," he says, "you are the same little girl

who always wanted everybody to be happy. You haven't changed."

A few minutes ago, her mother almost pushed her down that crevice that threatens to swallow her no matter how firmly she has planted her feet on either side of the yawning gap, each foot on solid ground, one in America, the other in the island of her birth. Now her father steadies her. *You are the same.* But much has changed in her life. She is not a little girl; she is a woman, a middle-aged woman who has learned the hard way that life is not always fair. She wants to remind her father that he knows this too.

"Lots of things have happened to me since I was a little girl, Daddy. I couldn't always make people happy. Not even myself."

A spasm of pain crosses his face and she regrets the memory she has dredged up.

"But I am still your daughter," she says, hastening to make amends.

He is pleased. He taps the side of the watering can. "Well, my fish are happy I got the frog out of their pond and this frog will be happy when I put him in the river."

"Do you still miss it?" she asks.

"What?"

"Fishing," she says. They are walking toward the front of the house, she following closely behind him. "You stopped."

"It's out of my system." He does not turn around.

"And hunting too?"

"I like watching the fish spawn and grow in the pond," he says.

They have reached the covered path near the driveway. The rosebushes are thick on one side and a stray branch, heavy with pink flowers, brushes against them. Her father reaches out and cradles a cluster of the roses in his palm. "Your mother has a green thumb," he says.

"Singh," she counters. "*He* has the green thumb."

He snorts. "Only under your mother's instructions."

How he supports her, she thinks. How he always takes her side! And because she has not been able to shake off the resentment that clouded her brain when her mother said, *You don't live here. You don't know*, she pushes him to return to the question she asked him. "Did Mummy make you give up hunting?"

"Why would you say that?" He releases the roses and they rock back to their place on the branch.

"I knew you stopped fishing when your friend died. But I never understood why you stopped hunting. I know Mummy didn't like the dogs or your hunting friends."

Outside, beyond the electric metal gate that encloses their house, beyond the paved street and the houses on the other side, the mountains loom in the distance. Against the blinding brilliance of the morning sky, they appear navy blue, as if all the green of all the trees climbing up their sides has been washed in dye.

Her father wanted to live on a hill. He wanted to look down on the green plains below, to see the silvered sea skirting the edges of the island, fanning out to the horizon where the sun sinks each night trailing embers, but he built his house here, on flat land, in a swamp. For the residential area where they live was a swamp before the land was cleared and filled with boulders and dirt.

It was her mother's idea, building the house in a swamp. Like Rio's favelas, the poor here live on the hills, five to a room, the poet says, the corrugated iron roofs of their shacks putting him in mind of that merciless ocean that swallowed thousands in the Middle Passage. The rich, needing space for the spread of their multiple rooms, chose flat land even if it meant clearing a swamp. But the mosquitoes have their revenge. In the wet season they return in hordes at night to reclaim their primordial territory.

"Those were the days," her father says. "I haven't seen those men I used to hunt with in a long time. I guess some of them may be dead by now." His voice drifts. "Most of my friends are dead," he adds, and his step falters.

This is not where she wants to take him. Unless she can do or say something soon, he will lapse into the morose mood that is becoming a habit with him since his eightieth birthday. Mention the past, mention friends from the past, and he will recount which ones have died. From there he will spiral downward.

"Everyone dies," he says. "No way to stop that. Everyone dies." He repeats the words like a mantra, as if suddenly discovering that humans are mortal.

She reaches for the watering can. "Let me take that for you, Daddy."

He pushes away her hand. "This is too heavy for you."

"Do you want me to come with you to the river?"

"I think you should stay with your mother," he says. "She's in the back, in the garden with Singh."

No, she tells him. Her mother is not in the back, in the garden with Singh. She has gone to her room.

His face does not register the least surprise when she tells him this.

"She gave me instructions for Singh."

"Oh?"

"She seemed tired."

"Hmmm." This is the only sound that comes out of his mouth. He asks no questions, though less than an hour ago he accused her mother of needing to be in the garden with Singh. Of needing to have someone to boss around, he said.

They have reached the driveway. He puts the watering can, with the frog secured inside by the block of wood and the stone, on the floor in the back of the car. His palm is on the handle of the front door when he hesitates. "You know why I am saving this frog?" he asks. And without waiting for her response, he says, "Same reason why I stopped hunting. You're too hard on your mother, Anna. I decided. I wanted to stop. Your mother had nothing to do with it." Taking less than a minute, he tells her that he stopped hunting because one day, as he had his rifle poised to shoot a deer, the deer looked straight in his eyes. "I saw life," he explains. "I saw that deer's desire to live, and I thought he was not much different from me. I want to live, why should he not want to live? What right had I to take his life? I put down my gun and never took it up again."

CHAPTER 3

So her mother had nothing to do with it. Her father stopped hunting because a deer looked in his eyes. Because he saw in the deer's eyes its raw, feral hunger for life. Because that hunger mirrored his own and he came face to face with the tenuousness of his life. A single bullet and the deer would be dead. But a single false move in the forest—stepping on a macajuel snake he mistook for a log—and he would be dead. Most of his friends are dead. He does not have much time left. At eighty-two, he has thirteen years left to reach the age his father was when he died, eighteen years the most, should he live to be a hundred.

This is why she is here, why she has decided that this time it will not be for a week or ten days, the usual length of her yearly visits. She will stay a month, thirty-one days. But she has counted her years too. Almost half *her* life is over. How many years are left for her?

She is not afraid of death . . . *death, a necessary end, / Will come when it will come*. What follows afterward is beyond her knowledge, beyond her control. It is futile, she thinks, to ponder too long on the inevitability of death.

It angers her father that life should end. Why? Why? he mutters, circling the house, his hands clasped behind his back, his head bowed. What's the point? Why work so hard? Why achieve so much?

And yet he has worked hard all his life, and yet he has achieved much. For what purpose? he asks Anna. He has been a museum curator, he says, collecting works of art to fill a building which has already been condemned to burn to the ground.

Anna offers him a more hopeful analogy. She points to nature, to the forest he loves so much. Plants grow and die in the forest and become food to nourish new plants, she says.

He is not consoled. Plants do not think, he says. They do not have consciousness. They are not aware of their death. They do not know what it is to have life and then to lose it.

Her mother has no patience with her father's anger. She wants to live, but she believes there is eternal joy and happiness waiting for her on the other side.

"Then if heaven is so wonderful, why do you want to live?" Anna had just returned from college when she asked her mother this question. She was bursting with the overconfidence and arrogance that knowledge without experience bequeaths to untried youth. "I would want to die right away if I believed, as you believe, there is so much happiness waiting for me in the afterlife."

"So you don't believe in God?" her mother asked.

"The god I believe in cannot be quantified, cannot be so easily described." She quoted Dylan Thomas: *"The force that through the green fuse drives the flower / Drives my green age; that blasts the roots of trees / Is my destroyer."*

Her mother did not understand.

"God is the creator and the destroyer," Anna said. "He is the force."

"The force?" Her mother stared at her, shocked.

"People make God in their own image. We give Him human attributes, ideal attributes to be sure, but human nonetheless, for this is all we know. We say God is a loving father because we have experienced, or we know someone who has experienced, a loving father. We say God will forgive us our sins because we hope our human loving father will forgive us our wrongdoings. God will protect us, we say, as our loving father will protect us. But God is not human. He's a . . ."

"A force? How could you believe that is all He is?"

"A supernatural force we should worship."

The taut lines on her mother's face relaxed. She breathed in deeply. "Yes, worship. That is what I tried to teach you."

"But not as you think I should worship Him. I don't believe in any of that, those chants and endless prayers. I believe in silence."

"Silence?"

"God is greater than us. We can only wait for Him to come to us."

"I believe in the power of prayer," her mother said.

Her mother is probably praying now. Twice a day she says the rosary, often directly after breakfast and then again after dinner in the evening. Anna planned a quiet morning reading, but her father has fanned the guilt that propels her now to her mother's room. She *should* be with her mother. *Should* was the word her father used. His response was an admonition, not simply a mild refusal of her offer to join him on his way to the river.

She knocks on the bedroom door. Three times she knocks but there is no answer. If her mother has been praying, surely she has finished now. Anna calls out to her. Still there is silence. She turns the doorknob. The door is unlocked. She opens it and enters. Her mother is not there, but the bathroom door is shut. She looks around the room. The bed has been made. A muted flower-print bedspread is stretched evenly across the mattress; two pillows in beige cases are plumped up against the mahogany headboard.

Lydia will clean the room later, dust the furniture, vacuum the carpet, but her mother makes up the bed.

Anna thinks this covering up, this haste to fix the bed, to smooth the bedspread over the sheets before Lydia comes, has more to do with sex than with her mother's obsession with neatness. Lydia cannot be privy to the intimacies of her mistress's life. Lydia may not be witness to evidence of the couplings of the mistress and the master of the house where she is employed.

Hamlet chastises his mother for marrying Claudius. What drives him to the brink of madness is the picture of their lovemaking that has blossomed in his head. *Nay*, he spits out at his mother, *but to live / In the rank sweat of an enseamed bed.*

Lydia cannot be witness to the enseamed bed. When she comes to clean the room, the rumpled sheets must have been flattened, the crooked seams straightened out.

Her father sleeps to the left of her mother, where he has slept for forty years. On his bedside table is a telephone and next to it, a small tray with loose note paper and a holder with the Parker pen and pencil set Anna gave him two Christmases ago. It bears a brass plaque with an inscription:

To the best Father in the World.
Love, Anna

The bedside table has one drawer. In the drawer are letters compiled neatly in stacks by the dates her father received them, a bundle of pencils tied with a rubber band, a leather-bound appointment book, her father's personal address book, a small glass dish with silver paperclips, a jar of white peppermints, each individually wrapped in red and white–striped transparent paper. There is also a calendar: a stack of thin papers, a sheet for each month, stapled to a cardboard backing. At night, on the calendar, her father crosses off the day that has ended—his obsession with mortality.

Everything is arranged carefully in the bedside drawer, the items lined up perfectly next to each other. Beside the table is a blue-upholstered chair with wood arms and legs. Sometimes her father sits on this chair to read his letters or rearrange his drawer. More often than not he sits on his bed, his legs outstretched on top of the covers. Visitors, though only close friends and family, sit on the chair.

Her mother has a matching chair on her side of the bed. Like her husband, she prefers to sit on the bed. Unlike him, she sits on the edge of it with her feet on the floor when she phones her friends or reads the books Anna brings for her. Only when her back hurts will she sit on the chair. She keeps the phone and the telephone directory on her bedside table. Next to it is a crucifix, about eight inches tall, held upright on a stand, and next to the crucifix is a worn prayer book. Anna notices that the silver rosary ring, usually next to the crucifix, is not on the table. On their visit to Europe three years ago, her father brought back a painting and her mother the silver rosary ring which had been blessed by the Pope. It is one inch in diameter, surrounded by ten silver beads crested with a small crucifix. Anna guesses her mother has taken the rosary ring with her to the bathroom. She presses her ear against the bathroom door but hears nothing. No sound of water running out of the faucet, no splash of the shower against the bathroom tiles. Her mother is praying. She will not disturb her. *Should* not. She is about to leave when her mother calls her name. Her voice is muted, almost a whisper. "Anna? Is that you, Anna?"

Unaccountably, Anna feels a pressing urge to escape. "I can come back later," she says. She is already at the bedroom door.

"No," her mother says, in the same muted voice. "Come. Come in. I want to talk to you."

Anna wants a peaceful morning curled up with her book in a cushioned wicker chair on the veranda that faces the lawn with a clear view of the two orange trees, their branches bowed down with the weight of fruit. She wants to be lulled by the twittering of birds squabbling among themselves for the sweet juice of the oranges. She does not want to talk. To talk with her mother is to stir up old wounds, to be reminded that at thirty-nine she is childless and single, to be reminded that it was she who chose to leave the island, to turn her back on all that could have been hers.

"Anna, can you hear me? Open the door, Anna."

But isn't this why she is here? She is here to talk, to reconnect, to be with them, with her father *and* her mother.

"Anna."

She turns the doorknob and enters the bathroom. Her mother is seated at her dressing room table, facing the door, her back to the mirror. Anna clasps her hand to her mouth when she sees her. Her mother's eyes are watery pools and the skin is ashy around her mouth.

"Mummy, what? What is it?" Anna steps quickly toward her.

Her mother brings a trembling finger to her lips. "Not a word." She is holding the rosary ring. It dangles on the crook of her thumb. "I don't want you to say a word to your father."

Anna comes closer to her. "What is wrong, Mummy? Are you sick?"

"Close the door," her mother says.

Anna stretches out her hand toward her mother, but she does not touch her.

"Do as I say, Anna." Her mother gestures toward the door. "Please, Anna."

Anna walks over to the door and closes it.

"Is your father here?" Her mother's voice is strained.

Anna's heart drops. "Is it something Daddy has done?" But her father is an old man.

"No," her mother says. "This is not about your father."

Why should she have thought otherwise? And yet the relief Anna feels is palpable. "Do you need a doctor?" Her heart has resumed its normal rhythm.

"No," her mother says. "I don't need a doctor. I need to know if your father has left."

"He's gone."

"Are you sure?"

"He found a frog in the pond and took it to the river."

"Good." Her mother stands up and puts the metal rosary ring on the dressing room table. Slowly, she pushes one and then another button through the buttonholes at the top of her dress. "I want to show you something." She frees another button.

Anna sees flashes of her white cotton bra in the opening under her dress.

"Unhook me," her mother says. She twists her body around, her back toward Anna.

Anna remains where she is, a safe distance away from her mother. She does not move. In their household, they do not expose their bodies, not to each other. Husbands and wives may have to bare their naked bodies to each other, but not mothers and daughters.

"Here. I'll help you." Her mother lowers her head. One by one her mother undoes more of the buttons on her dress, stopping just below her waist. She slides one side of her dress off her shoulder and down her arm and does the same on the other side. The top of the dress drops in folds at her waist.

"Can you reach the hooks on my bra now?" She is wearing a white half-slip. The exposed skin above it is creamy brown, not a single mark or flaw on it. The texture resembles leavened dough, soft, smooth, pliable.

"Go on, Anna. Unhook my bra."

Her lips have brushed her mother's cheeks, her hands have touched her body, but her hands have not touched the parts of her mother's body covered by clothes.

"Go on, Anna."

The panels on the bra have cut into the sides of her mother's back, pulling the flesh together. A canal forms along the path of her spine. Anna pinches the metal hook between her fingers and struggles to ease it over the eye of the fastener. Her fingers scrape against her mother's skin.

"Is it too tight? Do you want me to do it?" Her mother looks over her shoulder, but Anna has managed to unfasten the bra; the canal along her mother's spine spreads, relaxes. The leavened dough on either side deflates.

Her mother removes her bra. She turns around. "This is what I want you to see."

Nothing has prepared Anna for what her mother wants to show her. Nothing has prepared her for the lump pushing out beneath the skin on her mother's left breast or for the thin trail of partially dried blood beneath it. Anna gasps. Instinctively, with no time to think, she throws her arms around her mother's neck and buries her head in the well of her shoulders.

"Shhh." Her mother pulls her closer.

The muscles on Anna's throat contract. She cannot speak.

"Shhh."

They stay this way until self-consciousness returns—seconds later—both suddenly aware of what they have done. They have not embraced each other this way before, not within Anna's memory.

Anna is the first to back away. Her mother does nothing to stop her. "How long?" she asks. "How long have you had this?"

Her mother, calm now, lifts her arm. Under her arm is another large lump, her lymph nodes swollen, pushing against her skin.

"Oh, Mummy!" Anna clutches her neck and squeezes her skin to stop her head from shaking.

"I haven't told your father." Her mother rubs the spot on her shoulder where Anna had sunk her head. It is the only acknowledgment she gives of the intimacy that has just occurred between them.

"But Daddy . . . ? Didn't Daddy see it, both of them?"

"I prayed every night for it to go away." Her mother flops down on the bathroom chair. She does not cover her breasts. They hang down, two pendulous sacks against her chest, except in one a lump bulges out, hard, sturdy, full-blown. "The one on my breast just got bigger and bigger."

Anna averts her eyes. "Daddy must have seen it," she says.

"I wake up at night. At two in the morning. Your father is still asleep."

Anna stifles a moan. Against her will, her eyes are drawn back to the lump on her mother's breast.

"Every morning at two o'clock I come here. I pray. I say the rosary. It's on my mind all the time. In the day, I am busy and I forget sometimes, but at night I'm alone."

"But Daddy . . ."

"He sleeps like a rock. He doesn't hear me when I get out of bed. I say my rosary. I ask the Blessed Virgin to take it away."

"You need a doctor," Anna says.

Her mother shakes her head.

"I'll take you to the doctor."

"A doctor can't help me."

Her mother's mother died at fifty-six of breast cancer. In those colonial days on the island there was no chemotherapy, not for those without money, not for locals without connections. The tumor on her grandmother's breast just grew larger until it broke through her skin. It was bloody and ugly.

The prevailing wisdom among the women was that the tumor was a hungry beast eating away the flesh of its victims. If they fed the beast, if they satiated its ravenous appetite, it would eat the food they gave it instead of the woman's breast. So they put slabs of raw meat on the tumor on Anna's grandmother's breast. The tumor preferred human flesh; it kept on eating.

In the sweltering heat of the tropical sun, the raw meat decomposed and filled her grandmother's room with the putrid scent of decaying flesh. Beatrice Sinclair was revolted. She could not enter her mother's room without vomiting. The women gave her handkerchiefs soaked in cologne to press against her nose. The handkerchiefs were useless. She fainted at the door. Her mother died calling her name.

"Today," Anna says. "I'll take you today."

"A doctor was no use to my mother."

"Things are different now," Anna says. "Doctors know more. They can help."

"I pray every night. Sometimes I say six rosaries. Sometimes the sun is rising before I get back to bed."

"Last night?"

Her mother nods. "I couldn't sleep last night."

"Daddy must have . . ." Even if her father had not heard her mother's footsteps along the bedroom floor, twice he must have felt the mattress shift beneath him, once when she left the bed, the second time when she returned.

"Your father has his own way," her mother says.

Singh noticed. "Something wrong," he said. But her father did not blink, he did not show the slightest concern when she told him that her mother was not in the garden as he had assumed. And what about her? She had seen the dark circles under her mother's eyes.

"It doesn't hurt," her mother says.

Not yet. Not yet. Anna's stomach churns, the muscles in her chest tense, but no tears come. She does not cry.

They are a family who keep a firm rein on their emotions. Not all emotions, to be sure. Not indignation, outrage, anger. Pride gives rise to indignation; justice cries for outrage and anger. But the sadness that overcomes Anna now, the empathy she feels for her mother's suffering, the fear she has of losing her, these are emotions too close to the heart. Such emotions lay bare one's vulnerability, they threaten to loosen the control one deludes oneself into thinking one has over one's life. She will not cry.

"You'll have to tell Daddy," Anna says.

"Yes," her mother replies. "It's time we faced this."

"Faced?"

"Admitted it. Tell him it's time, Anna."

He knows?

"You tell him for me, Anna."

They are husband and wife, not mere acquaintances. They have lived with each other for more than forty years. They are not strangers.

"It's time," her mother says. "Tell him it's time."

CHAPTER 4

B ut her parents love each other. Her father can recall the first day he saw her mother. He can recite with impressive exactitude the date, the time of day, the weather, the exact spot on the street. He remembers what she wore, how she walked, every word she said.

He was walking on the sidewalk toward the black, marble-façade Treasury Building where Beatrice worked, in those days the property of the colonial government. It was ten past noon on the 10th of April, a particularly hot day in the dry season. The glare of the sun was so strong he had to pull his hat down low over his forehead to shield his eyes. That was why, before he saw Beatrice's face, he saw her legs, the backs of them, for she was ahead of him, having just left her office. He saw solid calves, tiny ankles, feet sliding in black pumps. Impressed and intrigued, he pushed back the brim of his hat to get a better view. The sight of her voluptuous hips swaying rhythmically to music he alone heard made him decide there and then he would have to speak to her.

A man in his part of town was either a breast man or a hips man. John Sinclair was a hips man. Breasts for him were functional objects that swelled with pregnancy and deflated once the baby was weaned. He had been breast-fed. He had seen his mother breast-feed his younger sibling. He had seen his aunts breast-feed his cousins. Now the wife of one of his friends was breast-feeding her son. It was hard for him not to think of breasts as not much different from the udders of the cows he saw in the fields, their calves sucking and pulling at their nipples. So breasts did not arouse desire in him. Not that John Sinclair did not appreciate an hourglass figure on a woman. It was just that the bottom half was the part that made his head spin. And to John Sinclair, Beatrice Forneau was endowed with a perfect bottom half, hips that flared from a narrow waist, a backside that rose and curved in a smooth arc behind her.

Never in his life had he seen a woman move her hips more seductively than Beatrice, he declared. He demonstrated her stride for his daughter. Placing his hands akimbo on his waist, he strode across the living room floor, swaying his hips from side to side while beating out a stripper's drum through his tightened lips. *Badoom, badoom, badoom.* Beatrice laughed so hard, tears rolled down her eyes. "No more, no more!" She had to struggle to recover her breath.

"That was how she walked," John Sinclair insisted. "*Badoom, badoom, badoom.*"

Her mother begged him to stop. "Enough, John!" But Anna could tell she liked this recounting of her first meeting with her husband-to-be.

"I almost knocked a man down following those hips," John Sinclair said. "I was a man on a leash."

"What leash?" Beatrice rolled her eyes and protested unconvincingly. "I didn't have a leash."

"Those hips! I was tethered to them," he said.

"You exaggerate."

"Exaggerate? *Badoom, badoom, badoom.*" Her father did his stripper's stride and her mother collapsed with laughter.

"But how did you get her to speak to you?" Anna asked.

"I came right up to her, tipped my hat, and said, 'Good afternoon, miss. You are the most beautiful woman I have ever set eyes on.'"

"And that was it?"

"Well, she didn't speak to me right away. I had to revert to that old trick of pretending she had dropped something. A piece of paper, I think I told her. She had a folder in her hand."

"In our day, a man didn't just walk up to a woman he didn't know and speak to her," Anna's mother says. "He had to be introduced."

"I couldn't wait that long," John Sinclair said.

"You must have been flattered, Mummy."

"Oh, I knew it was my hips he was after."

"And the face too, when I saw it. Those eyes, those cheekbones."

"Oh, John." Her mother's smile rippled across her face. Her eyes danced.

Anna was a teenager when they replayed their first meeting for her. She found them silly and sad then. Two middle-aged people approaching old age, the pleasures of youth behind them, reduced to finding compensation in memories. But now she is close to the age her mother was then and she knows that little ever changes in the heart, that the heart desires the same thing it desired when one was young, that the body, though aging, still wants to be held, comforted, appreciated, loved.

"Your mother is as beautiful to me today as she was on the first day I saw her," her father said to her not long ago. "I see no difference in her."

Their bodies have changed; the skin on her father's arms and legs, once muscled and firm, has loosened and the laugh lines on the sides of her mother's mouth have deepened. Time, that unrelenting chiseler, has carved ravines along her father's forehead and down her mother's neck, and yet her mother remains beautiful to her father, to him she is no different from the woman who dazzled him on that sunny April afternoon.

They must still make love, Anna is certain of it. But if they still make love, surely they have seen each other's naked bodies. Surely, her father has seen the lump on her mother's breast.

She waits on the veranda for her father to return from the river. When his car reaches the gate, she walks to the driveway despite the fact that he has a remote and doesn't need her to release the lock on the gate.

"You should have seen that frog swim away." He has turned off the car engine and opened the car door. "I bet he prefers it to my fishpond." He swings his leg out onto the paved ground. He is full of energy, sprightly even. His thin lips plump up when he smiles, his dark eyes shine, the hook on his long nose spreads and softens. He looks younger now that his face is animated.

In the morning, just out of bed, he seemed a shuffling old man, clutching the loose top of his pajama pants in a knot at his waist. But her father is no shuffling old man. He has not lost his senses, his incisive wit, his formidable intelligence. When he retired from the oil company where he worked as an administrator, labor unions and private contractors rushed to hire him as a consultant. At seventy-nine, he was still in demand for his unmatchable skills in labor negotiations. At eighty, he turned down retainers from four of the largest corporations on the island that still vied for his services. He was known for the ability he displayed with his wife at breakfast. She had forgiven him without his having offered her a word of apology. So it was with his opponents. Before they realized what they lost, they had already signed a contract.

Anna says something about the frog, agreeing with him that it made sense the frog would prefer the freedom of the river.

"And a better chance to mate too," her father says. He

takes out the watering can, the block of wood, and the stone from the floor of the backseat of the car. He crosses the veranda in the direction of the fishpond.

Anna walks behind him. "I talked to Mummy," she says.

"Good." He puts the watering can against the wall of the house, next to the faucet attached to the garden hose. "This should be Singh's job," he grumbles, bending down to open the faucet, "but he won't water the lawn, only the flowers. And only if your mother tells him to." He glances up at her. "Did you have a good chat with your mother?" But he does not wait for her answer. Before she can speak, he is back fussing about the brown grass. "The sun is really strong this morning. If I don't wet the grass, it will burn up and die." He unravels the hose.

Anna tries again. "Mummy isn't well."

He has opened the closure at the end of the hose. The loud hiss from the water gushing out muffles her voice. "What?"

"Mummy's sick," she says.

He makes a half-turn toward her and crinkles his eyes.

"She's in your bedroom," Anna says.

He turns back to the hose. In this position, facing the garden, she cannot see the expression on his face.

"Did you hear what I said, Daddy?" She is standing close behind him.

"Your mother is tired. She's been tired lately." He directs the hose to a brown spot on the lawn.

"Do you know why Mummy is so tired?"

"We're getting older, Anna. Both of us get tired. She gets tired quickly. I get tired quickly."

She blamed her mother's tiredness on the heat in the morning, but Singh was quick to expose her. "Is hot every morning, Miss Anna, and she does still come out," he said.

"Singh is here probably puttering around in the nursery, but he won't water the lawn." Her father is grumbling again.

"Daddy," she pleads, but he is adjusting the spigot on the hose and the water gushes out with fuller force.

"I must water the lawn. Me, not Singh," he complains. "Of course, we have to pay him just as usual. No difference in his pay when this used to be his job. That's your mother for you. She'll have her way."

"Daddy!" Anna raises her voice. The sharpness of her tone startles him. He swings around and the hose follows him. Water sprays all over her legs. "Look what you have done." Anna brushes away the water dripping down her legs.

He is immediately contrite. He turns off the spigot. "I'll get you a towel," he says.

"Wait!" She tries to stop him, but he is already on his way toward the bar in the veranda. "I don't need a towel."

He does not break his stride.

"Have you heard a word I've said to you?" She is walking behind him. "For God's sake, stop!"

But when he stops and looks at her, she softens. Intelligent eyes beg her to say no more. Yet her mother needs help. Her mother needs a doctor.

"Come." She puts her hand lightly on his arm. "Sit with me in the veranda."

"Your legs are wet," he says and moves away. "Let me help. I keep dry towels under the bar."

"No. I'm fine. I'm okay. The water will dry off in the sun." She takes his arm firmly now. "I have to tell you something about Mummy." She leads him to an armchair.

"Did you and your mother quarrel?"

"No. We did not quarrel."

"You always quarrel."

"Sit, Daddy." She is standing over him. "Sit."

He surrenders and does as she asks.

"We did not quarrel," Anna says again.

"Because I had hoped this time . . . I know your mother . . ." He is not looking at her as he says this. He presses his right leg hard into the knee of his left leg. He seems agitated, nervous.

Anna sits in the armchair next to him. She leans over and touches his hand lightly with the tips of her fingers. "Why didn't you take her to the doctor?"

He does not ask her to explain. He merely slides his fingers up his thigh. His fingernails leave an ashy trail on his skin.

"Why didn't you, Daddy?"

He looks down on his lap. "I saw blood on my vest," he says.

"And why didn't you say something?"

"She likes to sleep in my vest."

"Why didn't you ask, Daddy?"

"Last week, I saw it. My vest was in her hamper."

They have two hampers in their bathroom, one for him and one for her. They do not mix their dirty laundry.

"I took out the vest. That's when I saw the bloody spots."

"And what did you do?"

"The blood was on one side of the vest," he says.

"Where the tumor is." Anna will no longer dissemble.

"Where the tumor is." He echoes her words.

"So you knew?"

"I sleep with your mother every night," he says.

"And you said nothing to her?" She wants to keep her anger from vibrating through her vocal chords, but she feels herself losing control.

"Your mother is a very private woman." His legs are still

crossed. He bends forward. With one hand he clutches his right ankle, with the other he rubs his left knee. His body is twisted into a tight ball.

"Private?" She flings the word at him.

"Your mother and I respect each other's privacy. That is the way we have always lived our lives."

"You saw blood on a vest she wore. Blood, Daddy."

"I knew she would tell me when she was ready."

"But you must have known . . . ?"

"Yes." It is a simple acknowledgment of information he has kept to himself.

"Her mother died of it."

"Cancer," he says. "I knew it was cancer."

"Why didn't you . . . ?"

He raises his head. His eyes have lost their shine; they are infinitely sad. "She was afraid," he says. "I knew it was cancer but I also knew she was afraid."

CHAPTER 5

Schubert's G-Flat Impromptu. The music drifts into the veranda where Anna has been sitting for more than two hours now. The grief and pain the music expresses seem to her interminable, unending. It rises slowly, mournfully, and then soars upward to a crescendo, bursting in her heart. This is the music John Sinclair puts on the CD player when he comes out briefly from the bedroom where he has been with his wife since he left Anna on the veranda, dazed by his admission that he had seen the lump on his wife's breast, the blood on his vest, and has said nothing, has done nothing.

Two more times he comes out of his room. Two more concertos by Schubert. Did her mother ask for Schubert? Her mother loves the music her father loves, but she does not know the pieces by name. Did she hum a bar for him? Or does her father know which music she means when she says, "Play the music I love, John."

Does her father have access to her mother's private thoughts?

And yet her father says he respects her mother's privacy. She wears his vest to bed, for Chrissake! The bed is enseamed! She flattens the creases, straightens the crooked seams, but before Lydia comes to her room, the sheets are in disarray.

What price are they both willing to pay for privacy sold so cheaply in the country where she now lives? On national TV in America, Anna has seen grown men and women bare their souls, tell their darkest secrets, before audiences of millions.

She shuts her eyes and leans back in her chair. She has chosen this spot for the sweet citrus scent of oranges that permeates the air, she sits here to be soothed by the melodious whistles of the pretty-feathered birds in the trees, but neither the scent of oranges nor the joyful songs of the birds cool the anger that continues to simmers inside her. How can her father—how can *they*—listen to music at a time like this? How can he so calmly tell her that he knew her mother has cancer and yet has done nothing? Why has her mother waited this long to say something?

She senses a presence hovering close to her. It is Lydia. She has served Mr. and Mrs. Sinclair lunch in their room, Anna in the veranda. She has washed the dishes in the kitchen. "Can I get you something, Miss Anna?" Her hands are still wet from the dishes. She slides them over each other. "Something to drink? A glass of lemonade?"

"Oh, Lydia, no," Anna says. "I can get myself something to drink." She means this kindly, to spare Lydia the chore of serving her again, but Lydia's face drops and Anna realizes too late her mistake. She has offended Lydia. It may feel un-American to accept this kind of service in her own home when Lydia has work to do and she has none, but she is here on an island fresh with the memory of British colonial strictures; she is not in America. She is not even American. Isn't this what she has tried to force her mother to admit? Her absence over the years has not lessened her right to belong, her claim to the island, to her roots. She corrects her mistake. "If you don't mind," she says to Lydia, and Lydia's face brightens.

"Anything for you, Miss Anna."

Loyalty and affection keep Lydia here. "How can I leave your parents now when they need me?" she has said to

Anna. "Your father getting old. Your mother not the same like she use to be. She not as sprightly."

Anna asks for ice water and Lydia's face is wreathed in smiles when she returns carrying a glass with a white paper napkin wrapped around the bottom. In the warm air, the ice in the glass condenses and beads of water soak the napkin. "I boil the water for you and put it in the fridge," Lydia says. "This not water from the pipe."

Much has improved on the island. Lydia does not need to boil the water, but she wants to please, she wants to be of service. Tourists spread those false tales about the water. They make no distinction between one tropical country and the next, one place and the next that is not Europe or America. Don't drink the water there, they say. You'll get diarrhea, or worse, you'll die. Corporations smell money. Now even in Europe and America tap water is suspect and one has to pay dollars for a few ounces of it packaged in neat bottles.

"You're so good to us," Anna says. The napkin has slid across the damp surface of the glass and the paper separates. When Anna takes the glass from Lydia, pieces of it remain stuck to Lydia's fingers. She is embarrassed. She blushes, though the only way Anna can tell is by the shy cast of her eyes downward and the self-conscious smile that plays across her lips. Her dark skin conceals the sudden flood of blood to her face. "Sorry," she says and rolls the damp paper along her fingers.

"That's okay, Lydia." Anna extends her hand and takes the pieces of paper from the ends of Lydia's fingers. She squeezes the paper into a ball and gives it to her. Lydia puts it in the pocket of her apron.

"You know, Lydia, I don't like the way Mummy speaks to you. I want you to know that."

"I don't mind, Miss Anna," Lydia murmurs.

"I heard her giving you orders in the kitchen."

"I 'customed to her ways, Miss Anna. I know how she like."

But Anna insists. "I want you to know I appreciate all you do for them. I'm so far away. I can't be of much help. It's a comfort to me knowing you are here."

"I tries, Miss Anna."

"Mummy appreciates what you do. It's just that . . ."

"She belong to the old school, Miss Anna. I understand."

Anna looks away, humbled by the simplicity and purity of Lydia's generosity. The old school was not kind to people like Lydia and yet she has room in her heart for compassion.

"The water okay?" Lydia is still standing next to her.

Anna thanks her again, but Lydia does not leave. She is twisting and untwisting the ends of her apron over her leathered hands.

"I'll bring the glass to the kitchen when I am done," Anna says, but Lydia remains where she is. "You don't have to wait for me."

Lydia sighs, a deep release of breath that collapses her chest. "She not well." Anna knows immediately that Lydia means her mother. "I don't say nothing, but I see her." Lydia's voice is heavy with worry. "Sometimes she does have to lean on the wall to keep from falling. Sometimes I have to take her tea in the bedroom for her. Is four o'clock and she still resting in her bed."

"And did you ask her what's the matter?" Anna keeps a tight control on the pitch of her voice. She will not panic.

"Oh no, Miss Anna. I can't do that. Is not my place to do that."

Not her place.

Anna cannot place blame for *Not her place* solely at the

feet of the English colonizers. Not just the English and the Europeans, but Africans and Asians as well subscribe to social hierarchies. Even in hell, Dante tells us, there are stratified circles. In heaven, the best are nearest to God; in purgatory, the least without sin are on the mountain top.

Lydia, unlike Singh, will not call Mrs. Sinclair *madam*, as the old school required her to do. She will not call Mr. Sinclair *boss* or *bossman*. She will refer to Anna's parents by their proper titles. *Mr. and Mrs. Sinclair*, she calls them. But she remains aware of her place in relation to Mrs. Sinclair, and given her place, she cannot ask Mrs. Sinclair questions that touch upon the intimate parts of her life, that refer to the unclothed areas of her body. She cannot say to Mrs. Sinclair, I notice that your hips are not as wide as they were a few months ago. She cannot say, I see a strange swelling on one of your breasts. She is not privileged to observe Mrs. Sinclair's body. If she wants to know about Mrs. Sinclair's health, she must wait to be informed.

"You ask her, Miss Anna. You find out. She need help."

Help is on her father's mind when he comes out of the bedroom for his four o'clock tea. Mrs. Sinclair is sleeping, he tells Lydia. He takes the chair next to Anna.

Lydia serves them in the veranda. On a tray, she brings a pot of tea, two cups and saucers, two teaspoons, two knives, two dessert plates, a stack of paper napkins, a silver bowl filled with brown sugar, a small jug of milk, six slices of coconut sweet bread baked with cherries and raisins she made in the morning, a small dish of guava jelly, and a slab of white cheddar cheese. With slight variations—cake one day, butter biscuits another—she serves the Sinclairs this tea at four every afternoon. She puts the tray down on the coffee table.

John Sinclair tells Lydia that they won't need her for a

while and she returns to the kitchen. When she is gone, he gets up and pours a cup of tea for his daughter. "No sugar, right?" he says. "Just like your mother." His face is drawn; he looks worn out, wrung dry. He passes the milk to her. They use evaporated milk in their tea. When Anna told her parents that in America people drink hot tea with lemon, they wrinkled their noses in disgust. On their visits to her in America, they refuse to use the fresh milk that comes in cartons. Only canned evaporated milk will do for them, Carnation Evaporated Milk to be exact.

John Sinclair waits until his daughter drinks her first cup and has eaten a slice of the sweet bread. When she is done, he broaches the subject of his wife. "What do we do now?" The space between his eyebrows folds, the canals deepen.

"She should come back with me to the States," Anna says.

John Sinclair puts down his cup and rubs his eyes. "She won't do that." He slides his hands down the sides of his face.

"There are doctors who can treat her there," Anna says. "There are good hospitals in the States."

He shakes his head. "She's afraid."

"It doesn't look good, Daddy. I think the cancer has advanced pretty far. It's in her lymph nodes too. And the blood." She lowers her eyes as she says this, trying hard to hold back the accusation on the tip of her tongue. He saw the blood on his vest and he didn't do anything, he didn't say anything.

"She won't go."

"Breast cancer does not have to be a death sentence," Anna says, struggling to keep her voice even.

"She saw her mother suffer."

"There are new medicines, better surgeries . . ."

"That's not it," he says.

"Then what is it?"

"She wants to be treated here."

"They can't help her here," Anna says.

"Your mother won't go anywhere else. She says we have good doctors here."

"There are better doctors in the States."

"Your mother has faith in our doctors here."

"I'm not saying the doctors here are bad," Anna says, "but they are not familiar with the latest research."

"Your mother does not think so."

"And even if they have kept up with the research, you know the conditions of the hospitals here, Daddy. They use newspapers instead of sheets, for God's sake."

"We can bring sheets to the hospital."

"Patients are left in the corridors on gurneys for days. They don't have beds!"

"I can arrange that."

He is speaking to her in the patronizing tone of a manager subduing an overly anxious new employee. Anna glares at him wild-eyed. "You don't mean to let her have surgery here?"

"Your mother says we have the best oncologists here," he says.

"Oh God!" Anna buries her head in her hands.

Her father reaches out and winds his fingers around her wrist. "She'll be all right, Anna. Don't worry so much."

It is more than Anna can take. She pushes away his hand and bounds out of her chair. The words that earlier had trembled at the tip of her tongue come flying out of her mouth. "You are responsible!" she shouts out at him. "You let it go this far. You and your mumbo-jumbo about privacy."

"Anna, Anna," John Sinclair says soothingly.

"If you cared, if you really cared, you would have done something."

"I love your mother."

"Love her and you do nothing? You tell me something about privacy, respecting her privacy? Were you planning to respect her privacy until she died?"

"Your mother and I have no secrets from each other."

"No secrets? What do you call her not telling you about her tumor? What do you call your saying nothing? I mean, how do two people sleep next to each other, night after night, for more than forty years, and one of them not say a word about a tumor he can clearly see bulging from his wife's breast? And the blood? Oh, Daddy, how could you?"

"Clearly bulging? It was not clearly bulging to me as you seem to say, Anna."

"I saw it, Daddy. Even a half-blind man would have seen it."

"Your mother knew I saw it," he says softly.

Yes, that was what her mother had implied. "It's time we faced this," she said. As if she had planned this all alone. As if the plan was first prayers in the darkness of her bathroom, and when prayers did not yield the results she hoped for, then time to get the aid of her husband, time for both of them to confront what they already know.

"Your mother is modest," her father says. He brings his cup to his lips. The steam rises and shades his eyes.

"Modest?" Anna's tone is biting. She will not camouflage her anger. He cannot have forgotten that he told her how he met her mother. A modest woman does not sway her hips like a stripper. *Badoom, badoom, badoom.* "What do you mean, she's modest?"

"Privacy is not the same as intimacy, Anna," her father says quietly.

She does not understand.

"You make a mistake if you think I meant intimacy. Your mother and I are intimate."

Unexpectedly, she is embarrassed. Even when children become adults they still prefer the story of the stork to the truth about how they were conceived. She turns away from him. "What do you want me to say to you?"

"Don't oppose her. She has made up her mind. She will be treated here, in our country, in our homeland. She is proud of our doctors."

"And you? What do you say?"

"I support your mother, Anna. That is what I've always tried to do."

"You are giving her a death sentence," Anna says.

"You live in America. We live here. We don't think everything in America is good. She doesn't think everything in America will necessarily be the best for her."

CHAPTER 6

There is, her father says, a difference between intimacy and privacy. Her mother is modest, he says.

Intimacy: the condition of being intimate. *Intimate:* relating to one's deepest, innermost nature.

Privacy: the condition of being secluded from the presence or view of others.

Modest: a disinclination to draw attention to oneself, retiring, diffident.

In the intimacy of her parents' marriage, she was conceived. In the privacy of their bedroom, her mother and father protect each other's secrets with such fervor that neither will acknowledge what the other knows. Her mother will not admit to her father that she knows he knows about the lump on her breast and the blood on his vest. He will not reveal that he knows she knows.

Anna does not doubt her parents are privy to each other's deepest, innermost nature. But it strains credulity to think of her mother as modest. At breakfast, Anna was her father's ally as he threw darts at her mother, accusing her of bossiness, arrogance, snobbery, suggesting a lack of modesty. Now he has turned the tables on her, his daughter, hinting that she is the one who is immodest, the one who is the snob, the one arrogantly listing their island's inadequacies. But Anna is convinced her mother will die if she remains on the island, if she is treated by the doctors here, who are not as informed as the doctors in America. Her mother will not survive surgery in a hospital that does not have sufficient sheets for its insufficient beds, a hospital with equipment that is decades old, that is supported by a technology which has barely kept pace with the inventions of the previous century.

Why does her father give in to her mother? Why does he always submit to her will, to *her* plan, not his plan? For surely it was not his plan to wait, to simply stand by silently for a miracle, to find out if six rosaries said in the night would shrink the tumor on his wife's breast, make it disappear.

The lump on her mother's breast is as large as a lemon, the one under her arm not much smaller. Both of the tumors have festered for months. Years, perhaps. At what stage is the malignancy? Anna is certain it is close to the last stage, not far from terminal. Yet her mother refuses to have surgery in the States where she can be saved and her father says he supports her. It is all he has ever tried to do, he says.

How much penance is one required to do for one's sins? She knows bad things have happened between her parents. Her father was to blame. But how long will it take for him to earn absolution?

"Miss Anna, you speak to madam?"

Singh has come so quietly upon her, she is startled. Her shoulders jerk upward, her back stiffens, and her eyes skate down to the machete at the side of his leg. He is holding the handle loosely in his palm. The blade glints in the sunlight.

"I frighten you, Miss Anna?"

A reflex response she has learned from America. She is embarrassed, flooded with shame.

"You thought I was somebody else, Miss Anna?" Singh's eyes reflect puzzlement, but Anna detects a glimmer of amusement playing on his lips. "De bossman lock the gate. Anyhow, I have this." He lifts the machete, and with his other hand draws his finger along the thin sharp edge of the blade.

She is not in America, but there is crime here. NAFTA has made fishing and growing bananas and sugarcane in the Caribbean almost futile. Islands cannot compete with continents. There is oil on her island, under the sea, under the earth, but for the displaced fishermen and for the ones who cultivated the land, there is no work. The drug trade brings income. The islands are a strainer. Drug lords bypass the sentries at America's borders by shipping marijuana, heroin, and cocaine from South America here, packaging and smuggling them in domestic cargo bound for America. The most vicious of the drug wars get filtered out here. The crimes that happen in America are the remnants. Two weeks ago, a whole family—mother, father, and four young children all under the age of twelve—were beheaded, their heads cemented on pillars in their backyard, their bodies hacked to pieces. The Sinclairs protect themselves with electric gates, bolts on the exterior doors, and a wrought iron gate double-locked at night between their living and sleeping quarters. Anna fears these are not sufficient.

"People respect de bossman," Singh says. "Dey safe. Nobody do dem nothing."

"Singh." Anna says his name with a gaiety that does not fool him.

"Don't be frighten, miss."

"I knew it was you, Singh." Anna pulls down the edges of her shorts, which have bunched up on her thighs, and faces him.

Singh grins at her.

"You're worried about Mummy, no?"

"You speak to she yet?" Singh asks.

"Oh, Singh." This time she says his name with gravity. "We're going to need your help. She's sick, Singh."

"I did think so."

"She may have to go to the hospital."

"I did think so," he says again.

"She'll need you to keep up the garden."

"Madam know she can count on me."

"I'll tell her you said so."

"And de bossman?" Singh is looking straight at her. "How he taking it?"

"Daddy is okay," she says.

"He funny, de bossman. But he does feel things."

"I know, Singh."

"He don't talk, but he does see."

Anna is moved by his concern for her father. "Daddy is with Mummy now," she says.

"What she sick with?"

It is easy enough for her to answer, *Cancer*. The diagnosis has not been confirmed by a doctor, but the evidence is there. The lump on her mother's breast will not be benign. One in five women will be diagnosed each year. For a woman whose mother had breast cancer, the odds increase. Is she next? The statistics are there for her to read. It is no secret: for a woman whose mother has breast cancer and whose mother's mother died of breast cancer, the chances of her getting it as well are practically inevitable.

"You know what she sick with, Miss Anna?"

She is afraid and fear triggers the slight tremor that runs through her hands.

"Is something bad, Miss Anna?" Singh asks, his eyes on her hands.

It is something bad, but she will not say. She does not say for the very reasons her father has not said. He wanted to protect his wife's privacy. Now Anna finds that she wants to protect her own privacy. She will not give Singh access to her fears. She will not let him know that she is afraid that not only has something bad happened to her mother, but something bad is waiting to happen to her.

"I don't know," she says to Singh. "We won't know until we take her to the doctor."

This obsession with privacy.

"Nobody likes you to bleed all over them," her mother said. Anna had just turned eight. The doll she got for her birthday had slipped from her hands and fallen on the concrete walkway. Its brittle surface cracked and Anna screamed. She was inconsolable for days. "Crying excessively is a character flaw," her mother said.

In her parents' social circles, any weakness is a character flaw. Failure is a character flaw. Sickness is not to be discussed; death is not to be discussed. Sickness and death are the ultimate evidence of weakness and failure.

The problem with the lower classes, her parents' friends say, is their lack of control over their emotions, over their bodies. When their bodies fail, they cry out in pain. When family and friends die, they wail, they scream. They bleed all over each other.

It was a source of pride for one of her mother's friends that she did not shed a tear at her husband's funeral. How they praised her courage! How they said *doctor* in that peculiar way that everyone understood did not mean doctor in the usual sense of the physician who takes care of the body. "She's seeing a *doctor*," they said, when months later no one could persuade the widow to go beyond the gates of her home.

Self-control is the holy grail of the upper middle class. To lose control over one's self is to be humiliated.

Anna thinks it is the prospect of humiliation that makes her mother speak so harshly to Lydia. In the still darkness of her bathroom, the specter of a future when her limbs and muscles could fail her must shimmer brightly before her. Fear—and perhaps resentment too—makes her raise her voice, issue orders to Lydia. Boss her around, her father says. Always in the morning Lydia is bright-eyed. Always in the morning her mother finds blood on her vest. If the Virgin Mary does not answer her prayers, the time will come when she will need Lydia, when weakened by illness she will no longer have the strength to boss Lydia around.

Pride matters. Privacy matters. Her mother will not give Lydia the merest inkling of her fears. Her mother will make a silent pact with her husband: neither will speak of the tumor on her breast until she has given permission. Her husband will not expose her weakness, the failure of her body, even to his wife herself.

The discovery that she is not much different from her parents disturbs Anna. She has lied to Singh; she has once again dissembled. She will not admit to him that she suspects—no, she is convinced—a horrible disease is ravaging her mother's body. She will not admit she fears that the seed for the same disease may be lying dormant in her breasts, biding its time.

In America she is freed from these strictures of her social class so rigidly enforced when she is home. In America, she can bleed all over someone, she can cry, she can scream, and no one will say to her, "Don't. It's a character flaw."

But with this freedom comes another kind of confinement. For in America she is black, and in America the ways of black people have been defined, set in stone.

And when I am formulated, sprawling on a pin,
When I am pinned and wriggling on the wall,
Then how should I begin
To spit out all the butt-ends of my days and ways?
And how should I presume?

"Anna's not really a true West Indian," her colleagues at work explain.

Is a true West Indian the kind of person one sees on sitcoms on television, a Bert Williams with a modern-day gloss? Is a true West Indian woman one who plasters her face with makeup, layering her cheeks with rouge, her lips with bright red lipstick? Does she wear bright colors and shiny gold jewelry? Is she a dancehall girl?

Is a true West Indian man one who dangles gold bracelets around his wrists and thick gold chains around his neck?

Is a true West Indian one who listens exclusively to reggae, calypso, and steel pan music, one who finds no enjoyment in European classical music, who, indeed, derides it?

Does a true West Indian speak in dialect? Does he lose his *th*'s when he speaks? Does he says *dis* and *dat*, not *this* and *that*?

Does a true West Indian own his own home, but crowds six families into the rooms to pay the mortgage?

Does a true West Indian make education his religion but not for his self-enlightenment? Must he be a philistine, his goal monetary profit only?

"Anna does not speak like a true West Indian," some of her white colleagues contend.

"Anna isn't black," some of her African American colleagues counter.

The radio in Anna's car, the radio in her office, the radio in her apartment are tuned to QXR, the station for classical music in New York. She listens to Beethoven, Bach, Brahms, Handel, Mozart, Tchaikovsky, Sibelius. Opera is her first love. She does not know Italian, but she can sing by heart all the words from Act 1 of Verdi's *La Traviata*. She does not listen to reggae, she does not listen to calypso, but steel pan music fills her with nostalgia, brings her close to tears.

There are African Americans who accuse her of self-hatred, who say she is Eurocentric. Their only evidence is her manner of speaking, her taste in music and literature.

One and one make two. Two is not the same as one. She has ancestors from Africa, but from other places too.

. . . *either I'm nobody, or I'm a nation*. So says Walcott, the Nobel laureate from the Caribbean.

Geography, Anna believes, is a big part of destiny. Even if her African ancestors had not mated with other bloodlines, surely the geography of the islands would have changed them. Surely the psyche is affected when one is constantly surrounded by water; surely one's vision is projected outward. And if one interacts with the aboriginal Amerindians, and later with the Indians and Chinese who came as indentured laborers, one cannot be the same as one's ancestors from Africa. The European influence cannot be discounted, either.

She is all of these: African, Amerindian, Asian, European. She is Caribbean and not Caribbean, for she has lived many years in America. She is American and not American, for she has lived many years on her island.

She is critical of her mother's strictures, but her response to Singh troubles her. She worries that in spite of the years she has lived in New York, in spite of the years she has not lived on the island, she has not changed as much as she thinks.

Chapter 7

Her father is on the telephone when Anna sees him again. He is speaking to his friend, Dr. Neil Lee Pak, a specialist in internal medicine. Neil Lee Pak is Chinese, or sort of. He is part of the second generation of immigrants who came to the Caribbean fleeing tyranny and hunger in China and trusting in the promise of the British powers that life would be better in the colonies. The plan was that the Chinese would work in the cane fields that the Africans had abandoned after Emancipation, but the Caribbean sun proved an unbeatable foe for the Chinese. Under the broiling sun in the cane fields they died by the dozens. The survivors ran for shelter, built tin sheds, and made a living selling groceries. Most had arrived without female partners, so they took up with the black women. In two generations their children had gone from shopkeepers to professionals on the island: doctors, lawyers, engineers, teachers, entrepreneurs.

Neil Lee Pak is one of these children. His father was Chinese; his mother was a dougla—that is, she was part African and part South Asian Indian. Neil Lee Pak's cheekbones sit high on his face like those of his African ancestors. His eyes are attractively slanted like his Chinese forebears, his skin is a glistening brown with red undertones like his Indian grandmother. He is tall and slim, and his straight black hair is streaked with silver.

He never married, though he is close in age to Anna's mother. Beatrice likes him. He flatters her, tells her that she is one of the most beautiful women he has ever seen. She giggles like a schoolgirl when he tells her that.

Dr. Lee Pak never flatters Anna. When she was in college, he would ask her about her studies. When she began to work in the publishing industry, he would ask her about the books she was editing. He never comments on her figure or her face, but he notices the clothes she wears and is fond of asking her about the latest styles in New York.

Anna is certain Neil Lee Pak is gay. He demurs when he is asked about marriage or when the subject of children comes up. He has never had a steady girlfriend, though he is often seen with beautiful women, rarely with any one of them twice. The island has little tolerance for homosexuality and Anna thinks this is the reason why Neil Lee Pak pretends to have romantic interests in women.

Now Anna strains to hear what her father is saying to him, but his utterances are brief, most of them not actual words. He says "Ah huh" at least five times, each time nodding his head, his voice growing sadder and softer. He says, "Okay." He says, "Right." At last he says a whole sentence: "We'll be there first thing in the morning, Neil."

Anna does not know what her father said before his utterances were reduced to grunts, groans, and single words. She does not know how he explained her mother's condition to Neil, but her earlier anger flares up again. Neil is a friend; he is not the family doctor. In fact, her parents do not have a family doctor. They are never sick, and since they are never sick, they do not go to a doctor. Her mother has always laughed when Anna tells her that she has many doctors, that she goes to an internist once a year, that the internist refers her to an OB-GYN specialist once a year, that once a year she has a Pap smear, once a year she has a mammogram which her breast surgeon scrutinizes, and

once every five years, a colonoscopy on the recommenda-
tion of her gastroenterologist.

"You're courting illness," her mother once said with a
smirk, "going to so many doctors."

And there were many occasions when Anna has indeed
wondered if her mother was right. If she could have been
spared the many hours of anxiety she experienced each
time she waited for the results of a test to which she had
voluntarily submitted herself. "Preventive medicine," she
explained to her mother.

"That's why we have Neil," her mother said.

Though her parents claim Neil Lee Pak is not their doctor, he is their medical consultant. Over chess games her father and Neil play religiously every Wednesday night, he is
consulted about aches and pains. Without ever examining
her mother or her father, he writes prescriptions. Sometimes
her mother allows Dr. Lee Pak to press his thumb against
the vein in her wrist or to check her pulse at her neck, but
he is never allowed to examine her under her clothes, or,
God forbid, without her clothes.

"Your mother is a modest woman," John Sinclair says
with pride.

This practice her parents have of limiting themselves to
a superficial medical examination has worked for them so
far. Until now, until the tumor on her mother's breast ul-
cerated, broke through her skin, and bled on her husband's
vest, John and Beatrice have had no need of doctors.

"You're not taking Mummy to see Neil?" Anna asks her
father accusingly after he hangs up the phone. But when
he turns to face her, she regrets she has spoken to him so
harshly. His eyes are glazed, his shoulders are folded in-
ward, his lips have virtually disappeared. Just a straight line
appears where he has clamped his mouth shut.

"Neil recommends we see an oncologist," he says.

No more pretense that all is well, that her mother is merely tired, that it is merely the strain put on aged bones and flesh that has worn her down. The time has come. Her mother has decreed it so. The time has come to face the truth about the uneven swelling on his wife's left breast.

She wants to comfort him. "Neil is right," she says. "It's good that you called him. Did he give you the name of an oncologist?"

"He will make the appointment for us."

"Neil is a good friend." Anna squeezes her father's shoulder.

"Yes." He does not press her hand in return as he would have done at another time, under different circumstances. He does not smile.

"Medicine has advanced," Anna says, still trying to raise his spirits. "People survive with breast cancer." But her father has shrunk visibly before her eyes. His back is stooped; his head hangs low when he walks away.

At midday he comes out of the bedroom where he returned to be with her mother. For the second day, he instructs Lydia to serve them lunch in their room.

Lydia has to make two trips. John Sinclair does not like to have his food served on his plate. He requires separate dishes, each holding the different parts of his meal, the starch in one dish, the vegetables in another, the meat in another. So on the first trip to their room, Lydia brings plates, glasses, knives and forks, napkins, and serving cutlery; on the second trip, she brings the meal. When he serves himself from the dishes Lydia brings, John Sinclair puts the starch in one corner of his plate, and separates the vegetables from the meat. He maintains this arrangement on his plate while he eats. He has taught his daughter to eat her meal this way too, and like her father, Anna has difficulty sitting at the table with people who mix up the food on their plates while they eat. But unlike her father, Anna does not eat with a knife and fork. She eats the American way now, with a fork, letting her knife rest on the side of her plate. Her mother notices this, but does not remark on it. Her raised eyebrows are the only indication she gives that she is keeping score of the many ways Anna has changed, of how different she has become from the people who live on the island. But Anna has eaten too many meals in America. When she reverts to using the knife and fork, she is conscious of acting a part, of being a fraud, and it irritates her that in this instance her mother has won.

Before Lydia arrives today, Anna sets up the folding tables in her parents' room, in front of their armchairs. Lydia has made stewed chicken, rice, string beans, and the ground provisions that Mr. Sinclair likes: dasheen, cassava, and sweet potatoes. She says to Mrs. Sinclair, "I seasoned the chicken good. Plenty of garlic and thyme. Just a little bit of salt."

A weak smile crosses Mrs. Sinclair's lips.

Anna does not ask her parents if they want her to join them. They have not invited her to eat with them in their room. It is clear enough to her they wish to be alone.

Singh leaves at three. Before he leaves, he inquires again about her mother's health. Anna tells him her father will take her mother to the doctor.

"Tell madam to let me know if dere is anyting she want me to do. I come back day after tomorrow." He sticks his machete in his waistband, and then keeping his eyes lowered on it, he adds, "Miss Anna, I know about de orchids. Madam does tell me what to do, but I does already know what to do. I does just let madam talk. Madam like to talk."

Madam likes to boss you around, Anna thinks. Instead she says, "You're a good man, Singh."

Singh grins. "The wife say so."

Anna allows herself a moment of levity. "How much do you have to pay her to get her to say so, Singh?"

He laughs out loud. "Oh, Miss Anna, dat is funny." He swings his leg over the bar on his bicycle as if to demonstrate his youthful vigor. "Tell madam not to worry. I take care of de orchids for she."

Some time after three o'clock the phone rings. Lydia is in her room taking a nap. Anna answers the phone. It is Neil Lee Pak. He tells her that the appointment for her mother is at eight o'clock the next morning. To Anna's question about the qualifications of the oncologist, he answers curtly, "He was trained at Cambridge."

When Anna knocks on her parents' door to give them the message from Neil Lee Pak, her father invites her in. He is sitting on the edge of his side of the bed shuffling through a heap of papers. The drawer on his bedside table is open. Her mother is in her armchair reading a book. They both look up as she enters the room.

"Was that Neil?" her mother asks.

Anna gives her the time of the appointment.

"It would be nice if you could come with us, Anna," her father says.

"Of course I will, Daddy."

"Do you know where this doctor has his office, John?" her mother asks.

"Neil gave me the address."

"Well," her mother closes her book slowly, "it was just a matter of time. I had a long run."

"Don't speak like that." John Sinclair looks anxiously over at his wife. His hand is flattened against a tidy pile of the papers on the bed.

Anna is troubled by these papers. Her father has stopped working. He has no need for the sheaves of papers he once used to spend hours poring over. If these are not connected with work, what do they concern? Her heart sinks. They cannot be her mother's will! Now that they have finally faced the fact of her illness, they cannot be preparing for her death!

"It's time I faced reality, John," her mother says.

"*Death, a necessary end, will come when it will come*," her father replies.

Her mother looks at him inquiringly.

"*Julius Caesar*," Anna explains. It bothers her that her father should quote Shakespeare to her mother at a time like this. Why not say to her directly what he means?

"Oh," her mother says.

"It's time for both of us, Beatrice. Not just you. We both must face reality. We're not getting younger."

But her mother's reality is immediate and Anna wishes she can say to her that she should have faced it much earlier. She wishes she can say out loud that they would not have this crisis if her mother had gone to the doctor instead of sitting night after night cloistered in her bathroom, praying.

She is not an atheist. Perhaps an apostate. How many times has she prayed before stepping onto an airplane. That so many tons of steel could rise in the air is baffling to her, no matter the explanations about propulsion and jet engines. There are no atheists in foxholes.

Perhaps this is how her mother feels. Perhaps as she watches the tumor rise inexorably, swelling out her breast, prayer alone dams the panic that would send her running, screaming hysterically through the house. Prayer alone keeps her from bleeding over everyone she knows: her husband, her friends, Lydia, Singh. Prayer gives her the illusion of control when she has no control. As her fingers roll over her rosary beads, perhaps she believes that she has a direct link with the Blessed Virgin. That the Blessed Virgin is listening to her and to her alone, that at that moment she is interceding for her, persuading her son to answer the prayers that one Beatrice Sinclair, residing on such and such an island, on such and such a street, offers up to her.

Anna cannot begrudge her mother this illusion, this solipsism that to the religious is humility. She too turns to solipsistic prayer. There is no logical basis for her conviction that the plane she is about to board will crash if she does not say her special prayer. That *her* prayer, and her prayer alone, will save not only herself but all the other passengers.

She prays, but she flies, she travels by airplane. She wishes that her mother had done the same: that though she prayed, she would also have gone to the doctor when she felt that foreign hardness in her breast.

At four o'clock Lydia rings the bell for tea. She has set the table with place mats, dessert plates, cups and saucers, and cutlery. The knife is on the breadboard, next to the sweet bread, which Mr. Sinclair will slice for his wife. Lydia has learned the preferences of her employers and has prepared two small pots of tea in the kitchen. She knows Anna's father likes his tea strong so she puts three teabags in the hot water for him. Mr. Sinclair would prefer that she use loose tea, but Mrs. Sinclair likes the modern convenience of the teabags, especially since she wants her tea drawn much weaker than her husband's.

Anna comes into the kitchen to tell Lydia that her parents will have their tea in their bedroom. Like Singh, Lydia expresses concern. "They take lunch today in their room. Yesterday too. I hope is nothing bad."

Anna says her mother will go to the doctor tomorrow.

"I glad," Lydia says. She will make something special for breakfast in the morning for Mrs. Sinclair, she says. She puts the pots of tea, the coconut sweet bread, the guava jelly, the butter, the cups and saucers, and the cutlery on a tray and takes it to the Sinclairs in their bedroom. Anna has her tea at the table, in the breakfast nook.

At five o'clock Lydia leaves, but not before she has made sandwiches for the Sinclairs for their supper.

It is dark when John Sinclair emerges from his bedroom, though it is only half past six. But here, in the tropics, the sun drops suddenly out of sight drawing a thick curtain over the day. For too brief a moment the sky turns red, pink, orange, and purple, but soon it is an indifferent black. The greens, blues, and whites of the day disappear as if they had never existed at all. There is no twilight here, or the twilight merges so swiftly into the night that one can miss it completely if one has not stopped to notice. In the countryside, the birds are asleep in the trees by six; parents have called their children home.

Half past six is late for her father. Every evening, unfailingly at six, he appears at the table for dinner. He is a stickler for punctuality. Usually he is dressed and ready half an hour before it is time to leave for an appointment. He walks up and down the corridor, pausing only to announce to her mother how much time she has left before they must go. Her mother has told stories of the times he drove her around for blocks because they arrived too early for some event to which they had been invited. Often he would lose his way back, she said.

Anna is amazed that her mother has tolerated her father's obsession with punctuality. But her mother seems impervious to her husband's neurotic anxiety. She pays no attention to him. Sometimes she will say, "John, why don't you have a cup of tea?" Sometimes she will casually call out to him to help her with a difficult zipper. She is never flustered. She takes her time, but never more than the time her husband has told her she has remaining.

"You can never judge a marriage by what you see on the outside," Anna's father has said to her. "Only the husband and wife know what goes on behind the closed doors of their bedroom."

And so it must be true. Her parents' marriage has lasted forty years; her marriage to Tony lasted barely two.

Anna is editing the manuscript she has brought with her when her father comes out of the bedroom. She has a blue pencil in her hand and is leaning over the folding table in front of her, marking the top page of the manuscript. A smaller pile of pages is on the right side of the larger stack.

"Working?" her father asks as he approaches her.

Anna takes off the reading glasses that have slid down her nose and looks up at him. "Editing a new novel," she says.

"Seems it's going to take you awhile," he says, pointing to the shorter stack with the pages turned down.

"It's a new writer."

"Man or woman?"

"Woman," she says.

He sits next to her and stretches out his legs. "Seems like men aren't writing much these days. In my time men wrote books."

"They're still writing books," Anna says.

"You wouldn't know by what's in the bookstore."

"The laws of supply and demand," Anna says. She puts down the blue pencil. She can tell he is spoiling for an argument. He begins this way with her mother. His demeanor calm, his voice even, as he lures her mother into his web. "Women buy books," she adds, "and women want to know about women's lives."

"Men write about women's lives too," he counters.

"Women know more about women's lives."

He shakes his head. "I think it's all about that women's

movement. From what I can gather from the news in America, women have taken over."

"You can't be serious, Daddy."

"I'm just telling you what I read in those American magazines and what I see on American TV."

"You can't be saying there's some conspiracy cooked up by women to stop men from writing."

"From publishing," he says. "Not writing. How many male writers have you published in the last year, Anna?"

She knows if she tells him that last year only ten percent of the books on her list were novels by male writers, he would give her that self-satisfied, superior grin that usually quiets her mother. "Enough," she says. "I publish enough male writers."

"Ha!"

"I'm interested in good writing, whether it's written by a man or woman."

"What about this one? The one you're editing now. Is it good?" He raises his eyebrows and bends his head in the direction of the manuscript.

"It will be when I am done."

"Ha!" he says again.

He has caught her. She braces herself. He will say: If you can make this one good, why can't you improve a book by a male writer that is not so good? But she has him all wrong. He is not thinking about the plight of male writers. His mind is elsewhere. He slouches down on his seat and looks over to her. With the sweet tenderness of a loving father, he says, "You like your job, don't you, Anna?"

She melts.

She has not always liked her job, but she likes what she is doing now. She has pinned her hopes on this new writer. The manuscript is a literary novel and Windsor, convinced there is little profit in publishing literary work, is likely to pass on this one. But she believes she can help the writer shape her story to attract a wider audience of readers.

Yes, she says to her father. She loves being an editor.

"I used to love my job too," he says wistfully. "Now all that's behind me."

"You worked too hard," she says, her heart swelling with compassion for him. "You deserve to rest."

"I'll have time enough to rest when I am six feet under."

Anna draws her hand through her hair. Her father's comment disturbs her, but she does not betray her feelings. "How is Mummy doing?" she asks.

"She's sleeping. She didn't want dinner. I'm not hungry either."

"Lydia made sandwiches."

"I'll put them in the refrigerator," he says.

"No. I'll take care of that. Sit. Rest."

"Sit. Rest," her father repeats after her. "I'll be lying down, stretched out in a box, not sitting, when I rest six feet under."

"It'll be a long time before you are six feet under," Anna says patiently.

"I'm eighty-two. How many years do you think I have left?"

She gets it now. How foolish she was not to see what he wanted all along. He wants her pity. He is the old man who does not have long to live. She should have been suspicious when he ceded to her. His defense of male writers was just a detour. He hardly ever reads novels. She can't remember the last time he read fiction, except for P.G. Wodehouse, except to throw his head back and laugh at the antics of Jeeves and Bertie Wooster, secretly, she has always thought, getting perverse satisfaction, a sort of vicarious revenge, for the pomposity of the British colonial officers he was forced to endure. When he withdrew from their budding quarrel, she should have been alerted.

"It's Mummy who may not have long to live," she snaps.

He stares at her, alarm glazing his eyes. "Your mother. Of course, your mother."

A second later, her conscience would have warned her that she had judged him wrongly. A second later, she would have realized his talk of death was spurred on by his fears for her mother.

And even if it were not, even if just then he was bemoaning his own mortality, not thinking of her mother, didn't he deserve her sympathy?

Once, his days were full. Once, he worked late into the night, his head bowed low over stacks of papers. Once, the phone rang constantly for him. Once, important people stopped by the house seeking his advice. Then it all stopped abruptly and saving frogs intent on eating his fish became the highlight of his day.

CHAPTER 8

For more than twenty minutes now Anna and her father have been sitting in silence, she riddled with remorse for her harsh response to his innocent cry for her compassion. Surgery may save her mother, but nothing will add years to his life. *The moving finger once writ moves on.* Her mother is eleven years younger, eleven years her father will never see again.

"Life!" Her father scratches the top of his head where his hair no longer grows and lets out a loud guffaw. His eyes light up, but with a desperation that makes her look away. "It's so ironic."

"What's so ironic?" she asks, though she can guess his answer.

"Life. My life. It's so ironic."

Anna can pick out any number of stories he has told her about his life that would fit that description. Every time she comes home, he tells her the same ones. Sometimes within half an hour he has told her the same story twice. Always they are stories about his past. Always they begin this way: It's so ironic.

Anna believes he repeats these stories to keep his memory from slipping. He has, after all, built a reputation on an unerring photographic memory. He gave up his last consulting job when he was eighty because he had to use his notes, he said. He was a man known to defend his client in the Industrial Court on the island by speaking more than an hour at a time without once glancing at his notes.

Her mother, a practical woman, said he was foolish. Why give up the big retainer the company was offering for his services?

I forget sometimes, her father said. I'm not as sharp.

Her mother quoted to him from the Bible. Pride cometh before the fall, she said. Everybody forgets sometimes, she said. Now, you have a memory like ordinary people. Use notes like ordinary people.

But it was a matter of integrity with him, an integrity ingrained in him by a Presbyterian father whose own father had come to the island on a boat from Madeira, fleeing discrimination from the Roman Catholic Church. He will not lie. He will speak the truth even if it condemns him. He will say he saw blood on the vest her mother wore at night and admit he never confronted her. He will not try to pretty up his words with language that will spare his daughter the stark bluntness of his reasoning. He will say: Your mother and I respect each other's privacy.

He explained to her mother that he would not be as fast if he had to consult notes. Though he wasn't a lawyer, companies hired him because he was quick, he said; because he could rebut an argument that would take lawyers for the other side hours, if not days, to respond to, sorting through mounds of papers. It is a matter of integrity, he said to her mother when he turned down the retainers.

He will not read the letters Anna addresses to her mother; he will not allow his wife to read the ones Anna addresses to him. Anna can write in confidence to him; she can write in confidence to her mother. She can be certain that unless she stipulates it, what she writes will not be shared.

Her friends in New York are shocked when she tells them this. "Is it because your parents fight? Is it because they are so different from each other?"

It is because of her father's principles of integrity, honesty, and privacy, Anna tells them.

Anna's memory of the first harsh words her father said to her is from the day she read the card that was stuck in a floral arrangement her aunt had sent to her mother. She was seven years old. She had taken the card out of the envelope and, brandishing it above her head, skipped into her parents' room. "Look, Mummy. Auntie Alice sent a card from England." Her father snatched the card out of her hand and slapped her fingers. He never had cause to slap her again.

"We can't be prisoners in our own home. I won't be your jailer. You have the right to privacy. You have the right to know that what is yours is yours and that your mother and I will not interfere; we will not pry."

Letters lie open on the table and anywhere in their house. No one reads them unless they have been given permission.

Her mother has her own interpretation of her father's rule. "Don't be an eye servant," she used to say to her daughter when Anna disobeyed her in her absence.

To be called a servant of her mother's eye was the worst insult her mother could give her.

Privacy matters, her father said. Privacy matters so much he will guard his wife's secret even from herself.

"Yes, funny thing," her father is saying to her now. "Ironic. It was a lie that gave me my first job with the oil company, and it was a lie . . . No." His fingers brush the back of his other hand. "No. It was *a lot* of lies that got me to leave the government and work again for the oil company."

He is staring straight ahead into the darkness of the night. A frog croaks. A bird flutters its feathers. Two lizards scamper out of the bushes. *Swish, swish.* They race around the pond and disappear again in the grass. Lizards making love. The wind rises and sweeps past the tops of the orange tree. An orange drops on the ground. *Bup!* A cicada shrieks. Night sounds. Her father's voice drones on, mingling seamlessly into the nocturnal thrumming.

Anna leans back in her chair, closes her eyes, and listens. She can tell her father these stories herself, but it comforts her to hear them again, in his voice, to pretend that nothing has changed. That all is well. If she concentrates, she can delude herself into forgetting, even if only for an hour, that while her mother is sleeping in the bedroom not far from where they sit, a tumor is devouring cells in her breast.

Her father tells her that after he was accused of cheating on his Cambridge A-level chemistry exam, he lost faith in the promises of the colonial government. He packed his bags, intending to leave the city for good and try his luck in the oil fields.

Of course, the oil fields in the south of the island were owned by the British colonial government, he tells her, but the drilling was done by private companies from England, Europe, and America. He had learned that one of the companies was looking for an assistant to the chemist whose job it was to test the crude oil. Both his parents and the friend who told him about the job vacancy warned him it was highly unlikely the company would hire a local brown-skinned boy, but he was not dissuaded. "The foolish optimism of youth," he says to Anna.

Only one bus traveled to the village on the outskirts of the oil fields. It would drop him there around three in the afternoon and he would have to walk five miles into the fields to get to the building where the chemists worked. If he got the job, he would be given a place to sleep. If he did not get the job, he would have to walk back to the village and spend the night at the bus stop waiting for the morning bus. He was not worried. He was sure, given his knowledge of chemistry, he would get the job.

By the time he arrived at the weather-beaten wooden building that was the chemistry laboratory, he was hot, damp, and sweaty. His shirt was plastered to his back and rivulets of perspiration ran down the sides of his face. He knocked on the door. The Englishman who opened it took one look at him and shook his head. "The oil fields are further down the road, old fellow," he said.

John Sinclair explained he had not come to work in the fields; he had come for the job as assistant to the chemist. The Englishman lost no time informing him that the position had been filled. But perhaps because it was late (the bus had broken down and it was five o'clock by the time it was repaired, and past six and dark when her father arrived at the chemist's office, the sun having already descended below the horizon), or perhaps because the Englishman took pity on the crestfallen face before him, he decided to be generous.

"Tell you what, old fellow," he said, "there's a cot in the back room. You can spend the night. Leave tomorrow first thing and catch the bus back home."

It was all the opportunity he needed, her father says.

The Englishman took him through a long room where there were three large desks. The top of the desk in the front of the room was bare and it didn't take much for John Sinclair to conclude that the empty one and vacant chair behind it were to be occupied by the new hire. He knew the Englishman had lied, but accusing such a man of lying was dangerous in those colonial days, so he said nothing. The other two desks were crowded with all sorts of bottles, beakers, and tubes filled with foul-smelling thick, black oil. Sitting behind one of these desks was a young man, his skin tanned bronze.

"A French Creole," her father says. He does not hide his bitterness when he says this to Anna.

Technically, one had to have French blood to earn the title of French Creole. Technically, one had to be the progeny of the generation of French who brought their slaves from Martinique and Guadeloupe to the island when the king of Spain, distracted by the allure of gold in the Guianas, agreed that if the French cleared the bush, they could expand their plantations on his colony. But people had fallen into the habit of calling anyone who looked like a French Creole, a French Creole. Which is to say, someone with white skin, or, rather, someone with light brown skin that he could pretend was the result of generations of exposure to the sun. But everyone knew there were hardly any of these French Creoles left whose ancestors had not had relations with the Africans they had enslaved, relations not simply confined to the field, but extended to the bedroom, or, more often than not, to some dark corner between sugarcane stalks.

The man sitting behind the third desk was indeed a French Creole—his grandfather, an overseer on a slave plantation, being the only one who could claim pure French blood. When John Sinclair entered the room, the man did not say a word, but he swiveled his chair and followed John with his eyes as the Englishman led him to another room in the back of the office. There were two cots there. "You can sleep here with Anatole," the Englishman said.

It was not an arrangement that was acceptable to Anatole. When the Englishman left, Anatole made his position clear to John. "You don't expect we'd sleep in the same room, do you, old chap?" He pointed to the empty chair. "Make yourself comfortable."

"That French Creole thought he was hurting me," her father says, "but he did me a favor."

It turned out that later that night, unable to fall asleep on the uncomfortable desk chair, Anna's father began tinkering with the tubes of crude oil on the Englishman's desk. Soon he found himself completing the tests that the Englishman had left undone. In the morning, just before dawn, careful not to wake up Anatole, he left the building and began the long walk to the bus stop. The sun was beating down on his head when the Englishman tooted his horn and sped past him, sending a cloud of dust that settled on his clothes. Less than an hour later, as he was nearing the bus stop, he heard the horn again. This time the Englishman stopped his car. "I say, old fellow, still interested in the job?"

The Englishman had seen the test results. They were completed with such accuracy and with such detail he knew immediately that the work had been done by John and not by Anatole. He had hired Anatole as a favor to the head of the company who was married to one of his relatives. He soon realized his mistake: not only did Anatole lack the credentials, he also had no aptitude for chemistry.

"Strange, eh?" Her father chuckles in his peculiar way between laughter and astonishment. "I wouldn't have met your mother if I didn't leave the oil fields. And I wouldn't have been able to give her the comfortable life she has grown accustomed to if I had not taken the job in the first place and gone back years later to work for that very same oil company again."

They are quiet, he musing on his past, she drinking in the night air. A sudden loud noise startles them.

Plop! It is followed by another. *Plop!*

"Frogs!" Her father jumps up and walks swiftly over to the light switch on the wall of the veranda and turns it on. "Now they'll go after my fish."

"There are two in there," Anna says. The frogs are splayed out in the water, their moist dark green skin glistening in the electric light, their back feet scissoring, their front feet pushing them forward through the water.

"The male frog probably followed the female frog," her father explains. He grins. "Just like me and your mother."

"How romantic!" Anna says.

One of the frogs has stretched his front limbs over the back of the other frog and is mounting her. "Look!" her father says. "See that!" Anna peers down in the pond but the frogs, as if sensing an audience, disappear under the water.

"I'll take them to the river tomorrow." Her father makes a half step to turn away and then changes his mind. He glances down at the pond again. The frogs have resurfaced, one on top the other. "Life." He shakes his head. "It goes on and on and the old like your mother and me must make room for the young." He rubs his hand across his brow. "Poor Beatrice."

Life. Two frogs copulating remind him of how little time he has left, how even less time perhaps remains for his wife.

"I think Mummy always suspected it could happen to her," Anna says. "It happened to Granny. But Mummy will be all right. I know it. I feel it in my bones."

"It's just so strange. Don't you see?"

There is something in his voice that signals to Anna that they are not speaking about the same thing.

"The irony." He is chuckling again. "That same Englishman who didn't want to hire me because my skin is brown was the very one who, years later when I was working for the government, tried to do his best to get me to come back to the company. And guess why?" He grimaces. "Yep. Because my skin is brown. Imagine that, Anna."

He stands up. He's tired, he says. It's been a long day. "Ready to turn in?" he asks Anna. She says she will sit in the veranda a little longer. "Don't forget to switch off the lights," he tells her. She says she won't forget. He leaves, repeating under his breath in wonderment, "Imagine that."

CHAPTER 9

I *magine that*. Anna does not have to imagine. It was all too real for her. The Englishman came to their house and nothing was the same after her father accepted his offer—not their lives, not her life.

It is her father's story but it is her story too, for in the end she was left without a country, without a place she could call home. It was not hard afterward, after those years in the Englishman's country, to leave her island for America, to turn her back on all that was a part of her. Fruit, which before that time in the Englishman's country, she could identify blindfolded by their smell: mango, sapodilla, pommerac, chennette, five fingers, doungs, sieca figs. Wild flowers, which before that time, blindfolded, she could name by touch: crown of thorns, cup of gold, firecracker, morning glory bush, chain of love, shrimp plant, spider lily. Birds, which before that time, blindfolded, she could distinguish by ear: kiskadee, ramiea, picoplat, semp, chikichong.

"Pick a house, any house, it's yours," the Englishman said when he called. "Bring your wife and daughter. Drive around. We'll meet for tea at the clubhouse. My wife will come."

The Englishman's country was not far away from where her father got his first job. It was up a hill, five miles from the oil fields where black men in tall rubber boots sank knee-deep in the soil, their bodies splattered with the thick foul-smelling oil that no amount soap would remove. Five miles from where black women emerged at dawn, leaving their crying babies behind to make the trek up the hill to clean toilets, wash dirty laundry, and wipe snot off the noses of sickly babies, not theirs. Five miles from where little black children played on slippery sand. Five miles from where oil spread like a tablecloth across the surface of the sea and shimmered with rainbow colors. Five miles from where dead pelicans bobbed in the glistening waves.

Along the road to the Englishman's country the land was dotted with statuaries, giant iron dinosaurs, their stunted wings frozen in flight, cracks snaking down their sides, the spaces between them stained orange with rust.

"Pumps," her father said when her mother asked.

"Why aren't they pumping?"

"They shut down the ones that are close to the road," he explained.

"But why?"

"They could be dangerous. They could cause a fire, and the houses . . ." He pointed to the road in front of them. Above, where it climbed the hill, metal roofs glittered in the sun between a thick forest of trees.

"Ah," her mother said, blinded by the allure of the glittering roofs. "Ahhh."

But Anna was not blinded by the glittering roofs. She had read the reports in the newspaper. The pumps that were inactive were not only those close to the road; almost everywhere on the oil fields pumps were not moving. The drillers had hit hard rock. Motors caught on fire and burned out. There was no more oil on the island.

"Poppycock!" the Englishman said. "Why would we hire you if that were true?"

Her father did not argue with him.

"You'll be part of the administration," the Englishman said. "Personnel manager."

At the time, her father was working for the colonial government in the Ministry of Labor. He had left the English chemist years ago. Nine months was all he had managed to endure in the oil fields before he began to pine for the city, for the company of his family and friends, for a nightlife that offered more than shots of rum with the local drillers, crouched around a flambeau dug into the earth, the flames casting an eerie sheen on their oil-splattered bodies. He was young, just twenty. He wanted more.

He took the test for the civil service and passed with distinction. He was given a job in the Ministry of Labor, the first of the ministries the colonial government had opened to locals for positions in management, not a capricious decision. England is an island, miles away from the Caribbean; if trouble came, it would come from the workers. Local men in management would be a paean to appease the workers.

By the time John was hostage to Beatrice's swaying hips, following her like a lovesick puppy dog for blocks along the main street in the city, he was already gaining the admiration of his boss, a colonial nearing retirement age, for his talent at labor negotiations. He was in his thirties when he accompanied the Minister of Labor to the annual conference of the International Labour Organization in Geneva. He was not yet forty when he negotiated contracts between the workers on the sugarcane estates and their employers. When the oil field workers unionized, he was the one they trusted to mediate their contract.

He got noticed. Sitting around the table representing his oil company was the very Englishman who had lied to him. The position is filled, he had said. But by the next morning the Englishman was forced to admit that skin color had nothing to do with the making of a chemist.

Now he was offering to triple her father's salary. The perks? A house for his wife and a new car. "Not a Rolls

Royce or a Bentley, you know." He slapped John Sinclair on his back. "A Vauxhall, old man."

It was the car her father had planned to buy.

He would have a chauffeur too, the Englishman said. Mrs. Sinclair would be free to use the chauffeur whenever she wanted. After the chauffeur dropped Mr. Sinclair off at the office, of course.

Of course.

Now, in their new Vauxhall, the Sinclairs were on their way to pick out a new house. Past the silent pumps, the road wound around a bend and was then blocked by a long iron pole that ran across it. On one side of the road, the pole was attached to a lever operated by an officer in a stiff khaki uniform who sat on a white wooden stool. His partner, similarly attired, also sat on a stool, on the other side of the road. There was no covering above them, nothing to protect them from the full force of a fierce sun except for short-brimmed officers' hats that barely shaded their eyes. Their dark skin, blackened like burnt toast, glistened with sweat. There was a spreading tree nearby, and perhaps this was where they took shelter from time to time, but they were sitting on their stools when John Sinclair brought his car to a stop. Both got up immediately and approached the vehicle. One officer went to the driver's side, the other to the passenger's side.

"Your pass?" the officer on the driver's side demanded.

He didn't have a pass, her father explained. They were here to meet the Englishman for tea.

Her mother leaned across her father, her arm crushing his chest. "And to pick out our house," she said, barely able to contain her excitement.

The officer was unmoved. "You must have a pass." A trail of sweat trickled down the side of his face. "You can't go up the hill without a pass." He walked back to the wood stool at the side of the gate. Under the stool was a notebook. He picked it up, flipped through the pages until he found the place he was searching for. He read what was written on the page, looked over at the Sinclairs, rubbed his eyebrows, looked back down at the book, pursed his lips, and returned to the car.

Her mother had turned to the officer on the passenger's side of the car. She was still trying to explain their presence, their right to go beyond the pole. "You don't understand," she was saying. "We're going to live here."

The officer was not impressed. "You need a pass," he repeated.

The officer with the notebook was now standing next to her father. "Look here," John Sinclair addressed him in his best officious voice, "Mr. Hathaway must have left a note. You must have something in that notebook."

The officer drummed the notebook on his knuckles. It was closed except for the place where he had stuck his finger between the pages. He shook his head. "Like my partner say, you need a pass."

"Let me see what you have there."

"It have nothing in this notebook about you people coming to tea," the officer said adamantly.

"I can't believe . . . What does it say on that page where you have your finger?"

The officer opened the book. "If you want to know, if it go make you feel better, it have something about Mr. and Mrs. Sinclair, but nothing about you."

This was just the beginning. Even their own people knew they didn't belong. It was their island, but up the hill was the Englishman's country.

The Englishman brought his wife to meet them. She came with an armful of catalogs. "You'd want to select furniture for your house," she said.

"Yes, that's another thing," the Englishman said. "You can furnish the house however you wish. It's on the company."

"Scandinavian," his wife recommended. "It's all the rage here. Pick it out now and Hugh can order it. You will, won't you, Hugh?"

"The furniture will arrive before you move in," the Englishman promised.

That was the way life was for the Europeans who lived on the hill: a house, Scandinavian furniture, a brand-new car, a chauffeur, servants. Then there was the club, the swimming pool, the golf course, the tennis courts. None of this meant for the locals. But times were changing; there were rumblings about independence. The Europeans needed their local man.

The house her mother finally chose was a two-story concrete building with large rooms. There was a shaded porch on the first floor and behind it, the living room and dining room, side by side, separated by a corridor, and in the back, a well-equipped kitchen and a laundry room. Upstairs were the master bedroom with its own bathroom, a bedroom for Anna, a bedroom for guests, and a study for her father.

The house was almost twice as large as their previous home; it had more rooms than any of the houses of her mother's friends. But among the houses on the hill, it was not extraordinary. Her mother could have picked any house and the size would have been the same. What distinguished this one, however, was the sweeping driveway that began at a little-used road not far from the main road. Halfway up the driveway, on one side of the lawn, was a giant, spreading lignum vitae, tree of life.

"Used for syphilis," her father murmured, lobbing off an innuendo that did not pass unnoticed by her mother.

She clicked her teeth and admonished him. "That's unkind, John."

"We didn't have syphilis before they came," her father retorted.

Her mother was not to be dissuaded. "Look at the flowers. They planted it for the flowers."

Between dark green leaves at the tips of the branches of the lignum vitae, clusters of blue flowers bloomed in profusion.

"And for syphilis," her father declared.

On the other side of the driveway was a flaming flamboyant tree, its delicate orange blossoms blanketing the lawn. A wood bench circled its thick trunk and leafy wide branches formed an umbrella above it. Mrs. Sinclair said she could not have dreamed of a more perfect house, in a more perfect setting.

For four years the Sinclairs lived in that house on the hill, and at the end of those four years, Anna no longer had a country.

Two incidents: the first at the swimming pool.

They had just settled in. It was midday on a school holiday. The men were at work, the women and children at home. Anna was bored. Outside the sun was relentless, the air still and turgid. "Go for a swim," her mother urged her.

At the club, next to the pool, women with various shades of hair—blond, red, black, brown—sat at tables under the shelter of enormous patio umbrellas. They stared when Anna crossed the lobby of the clubhouse and walked toward the changing room. Chatter and laughter died down in waves. Only the squeals and shouts of children remained. "Canon ball!" Loud splashes. Laughter.

One woman got up. The heels of her shoes clattered noisily against the tiled floor as she made her way to a closed door at the back of the pool. She knocked and a brown-skinned man appeared. They exchanged words and then, leaving the woman behind, the man signaled Anna to approach him.

"Are you lost, miss?" he asked her.

"I've come to take a swim."

"The pool is for the residents, miss."

To be fair, he was gentle, Anna told her mother later. He didn't raise his voice or try to embarrass her. "Actually, I think he was embarrassed for me. Here he was a brown-skinned man having to put out a brown-skinned girl from the white people's club. Of course I told him who I was, and I said my name in a loud enough voice for the women to hear me."

Murmurs rose from the chairs nearby. *The new colored family.*

When Anna emerged from the changing room, the pool was empty. Not a single child, not a single adult, remained in the water. That night, they drained the pool and refilled it with fresh water.

The second incident.

"Must I change schools?" Anna's eyes were red from crying. "All my friends are in my school. I'll have no friends in the new school."

"You'll make new friends," her mother said.

The nearest high school to the Englishman's country was ten miles away. A company van collected the children of the residents on the hill and they were driven to this private school run by European nuns. There were twelve children in the van on the first day, ten on the second, four on the third, only a thin boy, short for his age, and Anna on the fourth.

The Englishman offered a solution. He did not admit, of course, that the problem was caused by the people on the hill. He spoke as a friend, a father who had a teenager of his own. "My daughter would be furious if I took her out of her school," he said.

He arranged for Anna to return to her old school in the city by the company's tiny twin engine plane. Each morning at six, a car arrived at the home of the Sinclairs to take Anna to the airport. At the airport in the city, another car rolled up to meet the plane and Anna was driven to her old school. At the end of the school day, the car returned. There was no time for friends. And even when there was a possibility of time—say, the hour classes broke for lunch—her classmates could not understand how a local girl came to be treated as an English girl, or a French Creole. They were suspicious. *Roast breadfruit*, they called her. Black on the outside and white on the inside.

Alone in the veranda, Anna sighs, remembering. In the background she hears the shuffling of feet. Her father has returned. "Don't forget to turn off the lights," he says.

"Couldn't sleep?"

"Your mother's asleep," he says.

She decides to take a chance and tell him about her mother's restless nights. "Mummy wakes up in the night, you know."

In the shadow cast by a pillar in the veranda, her father's face is distorted, half illuminated by the electric light, half in darkness. "She burns candles," he says.

"So you knew?"

"She's my wife," he says.

He is wearing an old pair of pajamas. They have faded with washings, but as he stands there, a sad-faced harlequin in patched-up clothes, Anna glimpses the man he was, the man he still is, a gentleman. A man of integrity, a man of uncompromising principles.

CHAPTER 10

Blinding sunshine and it is just quarter to six. Birds sing, leaves swish back and forth with the breeze, fruit fall to the ground. Beyond the gate, the sounds of cars rumbling by. They slow down at the speed bump on the road her father had petitioned the Ministry of Works to install. A car slaps heavily onto the asphalt after the rise and fall of the speed bump and the driver guns the engine in defiance. Young people. Music blares from the car, fades, and leaves a trail, like smoke, that insinuates itself through her open window.

Even at this hour, so early in the morning. Life.

Inside, her mother stirs, footsteps padding on the carpeted floor. It must be so, her father says: the old must make way for the young. Frogs copulate, make tadpoles. Tadpoles grow up to be frogs. The parent frogs die. He too will die. Her mother too will die.

Thou were not born for death, immortal bird / No hungry generation tread thee down.

There is much to resolve, Anna thinks, much to finish. Her mother's life cannot end now. There are new medicines, new procedures. Most survive beyond five years. But her mother's tumor is large; it has broken through her skin. It bleeds.

The bedroom door opens and shuts. Along the corridor, more footsteps. Her father's. He's dressed, ready to leave. His footsteps advance and retreat, advance and retreat, advance. He is nervous, scared.

The bell at the front gate rings. It is Lydia. She is early. "I come just in case she need me." Anna hears her say this to John Sinclair when he opens the gate.

Lydia is already in the kitchen, tying her apron around her waist, when Anna comes out of her bedroom. "What would Mummy do without you?" she says to Lydia.

Her father grunts. "Lydia likes working for us."

Lydia grins. Perfect white teeth against polished black skin.

"Don't you, Lydia?" John Sinclair presses her. "Don't you like working for us?"

Lydia continues to smile. She does not answer him.

"I'm sure Mummy will appreciate your coming so early," Anna says. "It's really considerate of you."

"I happy to do it," Lydia replies.

"You can leave early," John Sinclair tells her. "You don't have to stay till five."

Forever the labor negotiator. It is no longer his job, yet he still thinks in these terms: fair wages for fair labor.

"I make Mrs. Sinclair a good breakfast," Lydia says. "They have ripe oranges on the tree. I make her fresh juice."

When she is out of earshot, Anna chastises her father. "You could have been gracious. Lydia cares about Mummy. You could have thanked her for coming early."

"We pay her for eight hours," he says. "More than that is overtime."

When Lydia rings the bell for breakfast, Beatrice Sinclair comes out of her room. Not a shadow of fear or worry mars the smile on her lips. She is wearing white pants and a pretty white top made out of gauzy material that drapes softly over a solid white lining. Tiny red roses are scattered across it and down the middle is a row of tiny buttons.

"Mummy!" Anna rushes out of the kitchen to greet her in the corridor. "How beautiful you look!" The words fall back on her ears, false, exaggerated, her gaiety forced. Her mother is dressed for the doctor, a doctor who will confirm—there is no doubt—that she has breast cancer, perhaps inoperable breast cancer.

"You think so?" Her mother glances from Anna to her husband. She smiles, a coquettish expression inappropriate for a woman her age. So Anna thinks.

This is how the morning begins, her father officious, her mother coquettish, she throwing a bouquet of compliments, and all of them desperately trying to conceal an undeniable truth that they will soon have to face.

"Come, Beatrice," John Sinclair says. He is already seated in his place, at the head of the table. "Sit." He pats the back of the chair to the right of his own.

"Well, what do you think, John?" Beatrice is still standing. She twirls around. "How do I look?"

"You look as you always look to me," he says. "Beautiful."

"Chaa!" Her mother snaps her lips and waves him away but she is clearly pleased. "Your father gives me the same answer no matter what I wear," she says to Anna and sits down.

"That blouse really suits you," Anna says.

"I thought it would be suitable." Her mother fingers the tiny buttons that run down the front of the blouse.

Anna feels a knot rise in her throat. The buttons will make it easier for the doctor. Her mother will only have to slide them out of their openings. No wrestling with zippers, no tugging over her head, no mussing up her hair.

John Sinclair too is affected. He cannot miss what she means. But Beatrice has left him no room for pity. She has spoken in practical terms. Suitable, she said. And all John can offer is a weak smile in response and something about Lydia coming early to pick oranges.

"Is that true, Lydia?" Beatrice calls out to Lydia, who is about to leave the kitchen to have her breakfast in her room.

"Oh, Mrs. Sinclair," Lydia says, her voice tremulous.

"What's the matter with you, Lydia?" Beatrice's eyebrows merge. Anna cannot tell if she is irritated or pretending to be so.

"Oh, Mrs. Sinclair." Lydia turns away from her and faces the sink.

"What's the matter with Lydia?" Beatrice asks her daughter.

"She came early because she wanted to make fresh orange juice for you."

"Oh!" Beatrice says, almost in a whisper, as she takes in the full significance of Lydia's gesture.

"Here, I'll pour some for you," Anna says.

Beatrice takes the glass of juice from her daughter's hands. She looks across the room toward the kitchen. "Thank you, Lydia."

Lydia, still with her back turned, murmurs, "I did want to do it for you, Mrs. Sinclair."

Anna's father reaches for the bread. It is crusty, and when he cuts it with the serrated bread knife, it makes a wholesome grating sound that breaks the somber tension at the table.

"So," Beatrice says, buttering the slice her husband has passed to her on the breadboard, "what about Neil? Is he meeting us here or has he given you directions to the doctor? What's his name, the doctor Neil recommended?"

John Sinclair clears his throat. "Dr. Ramdoolal. Neil says he will meet us at Dr. Ramdoolal's office."

"What about you, Anna?" Beatrice turns to her daughter. "Will you come?"

"Of course, Mummy."

Her mother smiles wryly. "You didn't expect this on your vacation, did you?"

Anna swallows the knot that clogs her throat.

Neil Lee Pak arrives before they do. Anna's father is speaking to the receptionist when he emerges from a back room, clearly Dr. Ramdoolal's office. He has a grim expression on his face. He strides across the room and immediately starts a quarrel with her mother. "Beatrice, Beatrice. What can I do with you, Beatrice? All that nonsense about not wanting me to examine you."

"Not now, Neil." Her mother takes the chair her husband offers her.

"God knows I tried."

"Please, Neil." Her mother brushes him away.

"How many times have I asked you to come in for a proper examination?"

"You gave me a proper examination, Neil."

"Only what you'd let me do."

"Enough, Neil," her mother says firmly.

Neil Lee Pak turns to John Sinclair. "A stubborn woman," he says.

"Stubborn as a mule," he replies.

Her mother stands up. "Anna, come with me to the bathroom."

Anna has had three glasses of orange juice at breakfast, so she is happy to accompany her mother to the bathroom. It took them almost an hour to get to Dr. Ramdoolal's office, driving bumper to bumper through traffic that snarled around the bends in the highway. Anna knows that it is for her mother's sake that her father has not gloated. When he insisted they leave directly after breakfast, her mother protested. "What if Dr. Ramdoolal's office is closed? What shall we do then? Just sit in the car?"

Normally, the drive to the city takes twenty minutes, but John Sinclair correctly estimated that it would take longer in the morning when people were on their way to work.

"Then let's go later when the traffic dies down," her mother proposed reasonably. But John Sinclair, ever punctual, didn't want to take that chance.

"Come, Anna," her mother beckons her. She leads Anna across the room with the same calm self-assurance with which she entered Dr. Ramdoolal's office, her back erect, a smile plastered on her face. But no sooner does the bathroom door close behind her than her face crumples, her knees buckle. Anna grasps her shoulders and steadies her.

Her mother's eyes are welled with tears; her lips are trembling. "I . . . I . . ." she begins. She cannot continue. What follows is a bleating moan.

There is a stool beneath the sink in the bathroom. Anna pulls it out and lowers her mother gently onto it. "Tell me, Mummy. What?"

"I'm scared, so scared, so afraid." Anna has to bend down to hear her.

She wants to hug her mother, put her arms around her shoulders and comfort her. But they do not hug in her house. Stiff upper lip. Self-control. Discipline over the emotions. These are the values they believe in. Yet the trembling has increased on her mother's lips. No tears flow, but tremors course down the sides of her face. Her hands are shaking. Anna takes them and cups them between her own.

"I'm so afraid," her mother says again.

Anna knows what terrible shadows dance before her mother's eyes. "It won't happen to you like it happened to your mother," she says. "I won't let it." I, she says, as if she has the power to control her mother's fate. I, *Anna, will make certain that you will not suffer the way your mother suffered.*

"I don't want him to see," her mother is saying.

"Who, Mummy? What don't you want him to see?"

"The doctor. I don't want him to see it."

When the doctor removed the raw meat from her grandmother's breast, she howled like a wild animal caught in an iron vise. And the stench! "It was horrible, Anna," her aunt said.

Her mother begins to sway. The tremors on her hands and face increase. Anna stretches her arms across her mother's shoulders and presses her fingers into her flesh. It is the extent of an embrace she allows herself. "Shhh. Don't be afraid, Mummy. I'm here," she croons.

"He can't, Anna," her mother whispers. "I won't let him."

"It's not the same. Dr. Ramdoolal will help you."

"I won't let him touch me."

In the morning, her mother was in control, smiles all around at breakfast, a kind word to Lydia. She had prettied up herself, color on her cheeks and lips, red roses on a diaphanous white blouse with buttons down the front for the convenience of the doctor.

Stiff upper lip. Some say the people on the island have inherited this from the British colonial masters. Stiff upper lip that turned a tiny island into an empire, master of most of the world. Stiff upper lip that defeated despair when the Blitz almost destroyed their capital. But John Sinclair disagrees. The British left behind systems for a democratic government, for laws, for education, but he will not credit them for the discipline with which he has conducted his life. He has inherited this from his father, and his father from his enslaved African mother, and she from hers. His theories are Darwinian: "Do you think my African grandmother and the other Africans would have survived if they were not the strongest? Do you think they would have lived to bear children and their children to bear other children

if they didn't have discipline, if they didn't know how
to control their emotions, to keep them in check? If they
didn't know how to take the lash, the iron bit in their
mouths, and keep their pain bound and gagged, hidden
from those who waited for their fall, their collusion in the
slaver's demonic intent to turn man into animal? If they
didn't have the fortitude to will themselves to live another day?"

Anna was a child when he began telling her this.

"We were the seasoning station," he said. "They brought
the Africans here, to our islands, to be broken in, to be
tamed before they were taken to the American continent. If
the Africans they captured did not die in the blistering heat
of the sugarcane fields, the slave owners knew the ones that
remained were among the best, the strongest, the most re-
silient; they would survive the cotton fields in Georgia. We
are the ones they could not break. We are the progeny of the
ones they had to leave behind on the islands, the ones they
could not tame for Georgia, the ones who refused to die.
We know discipline, restraint, we know order. Discipline
is in our blood."

Discipline is in her mother's blood too. She puts on a
face to meet the faces she must see at breakfast: her husband, her daughter; Lydia, her helper. To them she signals
no fear. Optimism in fact. All will be well when she sees
the doctor. At the doctor's office, she brushes away the
simpering Neil, softening his guilt by passing it on to her,
chastising her for what he should have insisted she do. He
is a medical doctor after all. Enough! she says. Only in the
bathroom does she let slip that face she has so carefully prepared. Tears well, tremors snake up her arms.

"You have to show it to him," Anna says. "You can't hide
it anymore."

Beatrice Sinclair bites her lower lip. "Silly me," she says.

Stiff upper lip. "Silly old me." She emerges from the bathroom, her face restored.

The nurse comes in. Dr. Ramdoolal is ready for Mrs. Sinclair.

"Anna should go with Beatrice," Neil Lee Pak says to Anna's father. "Woman business." He says this as if John Sinclair has not known his wife's woman business for years. But John Sinclair yields to him. If he has noticed the tiny red tributaries crisscrossing his wife's eyes when she returned from the bathroom, he has decided to say nothing. Privacy is their code of honor, proof of their loyalty to each other. Proof of their love. He will stay with Neil Lee Pak in the waiting room, he says.

Anna is relieved when she sees Dr. Ramdoolal. He is not a young man, but she did not expect to see a young man. A middle-aged man perhaps, and perhaps he is. His face is unlined, his skin color vibrant; it has not lost that rich brown hue of many young Indians on the island. But his black hair has turned white, shocking white indeed, and there is not even the slightest hint of levity in his dark brown eyes. This is a doctor who has witnessed human suffering, she thinks. He will understand her mother's fears.

Dr. Ramdoolal takes barely a minute to examine Mrs. Sinclair. He asks her to unbutton her blouse. He sees the tumor, the size of a lemon, pushing out over her bra. He grimaces.

He does not need her to take off her bra, he says. He has seen all he needs to see. He asks if there is also a lump under her arm. Beatrice nods.

"Let's take a look." Dr. Ramdoolal stretches out his arm to help her remove her blouse. She recoils. Anna mumbles an apology and slides the blouse off her mother's arm.

"It's only on one side," her mother says. She lifts up her left arm.

The tumor is the size of a plum.

Dr. Ramdoolal grits his teeth. "You can button up," he says.

Her mother's trembling has subsided; her secret is out. "How long, doctor?" she asks. She rebuttons her blouse with steady fingers.

"It's cancer," Dr. Ramdoolal says, matching her directness. "But I suppose you know that."

"My mother died of breast cancer. How much time do you think I'll have?"

"It depends," he says.

"Depends?" Anna's mouth drops open.

"There are treatments, but your mother has let this go too long. You know that as well as I do, don't you, Mrs. Sinclair?"

"Two years," her mother says. "I've felt it for two years."

Anna feels faint.

"That would be my calculation," Dr. Ramdoolal says. "Maybe more."

"So what happens next?" her mother asks.

"I will discuss that with you in my office. It will be good if your husband is there with you."

"And my daughter?"

Dr. Ramdoolal nods his assent.

Anna needs to sit down. There is a chair in the room, but she cannot leave her mother's side now, not when her mother has managed to summon up her strength to look Dr. Ramdoolal fully in his face as he gives her that inconclusive answer. It depends, he said. It depends on what?

"Depends on how she reacts to the treatment," Dr. Ramdoolal says to John Sinclair when they are all sitting in front of him, in his office, Anna in the middle between her mother and father.

He is encouraging at first. Mrs. Sinclair is lucky. She has what is called a neglected primary. It is a slow-growing cancer. "I see many cases like this in postmenopausal women," he explains. "The ovaries have shut down. The baby-making hormones have dried up. There's nothing there to feed the tumor. It will grow, though, but it won't spread as fast as if it were aggressive. Some women last into old age with lumps bigger than your wife's still in their breasts. Something else kills them, not the cancer. The fact that the tumor has not killed Mrs. Sinclair in all those years she has felt it means it is not aggressive."

"*Two* years," Anna corrects him. Two years are already too many. She will not let him blame her mother for more. She will not let him get away with *all those years*.

Dr. Ramdoolal, who has managed to avoid eye contact with any of them as he speaks, looks directly at Anna, surprise, tinged with annoyance, registering on his face. "Pardon me?" He lifts his eyebrows. It is obvious he is not accustomed to being interrupted.

Anna turns to her father, pointedly addressing him: "Mummy says she has felt the lump on her breast for two years now."

John Sinclair lowers his eyes to his hands. He has not missed his daughter's unspoken accusation. How long has it been since he saw the protrusion on his wife's breast? *The size of a lemon!* The size of a lemon is too large for him to have avoided noticing the tumor on his wife's breast.

"Your wife is not exceptional," Dr. Ramdoolal says, sensing John Sinclair's discomfort. "Some women wait more than two years after a lump is visible before they come to see me. They pray."

John Sinclair frowns at his wife. Anna pats her shoulder.

"Yes, that's what they do instead of going to the doctor. They pray," he says drily. He is speaking to John Sinclair as if he already knows of Beatrice's nighttime vigil at her makeshift altar in her bathroom. "We live in a country that believes in miracles. I might as well not have gone to medical school." He shuffles through the papers on his desk. "Not a week passes before I see someone in my examining room who claims he has seen God. What's that thing, Mr. Sinclair?" He pauses and places his palm flat on the papers. "The name they have for the bleeding on the hands and feet? Yes, the stigmata. I had a man who came to see me. Big holes in his hands and feet. He had driven a nail through them, but he swore to me he had done nothing. He said he woke up one morning and he was bleeding. Like Jesus Christ on the cross, he said. Now people give him money to pray to Jesus Christ for them. But they won't come to me. They prefer to give their money to that charlatan. Then, when it's too late, they want *me* to work a miracle for them."

Dr. Ramdoolal is not a Christian. He does not believe in the Christian God. If he allows himself to believe at all in the supernatural, it is in the gods of the Hindu temple where he sometimes prays.

"And that statue in Arima that started crying? Did you hear about that, Mr. Sinclair? La Divina Pastora." Dr. Ramdoolal plucks out a sheet of paper from the pile on his desk and puts it aside. "Not that I have anything against prayers. I pray myself, but . . ."

"Miracles happen every day," Beatrice says quietly.

"Yes," Dr. Ramdoolal replies. "Yes, miracles happen. But that tumor has been growing for years in your breast, Mrs. Sinclair."

"Two years without medical treatment." Anna does not back down. "And yet she is here. Alive."

"Your mother is fortunate."

"The power of prayer," Beatrice Sinclair says.

Dr. Ramdoolal shakes his head. "I wish you'd come to see me earlier, Mrs. Sinclair."

John Sinclair is sitting at the edge of his chair. His spine is ramrod straight. The muscles in his neck are strained. He has left his wife and his daughter to do battle against Dr. Ramdoolal's implied accusations. But Dr. Ramdoolal was looking at him when he said he wished Beatrice had come to see him earlier. He was accusing him, not Beatrice.

"Can you help my wife now?" he asks, his only defense.

"There are some things we can do," Dr. Ramdoolal says. "First, she'll need chemo."

"Chemo?" John Sinclair's back gets stiffer.

"Chemotherapy. We give her the drugs intravenously. The chemo will kill the cancerous cells."

"And that is it?" Beatrice looks at him hopefully.

"Oh no, Mrs. Sinclair. That's just the beginning. This disease is systemic. The tumor presents in your breasts, but tiny cancerous cells may be flowing through your body looking to attach themselves to an organ and form a new lump. The cancer is in your lymph nodes. I saw that when you lifted your arm."

He cautions her that he can offer no guarantees. The chemo will reduce the size of the tumor. It will kill the bad cells but it will also kill the good cells, he tells her. It will attack her bone marrow, the factory, so to speak, where the red and white blood cells and platelets are manufactured. She will feel weak. He may have to harvest cells from her bone marrow and inject them back into her if she gets too anemic. The chemo will make her sick. She will vomit every time she gets the treatment. She will lose all her hair.

"My hair?" Beatrice has been listening attentively. She has been sitting still with her hands folded on her lap. Nothing in her expression has betrayed the slightest reaction she might have had to what Dr. Ramdoolal is saying, but when he mentions her hair, she brings her hand to her mouth and gasps. "All of it?"

"We don't have any other choice. The tumor is too large. You've let it grow too long, Mrs. Sinclair."

Anna tells Dr. Ramdoolal that she objects to his implication that her mother is to blame. "You've made that point already. I think you need to understand my mother was very frightened. Doctors made her afraid. They couldn't help her mother and what they did—"

Beatrice Sinclair squeezes her daughter's hand and stops her. "Let the doctor finish what he has to tell us, Anna."

"It's just that I want to be as honest with you as I can," Dr. Ramdoolal explains.

"Go on," Beatrice says.

"You need chemo first because it's dangerous for a surgeon to remove a tumor that is as large as the one you have. Bleeding, you know. It could be fatal." Dr. Ramdoolal does not sugarcoat his words. "When the tumor gets smaller, a surgeon will be able to do a mastectomy."

"And after the mastectomy?" her mother asks.

"Some more chemo for insurance. And then radiation. But I must repeat, Mr. and Mrs. Sinclair, there are no guarantees. This disease is insidious. Some cells cling to the chest wall. You can't be sure you have got them all."

"And after that? After the radiation?"

"We wait."

"For a miracle?"

Anna winces. The hope that floods her mother's eyes is the wishful faith of a child believing in fairy tales.

"For a miracle," Dr. Ramdoolal concedes. "For a miracle, Mrs. Sinclair."

Silence falls between them, no longer than a few seconds, but an eternity it seems to Anna. Finally, her father speaks. "Will you do the surgery, Dr. Ramdoolal?"

The doctor shifts his body in his chair. "I can do the surgery, Mr. Sinclair," he says. "I was trained at Cambridge. I have kept up with the latest techniques, but we don't have the equipment. None of the hospitals here have the equipment I will need."

"Then what?"

"I recommend the U.S. There are excellent hospitals in New Jersey. I can refer you to a surgeon, a friend of mine. He grew up here, went to the University of the West Indies. Paul Bishop. Do you know the Bishops, Mr. Sinclair? His father was a union man. Worked in the oil fields."

"Henry Bishop," John Sinclair says.

"The very man. His son Paul did well. He's the head of surgery at his hospital in New Jersey."

"Henry Bishop's son?" Beatrice asks.

"She's heard me talk about his father," John Sinclair explains.

"I recommend him. You'll be in good hands with Paul Bishop. Doctors hate to admit anyone is better than them, but I'll tell you quite frankly: Paul Bishop is a better skilled surgeon than I could ever be, even if I had the equipment. After the chemo has reduced the tumor, have him do the surgery."

Beatrice shakes her head. "No," she says.

"Mrs. Sinclair?" Dr. Ramdoolal wrinkles his brow.

"I want to have the surgery here," she says quietly.

"Go to the U.S., Mrs. Sinclair," Dr. Ramdoolal says with exaggerated patience.

"I want to stay here."

"I strongly recommend—"

"I will stay here, Dr. Ramdoolal."

"If you want to die, Mrs. Sinclair," he says, "stay here."

Beatrice draws in her breath. The sound is audible.

Anna does not believe the doctor means to be cruel. He is frustrated, and this makes him sound cruel. Yet he has scared her mother. "Look what you've done! You've frightened her," she snaps. She leans toward her mother and whispers, "You won't die, Mummy. You won't."

Blood drains from John Sinclair's face. "Die? What do you mean *die*, Dr. Ramdoolal?"

The doctor places his hands on either side of his head. He shuts his eyes and shakes his head. "Please, Mrs. Sinclair, Mr. Sinclair, I didn't mean to say—"

"Is it that bad?" John Sinclair asks.

Dr. Ramdoolal slides his hands down his neck and clasps them together under his chin. "Your wife has as good a chance as any. It's hard for me, you understand. I came back here after medical school—the government invited me to come back . . . they made promises, but they do nothing. They won't buy the equipment. This is no place to have surgery, Mrs. Sinclair. I tell you that as your doctor. As someone who has your best interest at heart."

"How can you speak this way about my country?" Beatrice says softly.

"It's my county too, Mrs. Sinclair."

John Sinclair reaches for his wife's elbow. "Not now, Beatrice." He turns to Dr. Ramdoolal. "We'll take what you say under consideration, doctor."

"I'm going to stay in my country," Beatrice says.

Dr. Ramdoolal picks up the sheet of paper he has put aside on his desk. "You'll have to decide about surgery soon, but for now you should start chemo. It's the best thing for you to do, Mrs. Sinclair." He looks at the paper. "I can make room for you. I'll tell my nurse to fit you in. Tomorrow, then?"

"Yes, tomorrow," John Sinclair answers for his wife.

* * *

At home Beatrice is quarrelsome, contradicting her husband at every turn. John Sinclair believes her nerves make her so. He thinks Dr. Ramdoolal has scared her. He is patient with her. He tells her that she will not be alone. He will sit next to her through each of her chemotherapy sessions. He will not leave her side. Anna will come too, he says.

"Oh, don't make such a fuss, John. I won't need two people," Beatrice responds, dismissing him.

"Then it'll be me alone."

"If that's what you want to do," she says.

"Beatrice, *till death do us part*, remember?"

"So now *you* also think I'm going to die?"

He has put his foot in his mouth. Anna bails him out. "Daddy just wants you to know he meant his vows."

"Humph!" Her mother flings her shoulder away from him and walks toward her bedroom.

Later, after lunch, Anna finds her father feeding his fish. He has some brownish nuggets in his hand and he drops them two by two into the pond. The nuggets float to the surface and swell out into plump balls. From all directions the fish come, the larger ones pushing aside the smaller ones. Concentric circles widen in the water and miniature waves ripple to the concrete edge. Where tiny fish jockey against each other for crumbs, the surface is dimpled as if peppered with raindrops.

Anna stoops down on the rough border. Before the concrete had hardened, Beatrice Sinclair instructed the workmen to sink brown and white pebbles into the wet surface. The border is pretty but the rough edges of the pebbles jab against the soft skin on the soles of Anna's feet.

When she was a child, on hot steamy days she loved to kick off her shoes and run through the grass. She could play for hours barefooted on the stony banks of a river or on the coral-strewn sand at the beach. Now, winters and dirty pavement in New York have forced her into shoes and softened her feet.

"Your fish were hungry," Anna says to her father.

"I give them enough to eat," he replies gruffly.

Anna trails her fingers in the water. "Maybe you need to give them more."

"What? For the frogs?"

Anna grins, and her father drops more nuggets in the water.

"What's that you are giving them?" she asks.

"Dog food." He reaches into a big bag leaning against the wall. There is a picture of a large dog, a golden retriever, on the front panel.

"Dog food?"

"I can't get fish food in this country," he says. He takes out a handful of the nuggets and throws them in the water.

"So what Dr. Ramdoolal said is true?" Anna has taken her hand out of the pond. Water curls down her fingers and drips to the ground.

"Dr. Ramdoolal? Oh yes, he's right about no equipment in the hospital. Just like I can't find fish food on this island no matter where I go."

Anna stands and wipes her hand along the leg of her pants. Her father is observing her. "Your fingers will smell of fish and dog food," he says.

She brings her fingers to her nose and sniffs. "Not too bad."

"Why don't you go in the house and wash your hands?"

But she does not leave. She trails behind him as he walks over to the opposite side of the pond. "Has it come to this? Is this what independence has brought us?"

"I don't think the English were any better," he says. "If that is what you mean."

It is what she means. "I don't remember hearing those kinds of complaints when they were here."

"Oh, they had good hospitals for sure, with the latest medical equipment and all that. But those hospitals were for their own use." He looks at her over his shoulder. "And, of course, for their favored few."

She flushes with embarrassment. How could she have forgotten? They lived on the hill, in the Englishman's country. They were among the favored few.

He has stopped at the edge of the pond. He slaps his hands together and flecks of the brown nuggets caught between his fingers sprinkle down on the water. Baby fish pushed to the outskirts of the pond in the feeding frenzy turn and zoom toward the tiny particles floating on the surface. "Good," he says. "Now they have all eaten."

"Dog food," she says.

"I won't deny it's frustrating. My God, if we can have dog food on the island, why can't we have fish food? I tell you, it's all about money and corruption. The more things change . . ."

". . . the more they stay the same."

"Human nature is the same no matter the color of your skin," he continues. "When the oil came back, money flowed on the island. We had our independence then. The English weren't in control here. So who do you think got the money? Not the people for sure. The politicians and their cronies. They pocketed the money. And the politicians were not English. None of them. Machiavelli was right. People are greedy. They always want more, and then more is never enough. They cheat and steal to have what they can never possibly use, not in the one lifetime given to them. They don't care if the medical equipment in the hospitals is inferior so long as when they are sick, they have money to fly to New York to go to a hospital there. Who cares about the ones who can't afford to fly to New York?"

There are no more crumbs of dog food left on her father's hands, but he is still standing at the edge of the pond, staring into the water.

"Do you know why we have dog food and no fish food?" he asks.

Anna shakes her head.

"Because on this island we need dogs. People with money need dogs to protect them from the people who have no money. The man in the street finds it hard to understand why, in a country that has so much money from oil, he has to live on a pittance. So he becomes Robin Hood. He steals from the rich."

But this Robin Hood keeps what he steals. He doesn't share it with the poor, Anna thinks. There is no need to say this to her father; he knows it well. He protects his home. He does not have dogs, but he has all the rest—the electric iron gate at the entrance of the house, the wrought iron door at the end of the corridor, between his bedroom and the dining room, that they lock at night, a heavy mahogany door outside of the kitchen that they bolt twice. They are thinking of installing an alarm system, her mother told her.

If she should mention these measures he has taken to ensure the safety of his family, her father will still offer a defense for the poor. He will talk about the drug lords who have turned poor people into addicts and criminals.

"Who needs fish food?" he asks her. "Fish can't stop a thief from breaking into the vault in your house. Dogs can. I'll tell you something." He jabs his finger in the air over the water, punctuating his words. "Henry Bishop was different. I admired him. He was a union man, a leader. He could have had a lot of power, but he put the interest of the people before himself. Now his son is a big-time doctor."

A fish, sensing the moving shadow of her father's hand and supposing he is about to feed it again, surfaces on the water, its head alone. It opens its mouth and sucks in air.

"Enough for the day," her father says, but other fish have gathered.

"Are they still hungry?" Anna asks.

"No, but they'll still reach for more."

And are the Sinclairs among the wealthy who have enough but still reach for more? Her mother has a choice. Money has given her the luxury of choice. She need not take the risk of surgery in a hospital where the equipment the doctor needs is not available. They have the money for her to go to America.

"Mummy must go to the States," Anna says.

"Yes."

"You have to make her, Daddy."

He groans.

"You must, you know, Daddy." Anna's voice vibrates with urgency.

"I haven't been able to make your mother do anything she does not want to do."

"Dr. Ramdoolal says she'll die if she doesn't go."

Her father walks away from her to where he has left the bag with the picture of the golden retriever on it. He bends over and folds the top down.

"This is serious, Daddy." She is standing behind him.

"Maybe," he says, then straightens up. "Maybe for a son of Henry Bishop. Maybe for him your mother will change her mind."

CHAPTER 11

The oil had not dried up as the Englishmen had supposed when they hired her father to smooth over their exit from the island. Not long after the Europeans left, the Americans came with newfangled drills that cut through the hard rock as easily as if it were limestone. Oil gushed out; wells started pumping again. The island went giddy with an oil boom that freed pent-up imaginations in a wild explosion of construction never before seen on the island. In the sedate residential area where the Sinclairs built their replica of an American ranch house, all sorts of architectural wonders mushroomed. A prosperous merchant constructed his vision of a Mexican compound, a scattering of adobes, one for each of his family members, with the requisite clay statues posted at each entranceway. The island, too small for Indians to be segregated into Hindu and Muslim enclaves, saw the two groups competing with each other in a show of religious fervor. Hindus flew colorful flags and built elaborate temples on their front lawns with their gods inside sitting cross-legged and intimidating, visible through the concrete latticework. Muslims, not to be outdone, molded their roofs into domes, painted them a glittering gold and placed the crescent and star on their tops. One family recreated a European medieval castle complete with moat and movable bridge. The movie *Jaws* had just been released and an architect designed a *Jaws* house for several of his clients. The front was shaped like the wide-open mouth of the shark, with pillars rising from a cavernous veranda in imitation of the teeth. The veranda, meant to represent the bottom jaw of the shark, slanted upward and was overshadowed by a smooth, solid mass—the shark's head apparently—punctured by two large windows, its eyes. Probably because it was impossible to carry the conceit much further without blocking out both light and air, the rest of the house resembled the hull of a ship with many portholes. Another man arranged his garage along the full length of the front of his house so he could display his Rolls Royces. He had five, each a different color: gold, silver, black, red, and blue.

This is what happened in the Sinclairs' neighborhood. But in the north of the city, flat land was scarce so developers dumped truckloads of soil and rock in the marshlands bordering the sea. Within a blink of an eye, they shut out the sun with towering apartment buildings. They tore down trees to make room for gated residential communities, setting down concrete houses cheek by jowl which they painted in pretty pastel colors mimicking a Disney World already perfectly mimicked in Bermuda. "Just give them time," the old people said, clucking their teeth and issuing a warning: "The sea and swamp will soon take back what belongs to the sea and the swamp. Matter of time."

The mountains too were not spared. Where there was green, there are now many colors, none of them from flowering trees, none from the flame of the forest, the frangipani, the lignum vitae, the pink poui, the flamboyant, the powder puff. The pinks, reds, oranges, yellows, blues, purples that now dot the mountains are solid and stiff, fashioned out of painted concrete, brick, clay, slate, and galvanize. These colors do not shimmer with a breeze, they do not flutter to the ground and curl in the sun. No matter the season, wet or dry, they remain the same, always blooming, fading sometimes with the rain and sun, but never dying, never disappearing altogether to bud and bloom again later except when repainted.

But before all this, before the oil boom, before the Americans came, the Europeans, supposing that that they had taken most of what they wanted out of the ground, and not having the stomach for a fight with natives clamoring for independence, began preparations for their escape. They would maintain the few wells that were still producing oil, but they would essentially close down the company. Most of the workers would have to be terminated.

A union man came from the city and fired up the workers with talk about slavery and colonial oppression. White people had used them to make money, he said. Now that they had almost drained the oil fields, they were getting ready to run back to their countries with their pockets full of money they made from the back-breaking sweat of black people. "Is *we* money, not *dey* money. Is we oil dey tief. And dey so greedy, dey want to keep making more and more money. I say if dey can't keep all the workers, all de workers should leave the oil fields. Why we go work de wells dey want to keep pumping and make more money for dem? I say we shut down dey whole production."

Only one man, Henry Bishop, had the kind of influence on the workers to shut down the whole production. The people loved him and would follow him anywhere. He had a golden tongue and was capable, the people said, of selling snow cones in Siberia. He was barely literate, however. Written contracts and agreements were impossible for him to decipher.

The union man said he would do all the reading for Henry Bishop if Bishop got the workers to go on strike. Henry Bishop agreed. Every day he and the union man gathered the workers in front of Chin's grocery shop and laid out their case for a strike. By the end of the week most of the workers had walked off the oil fields.

The directors of the oil company called on their man John Sinclair. He would diffuse the strike. He would speak to Henry Bishop, local man to local man, and drive sense into his hard head.

John Sinclair said there had to be compensation, severance pay for the workers the company had retrenched. "You have to give them something," he argued. "They will shut you down completely if you don't."

Three weeks of strike and heavy financial losses finally persuaded the company bosses. They gave John Sinclair a budget and the authority to determine how much severance pay each worker would get.

Anna knows the barest details about the agreement between Henry Bishop and her father. He told her that Henry Bishop was a reasonable man. He understood that if there was no more oil on the island, there could be no more work for the workers. "Now some of you have work," John Sinclair said to Henry Bishop, "but if all of you go on strike, none of you will have jobs and none of you will get compensation."

John Sinclair was a reasonable man too and Henry Bishop's counter argument made sense to him: Why should the Europeans take all the profit out of the company and the workers not get a share? Why should they get millions and we get pennies?

John Sinclair went back to his bosses. More weeks of strike, more losses and tough negotiations made them concede that the severance budget they had allotted to John Sinclair was not enough. It had to be increased tenfold.

John Sinclair had one condition for Henry Bishop: no severance paycheck would be issued solely in the name of a male worker. Checks would have to be made in the name of the worker and his wife. The bank would be instructed not to cash a check unless the worker's wife was present.

The same rule applied for unmarried workers. They could not draw from their checks until a percentage was paid to the unmarried mothers of their children, or to women who could prove that they lived in a common law relationship with the men.

Anna likes to say that her father was the first feminist she knew, and except for the one time he betrayed her mother, she never had reason to reverse this conviction.

Beatrice is also proud of what her husband did for the women on the oil fields. She has told Anna this. She has also admitted that though she had called her husband foolish, she admired his integrity when he refused to accept retainers from companies that didn't want to lose him even though his memory was failing.

Beatrice is proud too of Henry Bishop. She calls him one of a dying breed of men who put people before their lust for money and power. So this afternoon, as Anna sits with her mother and father in the family dining room for their four o'clock tea, she hopes her father is right, that for a son of Henry Bishop her mother will change her mind.

Lydia serves them but she does not retreat to her room as she usually does when the Sinclairs have their meals. This time she remains in the kitchen, busily rearranging the dishes in the cupboards. Anna thinks she is worried about her mother.

"Don't you want to have your tea in your room, Lydia?" Beatrice asks, unfolding her napkin and placing it on her lap. It is Beatrice's considered opinion that helpers are gossips who will try all sorts of tricks to eavesdrop on their employers' conversation.

Lydia shakes her head. "The dishes all mixed up in the cupboards," she says. "I have to fix them." Worry lines deepen on her forehead.

"Can't you . . . ?"

But John Sinclair pulls his wife's attention away from Lydia. He wants to talk about Henry Bishop. He hands her the platter of scones that Lydia baked in the morning and remarks that he isn't at all surprised that Bishop's son has done so well in America. "He was an ambitious man, that Henry Bishop. I remember when the men complained. They didn't like it at all that they had to share their money with their wives. And God knows they almost started a riot when I said they had to give some of their severance pay to the mothers of their children even if they weren't married to them. If it wasn't for Henry Bishop, I don't know if things would have worked out so smoothly. And now his son is a doctor. The head of surgery in a hospital in the States. Wasn't that what Dr. Ramdoolal said?"

"I like Henry Bishop," Beatrice says.

Anna waits. She is sure her father will seize this moment to find a way to convince her mother that she should go to the States for her surgery. Henry Bishop's son will take care of her. She can trust him; he is her countryman. But her father does not say that. Instead he says, "Ramdoolal too. He is a big man here. Neil Lee Pak told me his father used to buy tomatoes from Dr. Ramdoolal's father. Now his son is a doctor. No ordinary doctor, mind you. An oncologist."

"Every doctor is an Indian today," Beatrice says drily.

"Paul Bishop is a black man," John Sinclair replies and sips his tea.

"Paul Bishop and his father are exceptions," Beatrice says.

Anna glares at her mother. "Mummy, you don't mean that?"

"What I said about Indian doctors? It's true, isn't it, John? You've been away too long, Anna. You don't understand."

Anna fights against the heat mounting in her throat. Her mother is ill; she must be patient.

"They are clannish in the way black people here are not," her mother continues. "Indians are willing to sacrifice their own happiness to send one of their relatives to university. Did you hear what your father said? Dr. Ramdoolal's father used to sell tomatoes at the side of the road."

"I suppose he grew them on his family's land," John Sinclair says.

"On his five acres," Anna adds, emphasizing *five*.

Beatrice pretends she has not heard her. "I bet his whole family—his mother, father, brothers, sisters, aunts, uncles, cousins—all of them stood back and did without so he could go to medical school."

Anna is painfully aware that Lydia is listening to her mother. More than twice she has seen her glance in their direction. But Lydia shows no signs that she is offended. Worry lines still mark her face.

"Yet when that one relative comes back, he has to take care of the rest of the family," John Sinclair says. His cup rattles against the saucer when he lowers it to the table.

"Dr. Ramdoolal doesn't seem to mind," Beatrice says.

"How do you know?"

"He seems to be doing well. He has a big office."

"I don't think he likes sharing his house with his parents and a whole gang of brothers and sisters, cousins, aunts, uncles, and you don't know which in-laws," John says.

"You can't be sure he's sharing his house," Beatrice counters.

"You're right. I don't know for sure. But do you see how many families live in that compound at the end of our block? There must be three generations of Indians in those small houses that circle the big house there. And those five Rolls Royces in front of Maresh Ali's lawn? I would bet there are at least five families in that house."

Beatrice butters the scone on her plate with studied

care. "All I can say is that ambition is in their genes." Her eyes remained fixed on the scone.

Anna looks over to the kitchen. Lydia is no longer working on the cupboards. She is bent over the sink, noisily washing pots and pans. Anna knows she has heard her mother and is banging the pots against each other deliberately. She is upset but she dare not complain. Anna calls out to her above the clatter and the stream of water gushing from the faucet. She wants her to hear what she has to say. "Lydia, can you bring me the cheese? I like cheese with my scone."

Lydia turns off the faucet and the noise dies down. When she brings the cheese to the table, Anna says loudly, "Some of the most successful black people in the States are West Indians. I don't mean West Indians from middle-class families." She is addressing her mother, but Lydia is her intended audience. "I was at a West Indian dinner-dance in Brooklyn a couple of months ago. Many of the people there were no different from Henry Bishop, people who didn't go to secondary school, or if they did, they went to a trade school. But you should've heard when they began talking about their children. Sons and daughters who were doctors, lawyers, MBAs working at Fortune 500 companies, other children in university, some at Ivy League schools."

"And why are you telling me this, Anna?" Beatrice asks, the buttered scone balanced on her outstretched hand.

"It's not about genes, Mummy. Indians don't have the monopoly on ambition or success. Or brains for that matter."

"As I have to keep reminding you, Anna, you've been away too long. Look around the island. The Indians own the shops, the cinemas, the restaurants. Indians even have their own steel pan orchestras. Now isn't that a joke? I mean if it was something black people had, it was steel pan. After the war, it was black people who figured out how to take those empty oil drums that the white people threw away and make music out of them. Now, the Indians have taken over. I hear the best steel pan orchestra these days belongs to Indians. And it's not only steel pan. You want a doctor, he is Indian; you need a lawyer, he is Indian. You need someone to build your house, or to build roads, they are Indians."

John Sinclair, who so far has kept his lips firmly shut as his wife and daughter argue back and forth, says quietly, "It's the psychology of immigration."

Beatrice spins her head around toward him. "And what is that supposed to mean?"

"People act differently when they migrate," he says carefully. "They leave their homeland because they want to better their circumstances. They are willing to make sacrifices. To work hard."

"In America, there are people who say that West Indians are more ambitious than African Americans," Anna says. "I tell them, go to the Caribbean and they will see how many unambitious West Indians there are. African American businessmen living in the Caribbean quickly find out it's hard doing business with people who like nothing better than to party and drink rum."

Lydia giggles. In the heat of the argument, no one has noticed that she has not returned to the kitchen and is standing not far behind John Sinclair, taking in every word.

"Lydia, really!" Beatrice Sinclair snaps. "If you don't have something to do in the kitchen, why don't you have your tea in your room?"

Lydia leaves but with a wide smile on her face.

Beatrice waits until Lydia's footsteps fade, then she says to Anna, "What you say does not disprove my point that the Indians are different. I still say ambition is in their genes."

"But it *does* disprove your point, Mummy. The Indians were immigrants."

"Psst. They were born here."

"Their grandparents and great-grandparents came from India."

"And black people's grandparents and great-grandparents came from Africa. So much for your immigrant theory," Beatrice says triumphantly.

"You forget the essential difference, Mummy. I'm sure I don't have to tell you."

"Slavery. She is talking about slavery, John." Beatrice throws open the palms of her hands and gestures in exasperation to her husband. "Everything is to be blamed on slavery. Well, Africans weren't the only people who were made slaves. Almost every country at one time had slaves. The Chinese had slaves, the Indians, the Amerindians, the Arabs. What about the Jews, the Israelites? Should they blame their problems on the slavery that happened to them years ago?"

"It was not the same."

"What was not the same?" Beatrice's tone is scathing.

"The experience was not the same," Anna says.

"You mean suffering is different depending on whether you were Chinese or African?" Her mother does not conceal her disdain. "You mean the experience of being whipped and chained and forced to work for no money for someone who owned you is different depending on the color of your skin or where you came from? Is that what you are saying, Anna?"

It is not what she wants to say. What she wants to say is that human suffering is human suffering. We are all the same. We all share the same desires, the same fears. We all want to survive, we all want to be happy. This is what she believes. "But . . ." she begins.

Her mother, the inquisitor, does not allow her to continue. "But?" She narrows her eyes. "So tell me, Anna, how is it different?"

"It's different when you are treated as chattel."

"Chattel? What's chattel?" Beatrice's eyebrows converge.

"Property, Beatrice," John says. He glances at Anna and brings his lips together in a tight round *O*, signaling her to stop, to end their quarrel.

But Anna does not retreat. She will redeem herself. She will not stop now. "Only African slaves were treated as chattel," she says. "Only African slaves were treated as if they were not human beings, as if they were a subset of homo sapiens, not the real thing. The slave owners bred the Africans like cattle, they separated them from their families. They used them whenever they wanted to, just as they would use their cattle. They branded them with hot irons."

Beatrice sucks in her breath. "Branded?"

"This is not conversation to have at teatime," John Sinclair says and places his hand on his daughter's wrist. "Let's talk about something else." He looks over at his wife. "Okay, Beatrice?"

Beatrice is still struggling with the image Anna has planted in her head. "And they did that too? The freed slaves who had slaves?"

Anna is surprised by the question. "You knew about that?"

"Your father told me. Didn't you, John? Didn't you say that even the Africans who were enslaved in America enslaved other Africans once they were freed?"

"Only a few of them did that, Beatrice. It was not common practice. It was the rare freed slave who did that."

"And the ones who did, did they brand their slaves?"

Anna knows of no evidence that African slaveholders

in America did not brand their slaves, but neither does she have evidence that they thought of their slaves as a species that was essentially different from themselves. How could they?

"They didn't treat their slaves as chattel," she says softly. "They didn't treat them as if they were not human."

Beatrice lowers her head and focuses on the food before her. Only the sounds of metal knives and forks against the dull, hard surface of the plates break the quiet around the table. Anna thinks her mother has accepted her answer. Their argument is over. Then, abruptly, her mother looks up. "The Indians didn't have it much better," she announces.

She has misjudged the silence. Her mother has been thinking of a response all along; she is not ready to give in. "They *chose* to come, Mummy. That is the difference."

"Still," Beatrice murmurs.

"You can't deny that being brought forcibly in chains on a slave ship is not the same as choosing to leave your country of your own free will. The Indians were dying of poverty in India. When the British came with their offer of five acres for five years of indentured servitude on the cane fields, they jumped at what seemed to them like an opportunity of a lifetime to change their lot. Dr. Ramdoolal's father may have sold tomatoes at the side of the road, but his family had five acres the British gave them and they had a chance to make something out of it."

"So what you are trying to tell me is that immigration . . ." Beatrice turns to her husband. "What is it you said, John?"

John surrenders. He has not managed to convince either of them to change the subject. "The psychology of immigration," he says and spoons sugar in his tea.

"So the psychology of immigration is in their genes? Is that right, Anna?"

"When slavery ended, Africans had nothing, no money, no property. Nothing. They were set free, but to do what? To live where? Certainly not to go back to the cane fields where they had suffered. The Indians had land. They could build a house, even if it was a shack made out of mud and coconut fronds. It was *their* shack, on *their* land. They owned it. The Africans owned nothing. Indians could plant yams, edoes, cassava on their land. They could grow their own food. They could sell tomatoes and make some money. The Indians had an advantage Africans never had. Before the race started, they were put far ahead on the race track."

"Race track?" Beatrice feigns puzzlement. "Are we talking about horses now, Anna?"

Anna is not fooled by her mother's pretense at ignorance. "You understand very well what I mean, Mummy. I don't have to explain. And like Daddy said, you also have to take into account that immigration affects the way people see the world. It changes their mindset. Indians were immigrants. They came here of their free choice, with the sole intention of working to make a better life for themselves than they had in India."

Beatrice sits back in her chair. "That was a long time ago," she says. "Three or more generations back. I don't see much difference between what you and your father are saying about the psychology of immigration and my saying that ambition is in their genes."

"It's racist, Mummy."

"There you go with all that black and white talk from America."

"Racism affects the very lives of black people in America," Anna says quietly. "It affects where they live, what kind of education they get, what jobs are open to them, whether they go to jail or not. In America, it matters a lot if you are black or white. It matters if you would be given the right treatment from doctors or hospitals . . ."

As her last words reverberate in her ears, Anna sees her mother's eyes shoot wide open. But the words have left her tongue; she cannot take them back.

"Not that . . ." she begins. "Not that this happens to all black people."

Too late. Her mother's hand jerks forward and the tea-cup she has brought to her lips misses its mark. Tea spills down her chin. She grabs her napkin and presses it against her mouth.

Anna tries again. Unwittingly, she has fanned her mother's fears. Since they left Dr. Ramdoolal's office, they have not spoken about her mother's refusal to go to America for surgery, but Anna realizes now, and too late, that while she has been pontificating—for that is what she has been doing—her mother has been thinking of little else.

"I knew it. I was certain of it. The doctors . . . the hospital. In America . . . I knew it was like that. That's why I won't go there. I won't, John." Her mother's voice wavers.

John Sinclair reaches for his wife's hand. "It's your best chance, Beatrice," he says soothingly. "Neil agrees with Dr. Ramdoolal. He told me so. He says the hospitals there are the best."

"I won't go," Beatrice repeats, so softly Anna only guesses that this is what she has said.

"It would be best, Beatrice."

"They see only skin color there. I know it. Anna has just said so herself. I won't be treated the way they treat black people there. I won't be treated as if I am not a human be-ing, as if I am a subset . . ." Her voice rises from a whimper to a whine.

Anna is stunned by this sudden transformation in her mother. She is ridden with guilt for her part in it.

"I won't, John. I won't."

"It'll be all right, Beatrice. I'll be there," Anna's father croons.

Her mother begins to cry. She shoves away her plate and plants her elbows on the table. "I won't. I won't." She brings fists to her eyes. Tears drain down her cheeks. "I won't."

By late afternoon, alone in the veranda, Anna has stopped blaming herself. She knows it wouldn't have made a difference no matter what she had said. Her mother's views are firmly entrenched. She cannot change her. Her mind was already made up in Dr. Ramdoolal's office, made up years before from the collage of images on the news from America beamed nightly on her TV into her bedroom: black people relegated to slums in the richest country in the world; black people on drugs in the richest country in the world; black people a minority of the population but filling the jails of the richest country in the world.

She won't go, her mother says. But Anna knows she must.

From the corridor leading to her parents' room she hears Lydia calling out to her parents. "Goodbye, Mrs. Sinclair. Mr. Sinclair." Lydia's footsteps retreat to the backdoor and Anna hears more voices. She gets up to look and she finds Singh standing near the backdoor, his hands gripping the handlebar of his bicycle, holding it steady.

"Singh!" Anna is surprised to see him so late in the afternoon. He arrives at dawn but he is always gone by three.

"I come back," Singh says sheepishly.

"How long have you been here?"

"I let him in," Lydia says.

"Does my mother know you are here, Singh?"

"I didn't want to disturb her," Lydia answers for him. "I know she sick and all. And she was crying at teatime."

"That's okay, Lydia. You did the right thing. It's just that you came in so quietly, Singh. You usually ring your bicycle bell."

"Lydia see me before I did have a chance to ring de bell."

"You have a message for my mother?"

"I bring she some orchids."

"Orchids?"

"Two plants. I put dem in de back."

"She was expecting them?"

"No, the wife send me. She say madam like orchids and I must bring she two new plants since she sick. De wife say it make she feel better."

Anna is so touched she can barely speak. "Thank you, Singh," she manages to say. "Thank your wife for me and my parents." She wants to say more but language fails her.

"I know madam from a long time." Singh's eyes scan the ground. "I work for she many years now. De wife don't know she, but me and de madam go back years." He pauses, and when he speaks next, he is looking straight at her. "She have a good doctor?"

"The best," Anna says.

"My wife say she should go to Dr. Ramdoolal. He's de best doctor."

"It's Dr. Ramdoolal, Singh. That's who Mummy is seeing."

All that talk about Indians and Africans, and Singh and his wife thinking no more about her mother's color than about the color of any other frightened, sick woman, bringing her a gift because they think it can ease her pain, her fears. Caring nothing about whether she is Indian as they are, or African, or whether, like so many on the island, she is unable to distinguish which threads, from which ancestors, from which parts of the world, from which cultures, have woven together to form her physical features.

CHAPTER 12

But the convictions persist. There is something about Indians, something in the genes that has made them so successful.

Anna paces the path between the rosebushes and the stone façade of the house. Singh has gone; Lydia has gone. A peaceful quiet has descended over the house. The sun is setting, sinking slowly behind the mountains, leaving a palette of reds that will be erased in minutes, replaced by an ink blue sky. Inside, her parents talk. Can her father convince her mother? Can he persuade her that the news on television and in the newspaper tell only one side of the story in America, mostly the worst side? *Can she?*

For the third time Anna passes the same rosebush. This time she stops, and like her father had done the morning before, she slips her hand under a pink rose. It is in full bloom, already poised to give way to the buds clustered on the stems around it. Its petals, loosely attached to the center, fall apart in her hands. She brings them to her nose and inhales. Her head swirls, her thoughts flitting from the dying rose to her sick and aging mother. Why couldn't she have let her mother win their argument? Why couldn't she have been more considerate? How painful it must be for her mother to confront the possible end of her life, the cancer gnawing away at her flesh.

But her mother is wrong. Genetic explanations for differences among people are dangerous. They led to the European and American enslavement of Africans for more than four hundred years, to the horrors committed under Hitler, to the horrors in Rwanda, to the horrors in the Congo and the Sudan, to the horrors in Iraq and Bosnia. Yet her father's theory about the psychology of immigration does not sufficiently explain why the Indians have done so well on her island. They came from India with nothing, just the clothes on their backs, a few rags tied up in bundles. Perhaps some came with family heirlooms, gold bracelets and trinkets, but these had personal value to them; they would not sell them. Still, Anna will insist, they were given advantages. The English gave them land, permitted them to keep their families, their culture, their religions, intact. The Africans were stripped of everything. Even their bodies were not their own. The Indians were never chattel.

Anna remembers the pretty Indian young woman from South Africa, an intern assigned to her at Equiano Books. Everywhere she went, everywhere she turned, there she was with a smile, a wave, a greeting. Good morning, Ms. Sinclair. Good day, Ms. Sinclair. Good night, Ms. Sinclair. Can I get something for you, Ms. Sinclair? Can I do something for you, Ms. Sinclair? So polite, so ingratiating. A sycophant. She suspected her of ulterior motives.

Anna had recently been appointed to head Equiano Books, Windsor's imprint for its books by writers of color. She had to answer only to Tanya Foster, the publisher of Windsor, who promised that this requirement was merely a formality. Equiano Books would be independent of Windsor. Anna would be free to acquire new titles and to determine the amount of money given as advances to writers. She would be given a special budget for marketing, money for brochures, money for advertisements in major print media, money to send her writers on tour. The fantasy dream of editors. She would have more autonomy than even many of the senior editors in the company.

This was no altruistic, charitable, goody-two-shoes move on the part of Windsor, Tanya Foster explained. It made practical sense, good horse sense, for Windsor to launch Equiano Books. "Profit. That's what I am talking about, Anna. We smell money in an untapped market."

The untapped market was the market of people of color, African Americans in particular, but also the newly arrived immigrants from so-called underdeveloped countries.

"To my way of thinking," Tanya Foster had said, "Pat Robinson is so far to the right, he has fallen off the scale, but he has a point. White people are not making babies. There are places in Europe with zero population growth. Zero! Italy, Norway, places like that. We don't want to be caught unprepared here at Windsor. We want to be at the head of the line. Equiano Books is a sound investment. Publishing, you know, is about the bottom line. Yes, we have to say all those high-minded things about literary expression, continuing aesthetic traditions, advancing the culture, promoting values, but at the end of the day what matters is profit. We are a business. We are not some sort of affirmative action program. We buy—in our case, books—and we sell. We buy because we think we can make money when we sell. And we think Equiano Books can increase our bottom line, bring us profits. There are readers out there we haven't reached. People of color we have not tapped. We need to reach them, Anna, and we will with Equiano Books. Some people may not like what I say, but I'll tell you this, in the next fifty years America will not look the way it looks today. People of color will be in the majority and Windsor must be ready to take advantage of this fertile new market."

Equiano Books was named for Olaudah Equiano, the author of the runaway eighteenth-century best seller *The Interesting Narrative of the Life of Olaudah Equiano, or Gustavus Vassa, the African, Written by Himself*. The title of the imprint was a main factor for Anna in sealing her decision. She convinced herself that a publishing imprint named after an African with the fortitude to survive the brutality of slavery and the intelligence to write one of the most incisive literary works about that dark period in America's past had to be one whose motives, understandably profit driven, were surely also based on a genuine interest in people of color. It soon became clear to her, however, that Windsor's choice of a name for its new imprint was simply a marketing strategy, the bright idea of some loafer-tasseled young Ivy Leaguer who remembered the name from an African American Studies course he was required to take, and liking the sound of its multiple vowels, recommended it to Windsor. The word was mellifluous, he said. Besides, it had the advantage of proving that the publishing company was sensitive to African American culture.

Windsor published two novels to test the market for the sort of books it had in mind for Equiano. One novel about gang warfare in the Bronx—or the 'hood, as Windsor boasted on the jacket cover—pitted blacks against Latinos. The other novel told the story of a woman struggling to raise three children fathered by three different men, all who abandoned her. The novels were a hit. They quickly became best sellers, making large profits for Windsor. Anna's job was to publish more of the same. The company's position was that only people with dark skin had the ability to capture in words the authentic experience of people of color, and only people with dark skin were able to guide these writers into producing such work. Black people had "soul," Tanya Foster declared. White people did not have access to "soul," a theory apparently based on the inherent powers of skin color. So, after four months on her new job, Anna was not the least surprised when, barely able to suppress her glee, Tanya Foster said to her, "You're going to be real pleased with me, Anna. I've found you an assistant. All the way from Africa. From South Africa."

Tammy Mohun was African indeed—South African—but she was not a black South African. She was a "colored" South African, an Indian with flawlessly milky brown skin, big, saucer-shaped dark eyes that she made seem even larger with the black ghee she pasted on the top and bottom of her lids, a tiny mouth, a nose prominent on her small face, and thick shining black hair caught in a braid that fell down the length her back.

"My family's been in South Africa since the eighteenth century," she said to an astonished Anna. "Africa is my home."

Anna could not explain fully to herself why she felt a strong resentment toward Tammy Mohun. She was a sweet girl, anxious to please, always with a smile for her, a compliment for a blouse she wore, a skirt, a suit, the way she fixed her hair, willing to bring her sandwiches from the deli at lunchtime, to make tea for her in the afternoons. And she was a hard worker, not objecting when Anna asked her to review a manuscript the fact-checker had already worked on or to research some arcane detail. Without a murmur, she took stacks of manuscripts home on the weekends and returned each Monday with extensive notes on what she had read. That she felt somehow tricked by Tanya Foster did not fully explain Anna's simmering hostility toward the girl. But there it was. Each time Tammy approached her, smiling as if she never had a care in the world, Anna would become irritated for no reason at all. She would begin pushing papers across her desk or would speak roughly to the poor girl about some minor detail she had overlooked.

And then, one afternoon as Tammy handed her the usual cup of tea, steaming the way she liked it, with just enough milk but not so much that it was tepid, Anna no-

ticed, or thought she noticed, a slight trembling in the corner of Tammy's mouth. She did her best to pretend she had
not seen it, but her assistant stood in front of her, her arms
crossed over her tiny waist, her eyes trained on the floor,
rocking back and forth on her heels.

Anna had to pay attention. She shut her office door,
pointed to a chair, and invited Tammy to sit and tell her
what was making her so unhappy. Is it something I have
done? She had not treated Tammy well. Perhaps she was to
blame.

No, nothing you have done, Tammy said. You have been
more than good to me. So kind.

Then what?

I'm so ashamed.

Ashamed?

I lied to Tanya.

Lied?

I told her I needed this job. I don't need this job.

Anna did not understand. Is that why Tanya hired you?
she asked. Because you said you needed a job?

Not exactly. I applied for the job and she chose me because I was qualified.

Was it your resume then? Did you lie about your qualifications?

No, I didn't.

Then what?

I'm rich. My family is filthy rich.

Anna winces as she recalls how relieved she felt, how
vindicated. There was something about the girl. Smiling as
if she had no care in the world!

A tear dripped down from Tammy's saucer-shaped eyes.
I live in a penthouse near Lincoln Center, she said. I have a
summer home in the south of France. My family has mansions in South Africa. The tear grew fatter. More followed,

long wet lines trailing down her cheeks, pearling on her chin before they fell drop by drop onto the collar of her blouse.

Anna handed her a tissue.

Tammy blew her nose and wiped her eyes. Do you think what I did was wrong?

Anna shrugged. There are no laws against rich people applying for jobs, she said.

You know what I mean, Tammy sniffed. I mean, do you think what we did was wrong?

We? But Anna already knew who she meant. The coloreds, the ones neither black nor white in South Africa.

In Robbens Island where Mandela was imprisoned, black South Africans were forced to wear short pants even in the dead of winter. Indian South Africans were given long pants.

If we didn't do it, someone else would have done it, Tammy said.

In the dead of winter, black men trembled like frightened little girls, bodies betraying strong minds, bare hands rubbing bare calves, useless to stop the trembling. Black men are boys, Verwoerd and his henchmen declared. Boys wear short pants. Boys who have not yet reached the age of twelve, who have not yet matured into men, wear short pants.

Knees froze, hands froze.

My father said we did the blacks a service. Tammy folded her hands on her lap. She had stopped crying. How else would they get the goods they needed? They couldn't shop in Johannesburg. They had to come to us. She spoke with confidence now. We were fair. We did not overcharge them. Not one penny. We gave them a fair price for the goods they bought from us. We had to calculate the cost to us, of course. We could not charge the same amount you would pay for sugar in Johannesburg, of course.

And for milk?

The merchants in Johannesburg charged us more. We

had to pass on the costs. Then there was transportation. We needed lorries to bring the goods. And the risk . . .

The risk?

I don't know what you know about South Africa in those days, Anna, but it was not a safe place. People got killed. Women got raped.

I thought that happened to the black South Africans.

I mean us. If they caught one of us . . .

One of us?

A white person was not safe in the black district.

But you are not white.

Oh, I know in America I am black, but in South Africa I am colored, and colored people in my parents' day, during apartheid, could be attacked by the blacks just the same way whites were attacked by blacks.

Why would they do that?

Attack us, you mean?

Yes, why?

Because we are coloreds.

Yes, but why because you are coloreds? Anna fought against a sickening sensation rising in her stomach.

Because we had certain advantages.

Five acres. That's what the English colonizers gave the Indians on her island. The French Creoles, of course, got land too, many times five acres. With Emancipation, European slave owners had lost the free labor that had made them rich. There had to be reparations. They had to be compensated. The blacks? They got nothing. Wasn't their freedom reparation enough?

Was it our fault? Tammy shifted her body to the edge of her chair. She pressed her body forward, closer to Anna. It was the whites who made that system, she said. They were the ones who prevented the blacks from shopping in the white stores.

In the prison, facing a common enemy, the Indians rallied to support the blacks. If the blacks must wear short pants, they said, we will wear short pants too. Fearing a riot, the white South African guards caved in. But outside, in the real world, it was different. After Independence, Indians latched onto their British passports and immigrated in droves to England. Idi Amin was a cruel, brutal dictator and the choice he had given the Indians between keeping their British passports and filing for a Ugandan passport was really no choice, but in every former colony large numbers of Indians made the same decision. Fearing reprisals? Perhaps it was a fear that was well founded. They had been treated better, made to think of themselves as superior, the blacks as inferior to them, deserving of their scorn. Yet even in America and in Canada, where they have no reason to fear reprisals, Indians from the Caribbean choose to live apart from black West Indians.

Anna requested a transfer for Tammy. Guilt and resentment, not fully articulated but solidified, had formed a hard stone in the chests of both women which neither was able to loosen.

And why resentment on her part? Did she, like her mother, resent the success of the Indians in the detritus of the postcolonial worlds the British had left behind? What else was Tammy's family to do? Walk away from an opportunity? Did it matter that their opportunity came on the backs of black people, from the humiliation and suffering they were forced to endure?

All in the past, Anna says to herself. All in the past. And she makes her way to the back of the house, to the garden, where Singh has left two orchid plants, a gift his wife has urged him to bring for her mother.

It is a new day on these Caribbean islands, and perhaps in this her mother is right: Perhaps it is America that has taught her this sensitivity to race. Perhaps it is America that has made it impossible for her to forgive an innocent girl whose offense was no more than bearing the burden of her parents' past.

Here, where she is now, where she was born, where she once belonged, where she longs to belong again, the children of this past make peace with what had happened before.

Is it geography that makes this forgiveness possible? Do tiny landscapes surrounded by water force intimacy among people who do not look the same, who have brought with them cultures that are not the same?

Dr. Ramdoolal, an Indian, advises her mother, refers her mother to Paul Bishop, whose great-grandparents came to the island bound in chains from Africa. A doctor now, Dr. Bishop has surgical skills that Dr. Ramdoolal, without need of prompting, acknowledges are better than his own.

Dr. Neil Lee Pak, whose father is Chinese and mother is African and Indian, is her parents' good friend. Singh, an Indian, barely eking out a living from the land, feels sympathy for her brown-skinned mother who counts among her foreparents indigenous Amerindians, Europeans, and Africans.

America, the melting pot, and everywhere cities are divided into the distinct patches of an elaborate quilt. From the center the colors fan out, black turning to shades of brown, café au lait, then white as the colors reach the suburbs.

What is it? What is it that makes the island of her birth so different, so truly cosmopolitan? For if geography were all, if that were all it took to explain her island, to explain Ranjit Ramdoolal, Paul Bishop, Neil Lee Pak, and the many bloods that run through her parents' veins, then Manhattan, itself a tiny island, connected by bridges to the rest of America and to the world by an ocean, should be a true melting pot.

Not so. At lunchtime in the primary schools throughout the five boroughs of New York City and across the country, children, not yet adolescents, congregate in groups around tables, skin colors as defined and circumscribed as the black-and-white squares on a checkerboard.

It is late. Anna leaves the orchid garden. The busyness of the day is over and the evening air vibrates with quiet anticipation. Night is yet to come and now it is time for family, time for dinner around a table with husband, wife, and children. Time to resolve petty arguments. Time for her to put aside her quarrel with her mother.

She climbs the steps and opens the kitchen door. Her father is waiting. "It's half past six," he says.

Time for dinner, time for the sandwiches Lydia has prepared.

CHAPTER 13

Dinner, such as it is—chicken sandwiches and lemonade—passes uneventfully. Anna and her parents are polite to each other. They make no reference to their disagreements at teatime. After dinner her father goes to his bar in a corner of the veranda and packs the empty soda bottles inside a carton. Tomorrow he will exchange them for a carton of new ones. Her mother retires to the den. Anna washes the dishes. When she is finished, she walks past the den on the way to her room. The TV is on. She hears voices. A man shouts angrily. A chorus behind him responds.

"Anna," her mother calls her to the den. "Come, see this."

She hesitates. She knows without looking what her mother wants her to see. Their argument at teatime will resume if she responds. She does not want to be dragged into a quarrel again.

"Come. Look, Anna!" Her mother is insistent. Anna has no choice. She must go.

She enters the den. Her mother points to the TV screen. The channel is turned to a cable station in America. The nightly news from New York.

"See! See! Listen," her mother urges her.

Anna sees, she listens.

"How long?" a gray-haired black man chants. "How long will we continue to take this abuse, this attack on our people? This morning, just hours ago, a good man, a decent man, a father, a husband, killed by the police. Murdered in cold blood."

The man is wearing a dark suit. He is standing behind a podium erected in front of a limestone building. A multitude of microphones, like daggers, are pointed toward him. To the man's right is a taller gray-haired black man. He is wearing a black Nehru jacket. To his left is a soft-skinned, plump black woman. Her eyes are blank, her mouth slack. She is already dressed in black, already in the mourning clothes for a husband dead only hours.

"Murdered!" the man in the dark suit shouts.

Behind the two men and the woman, a crowd. Anna glimpses one or two white faces, no more.

"How long?" the man chants again. The crowd roars.

"Shot down like a dog by the NYPD! His poor wife."

The woman wails. Her cries rise above the shouts of the crowd, a knife cutting a bloody swath through the night air.

"Like a dog. Like a common dog!"

"Black men are under attack in America!" someone from the crowd shouts.

"All black people are under attack!" another person yells. The crowd roars again. Their words are indistinct, but their anger is palpable.

"Well, we are not going to take it anymore!" says the gray-haired man. "We won't sit still while they gun down our sons and daughters, our men and women. We won't stand by and do nothing!"

Her mother cranes her neck forward. She is looking intently, listening intently. "See. See what I told you, Anna."

"Remember MLK!" a man yells.

Anna walks toward the TV. "Mummy, let's go to bed," she pleads.

Her mother leans back on the couch. She presses her

hand to her mouth and looks up at Anna. Her eyes are watery. "I told your father," she says. "I won't go there. I won't."

Anna switches off the TV.

CHAPTER 14

D r. Neil Lee Pak arrives early in the morning to accompany them to Dr. Ramdoolal's office for the first of Beatrice Sinclair's rounds of chemotherapy. Lydia pushes the button that opens the electric gate and Neil drives up the driveway and parks behind John Sinclair's car. He comes into the house by the back way, through the family entrance. The Sinclairs are having breakfast, seated at their usual places around the table.

Beatrice greets him. "Oh, Neil," she says, "you needn't have come through the backdoor."

Neil grins good-naturedly. "So I'm not family anymore? You want to treat me like a stranger?"

"Silly man," Beatrice says.

She is cheerful this morning, no hint of the terror the evening before that stretched her eyes wide open and made her clasp her hand to her mouth so that the words when they came out were muffled: *I told your father. I won't . . .* But John Sinclair has confided to his daughter that her mother has spent most of the night praying in the bathroom. She has not slept a wink, he said.

Anna would never have guessed it. There are no dark circles under her mother's eyes that would surely be under *her* eyes had she not had sufficient sleep.

Her mother's hair is meticulously coiffed, the sides brushed back and the ends flipped up stylishly at her ears. She is wearing a rose pink linen dress that highlights the red undertones of her skin. The dress, her color, both give the impression of a woman who is well rested, healthy. It seems impossible that under that dress, in her mother's left breast, a demon is multiplying, eating away her healthy flesh.

Neil places his hand lightly on her mother's shoulder. "Beatrice, I must say you look lovely this morning." He does not kiss her. Like most of Beatrice's friends, Neil knows her mother does not like to be kissed. She squirms when she is kissed and will often offer her hand instead of her cheek before you can get too close to her.

"Ready to face the fire," she says.

"It's not going to be that bad, Beatrice." As usual, Neil is impeccably dressed: white golf shirt, tan pants, fashionable brown leather belt, and matching loafers. He looks more like an aging fashion model this morning than the doctor he is.

"Well, however it is, I am ready to face it," Beatrice says. "Come, sit down. Join us for breakfast."

The Sinclairs are having smoked herring and hardboiled eggs. The platter is a carnival of colors. Lydia has stripped the brown herring into small pieces, drizzled olive oil over them, and added chopped raw onions and cubed bright red tomatoes. She has sliced the hardboiled eggs so that they make perfect rounded shapes, the yellow enclosed in glistening white. She has placed thick slices of yellow and green avocado around the herring and the eggs.

"What a beautiful arrangement," Neil says, and takes the chair next to Beatrice.

Beatrice is pleased with the compliment. She passes the platter to him. "Would you like some bake too?"

Lydia has also made a bake, with flour, yeast, sugar, margarine, and freshly grated coconut. She put the dough in the oven while the Sinclairs were dressing for breakfast, timing it so it would be piping hot when the Sinclairs came out of their room. She knows John Sinclair likes his butter to melt in the bake. They have been eating for ten minutes now and the bake has cooled.

"Lydia," Beatrice Sinclair calls out to her, "warm up the bake for Dr. Lee Pak."

Neil puts up his hand and stops Lydia just as she is about to take a step toward the table. "That's kind of you, Beatrice, but the bake is fine for me the way it is. You are a lucky man, John. You have this every morning?"

"You should get married," John says. "If you had a wife, you'd have this every morning."

"You mean a wife like Beatrice," Neil says.

Anna can't help thinking: *You mean a maid like Lydia.*

"He means a wife," Beatrice says to Neil.

Neil's compliment should have been directed to Lydia, but her mother has accepted it as hers, rightfully earned. How many times has she explained to Anna that had she not trained Lydia, Lydia would not be as skilled at cooking and baking as she is now?

"Isn't it time you got married, Neil?" Beatrice asks.

"Marriage is not for everyone," Anna says, thinking to spare Neil, but she realizes too that she has opened a space she has been careful to keep closed from her mother. Her mother will undoubtedly pounce on it. She will say something about her daughter's spinsterhood, her inadequacy, her failure to keep a husband. They have not talked about Tony since her arrival on the island. Surely her mother will make a remark that will let it be known she does not approve of her daughter's single status. Men may have a choice, but women need to marry. A single woman living alone sends the wrong message to a predatory man. That is what Anna thinks her mother will say.

But Beatrice does not go through the door Anna has foolishly and carelessly opened. She is preoccupied with fears of her own. She must face the fire. She cannot back down now. It has all been arranged. In a few hours, needles will be stuck in her veins. She will be hooked to tubes. Poisonous chemicals will course through her body. If she is lucky, the poison will find the malignant cells, kill them before they can send out tentacles. If she is lucky, the healthy cells will get out of the way while the battle wages.

"Well, marriage is for me," John Sinclair says and beams at his wife.

Beatrice flushes. Addressing Neil, she says, "I wouldn't know what I would do without John if I had to face this alone."

After breakfast, the two men retreat to the fishpond to give Anna and her mother time to freshen up. *Freshen up*, her father says, as if they are off to some merry event, a visit to a friend or to one of the endless cocktail parties John Sinclair's former corporate clients continue to invite him to in the hope—which John insists is futile—that he will change his mind and help them sort out the many complaints they get from both workers and the newly formed independent government.

She is not being fair. Anna realizes just how unfair she has been when she looks across the fishpond and sees her father, his back bent as though a great weight is pushing against him, his forehead cupped in his hands. Neil Lee Pak is speaking to him. Neil's hands are drawn behind his back; his lips move rapidly. Her father shakes his head. Neil speaks again. Finally her father lowers his hands; he looks up. From where she stands, Anna can see the deep ravines between her father's eyebrows.

Anna goes to her room to freshen up. Almost immediately her mother knocks on the door and enters the room without waiting to be invited.

Anna is shocked by the drawn pallor of her mother's

skin. The lipstick and rouge she has applied to her face look clownish. "Mummy, Mummy," she croons. Her heart swells with pity. "It'll be all right. Dr. Ramdoolal says it'll be all right."

Her mother shuts the door. "I don't want you to come with me, Anna," she says. Her voice is firm, belying her pale exterior.

Anna is taken aback. "But why?" In the bathroom, in Dr. Ramdoolal's office, her mother confided in her. In the examining room, she needed her.

"I don't want you to be there." Her mother's lips are set in a determined line.

"But I want to be with you."

"No!" Her mother's resolve is indisputable.

She's still afraid, Anna thinks. The pink dress, the casual greeting to Neil Lee Pak, the banter at breakfast about marriage, all a pretense.

Anna comes closer to her. "You don't have to be so brave, Mummy."

Her mother backs away.

"The chemo won't be painful," Anna says.

The line along her mother's lips cracks, her bottom lip trembles. "I'm not afraid of pain."

"Then what?"

"What could happen."

"Nothing will happen," Anna says.

"If this does not work . . ."

"It will work," Anna says.

Her mother leans against the closed door. She shuts her eyes. "I don't want you to be there."

"But . . ."

"Your father will be with me."

"I will be with you too," Anna says.

"You are my daughter." Her mother opens her eyes.

"Mothers take care of daughters. Daughters don't take care of mothers."

"It's my turn now," Anna says.

"No!" Anna is startled by the firmness of her mother's voice. "No. I want your father to help me. We will drive behind Neil and then Neil will go to his home. I want only your father to be with me. This is between the two of us. Between your father and me."

Once, a long time ago, when she was in pain, a different sort of pain, not a pain to the body, a pain to the spirit, for her heart was broken, her mother said these same words. "This is between your father and me," she said, and she shut Anna out.

Her father and Neil Lee Pak are waiting for them in the driveway. Her mother comes out alone. Through the kitchen window, Anna can hear Neil Lee Pak ask, "Where's Anna? Isn't Anna coming too?"

"No," her mother says.

Anna cannot see their faces. She does not know if her father has made a sign to Neil Lee Pak to say no more. Whether he put his finger to his lips or shook his head. She knows only that he says nothing. That he does not try to persuade her mother otherwise. The next sound she hears is the car engines accelerating.

It is almost teatime when her parents return. Her mother's face is drained, her skin gray, her eyes dull. She feels weak, she says. She wants to rest.

Dr. Ramdoolal has warned them that her mother will be ill after the procedure. *The procedure*, he said, as if the methodically timed invasion of her mother's body with poisonous drugs is no more than the steps to be taken to solve a management problem.

Your mother may be nauseous, he said. Give her lots to drink. Nothing to eat except crackers until her stomach has settled.

But her mother is not nauseous. She asks Anna for a glass of water and goes to her bedroom with her husband. When Anna brings the water, her mother is stretched out on the bed. Her eyes are closed. Her father is sitting on the chair next to her mother reading the newspaper. Anna hands her mother the water. She takes two sips and gives the glass to her husband. He puts it down on the bedside table. "Go," she says to him. "I want to stay," he says. "No," she says. "Go. You too, Anna. Go." They try in vain to persuade her to allow them to stay, but she tells them she wants to sleep. "Keep Anna company," she says to her husband. John Sinclair picks up his newspaper and tucks it under his arm. He signals Anna to follow him, but as Anna is about to leave, her mother calls her back. "Anna. A minute." John Sinclair hesitates; he looks inquiringly at his wife. "I just want a minute with Anna," Beatrice says to him. He closes the door behind him.

Anna approaches the bed. Her mother's eyes flutter open, close, and then, with effort, they open again. "Your father was wonderful," she breathes. "He sat next to me all through the chemo."

"I knew he would," Anna says.

"He prayed for me."

"Yes."

"He has his own way of praying, your father."

Anna nods.

"I saw him," her mother says.

The bed cover has slipped off her mother's shoulders. Anna pulls it up. "I did, Anna," her mother says when Anna does not respond.

"Daddy loves you."

Her mother takes a deep breath. "I didn't mean it that way, Anna," she says softly.

"What?" Anna leans over the bed, closer to her. "What?"

"When I said I didn't want you to come."

"Ahh." Anna straightens up. "Put that out of your mind, Mummy. Rest. You need to sleep."

"It's just that I wanted him with me. *For better or for worse.*" Her lips part into a weak smile.

And not knowing what else to say, Anna repeats what her father said earlier, "*Till death do us part*, Beatrice."

"I am lucky," her mother says, and drifts to sleep.

Anna finds her father in the garden in the back of the house. He is examining the two orchid plants Singh has left in a corner, near the fence. He has taken off the tan slacks and blue shirt he wore for her mother's sake when they went to the doctor's. Now he has on shorts that end at his knees and a blue knit shirt stained with brown spots, most likely coconut juice.

"Singh brought them for Mummy last night," Anna says, walking toward him.

"He was here?"

"He came to drop them off."

"I guess your mother ordered them."

"No. Singh said they are a gift. From his wife and him."

"Oh." Her father bends down and picks up the bundle of plants. Singh has covered the roots with burlap. The thick dark green leaves of the orchids spread elegantly above the burlap. There are buds on the stalks that Singh has propped up with thin bamboo sticks. On one of the stalks, an orchid is flowering. The petals are bright white, rare even for the Caribbean. Her father strokes a leaf on the flowering orchid and says, his voice brimming with wonder, "He brought this? He came just to drop this off?"

"He was concerned about Mummy."

Her father sighs. "I complain she's bossy with Singh and Lydia, but you know, Anna, she is also kind to them."

"I'm sure she is, Daddy." She wants to please him. He is worried about his wife. She will not upset him. She will allow him the fantasy he seems to need.

"When Singh got married again, your mother made me give him a month's salary as a wedding present."

Anna is not impressed. "That was good of her."

"Do you know Lydia has a granddaughter?"

"Yes, I know that Lydia has a granddaughter."

"Your mother makes me pay her school fees and buy her school books."

"Mummy?" Anna is unprepared for this new information.

"Every year, for four years now," her father says.

"Four years?"

"Lydia's granddaughter . . . What's her name?"

"Jennifer."

"I keep an account for her at Zanzibar Books and at that clothing store, Murray's. She goes there and purchases what she needs. It's put on my account."

"Four years? Mummy's never said a word. And Lydia . . ."

"Your mother has forbidden Lydia to tell anyone what she has done for her."

"Forbidden?"

"Your mother says if she gets her reward here, she will not get it in heaven."

Her father says this in all seriousness. There is not a hint of mockery in his tone. He converted to Catholicism for her mother. The priest had refused to marry them otherwise. There was the question about their children. The children had to be Catholic and the priest wanted more than a commitment in intentions. He would believe her father's intentions to raise his children as Catholics if he himself became one. Her father loved her mother; he did what the priest asked.

When Anna was a child, she did not think of her father as a religious man. She does not think so now. Her mother says she saw him praying as the chemo drugs coursed through her veins. Anna thinks *saw* is the operative word. But her mother could not see into her father's soul. She could not see whether in his soul he prayed.

"She has amassed a fortune in heaven," her father says. "I am way behind her."

After dinner, when she was a child in their house, she and her mother said the rosary together. They knelt at the side of the bed and each took turns leading the prayer. They would go through the ten decades, each one beginning with the Our Father, followed by ten Hail Marys. Each night another mystery: the Joyful, the Sorrowful, the Glorious. Her father would find something to do while they prayed: a chess game with Neil Lee Pak, work he had to finish in his office, a friend he needed to visit. But there were some nights too when he sat in the study. What was he thinking then? How did he distract himself? For Anna is certain their voices filtered through the slit below the door. *Lead us not into temptation.* Was this his prayer too?

He always accompanied them to church on Sundays. He stood in the back; they sat in the pews in front. He waited dutifully until the Mass was over and drove them home afterward. He never complained.

When he is exhausted, her father says, "O Father me!" He sighs and groans. "O Father me!" A sort of prayer, perhaps, until one day she decoded it. *O Father, save me. O Father God, lead me not into temptation. O Father God, forgive me.* These are his true intentions, the purpose of his prayer.

For a few years now, on her visits back home, Anna has noticed he no longer stands in the back of the church. He sits next to her mother in a pew in the front. When the priest sings "Alleluia!" he stretches his hands upward, his palms open wide. All that display of religious fervor embarrasses her Catholic mother, but her father's Protestant childhood is fused in his bones. "Alleluia!" he sings with the priest.

He receives Communion now. But Anna is not fooled. He has not changed. This talk of the fortune her mother has amassed in heaven and the prayers he hopes she says for him is a camouflage. If he believes in heaven and hell—and she is not sure he does, for she has never heard him speak of an afterlife—this faith has not been enough to comfort him. Her mother is comforted by the hope of salvation. The inevitability of death still fills him with anger and resentment. Neither religion nor Anna's attempts at reminding him of man's part in the cycle of life seem to assuage his resentment. Anna accuses him of solipsism and he responds that the individual may not count *more* than the community, but without the individual there is no community.

No, Anna is not fooled when he follows her mother in the line for Communion, when he stands next to her at the altar and stretches out his tongue. She is convinced this change in him has not come because he is old, because he knows the time is drawing near when he shall meet his Maker. She thinks he has changed to impress her mother. He wants her to witness, to have proof of the condition of his soul. For the soul must be as white as snow before the sinner can receive Communion, before the Body of Christ can be placed on his tongue.

"I hope it will be a long time before your mother collects that reward," her father says, and puts the orchid plants back down on the ground.

Anna hopes so too. Her father has made his peace with her mother but she needs time, for there is much left for her to resolve.

CHAPTER 15

"Why didn't you come back?" her father asks.

It is night. Her mother is still asleep. Anna and her father have just had their first full meal of the day, pelau Lydia had prepared the way her father likes it: the rice grainy in the casserole, not cloying in lumps to the pigeon peas and chicken. The pelau was already cooked when her mother and father returned from the doctor, but John Sinclair is a creature of habit. He had tea, biscuits, and jam in the afternoon and waited until six to have this meal.

Anna is in the kitchen washing the dishes when her father asks this question. Though Lydia would gladly wash the dishes in the morning, her mother will not go to bed if there are dirty dishes left in the sink. Her mother is scrupulously clean, in her person and in her home. She will not appear at the breakfast table unless she has showered, fixed her hair, and, unlike her husband, put on clean clothes that have been carefully pressed. By teatime she has changed again. She claims the heat of the day makes her damp and sticky. (She will not use the words *sweat* or *perspire*). This is the excuse she gives her husband for needing a woman to come to the house twice a week to iron her clothes. She will find the places Lydia has missed when she polishes the furniture and will follow her with disinfectant to check that the bathrooms have been cleaned to her satisfaction. Acknowledging her own practice on the night before her weekly cleaning woman comes to her apartment in New

York, Anna once joked with her mother that she cleans up her bedroom to impress her cleaning woman.

Her mother responded indignantly, "I don't wash the dishes to impress Lydia. I wash the dishes because I do not keep a dirty house."

So while her father goes to the study to put on a CD, Anna washes the dishes from the dinner they have just eaten.

He has put on Vivaldi, *The Four Seasons*, and has turned down the volume, but the music seeps through the house, out of the study and into the kitchen, and, Anna has no doubt, along the corridor to the room where her mother is sleeping.

Is it for her mother that her father has put on Vivaldi? Does he hope that Vivaldi might penetrate the veil of sleep, calm her mother's nerves even as she sleeps?

"Why not, Anna?" he asks. "Why didn't you come back?"

The violins grow quiet; the pace slows down. *Spring.* When he first played *The Four Seasons* for her she knew only two on her tropical island, the wet and the dry. Now, *Spring.* In America it came alive for her. It was as she had imagined as a child: buds opening, breaking through the late winter's frost.

The music soars. The allegro, a pastoral dance. Flowers bloom. Colors blaze across a landscape reawakened at last from a wintry slumber.

"Vivaldi," she says.

Her father does not lose his focus. "After college," he repeats his question. "Why did you stay?"

She puts the last of the dishes on the rack to drain. "There was graduate school," she says.

"And after graduate school?"

"I came back," she says.

"You stayed six months."

"I couldn't find a job."

"So that was it? If you were able to find a job, you would have stayed?" He is standing in the rectangular archway, in the space between the kitchen and the family dining area, twirling the plastic CD container in his hands.

"I don't know how to answer that question," she says. "Getting a job was not a possibility open to me."

"You didn't give yourself time. I'm sure something would have turned up."

"There were no decent jobs for women when I came back with my master's degree," she says. "If I wanted to be a secretary, yes, there would have been a job for me."

"You're not being fair, Anna."

"Those were not fair times."

"We had our independence from England when you came back."

"Replaced by neocolonialism," she says, and turns away from him.

"Frantz Fanon." He tugs his ear.

They have had this argument before, once bitterly when she came for a visit after she had returned to America for good. She brought him Fanon's *Black Skin, White Masks*. "There. Read what Fanon says." She handed him the book. "That's the problem with the island now. We have been brainwashed to think like the colonizers."

"It was a man's world when I came back," Anna says now. "Except for white women. They were given the status of honorary men."

"Anna, Anna," her father pleads, but she is not mollified.

"I just wanted to teach," she says. "I didn't care what level. I had a master's degree, but I couldn't find a teaching job anywhere in the city. Yet there were teaching positions for white women, English women, Canadian women, foreign women. I guess black women were not considered bright enough, smart enough."

Her father cringes. In the background the mournful violins of the Largo begin.

"Things have changed," he says softly. "It's not the same now. Local women are in important positions today, in the government, in the private sector."

"Things changed too late for me."

Her father inclines his head toward her. "Come, sit with me in the veranda. It's a beautiful night."

He does not want to talk politics, and in truth neither does she. For it is a beautiful night. Not a cloud spoils the clarity of the midnight blue sky.

How many times a sky like this one was a reference for her when navy blue was not what she wanted but was the only blue the salesperson in the department store in New York understood when she asked for dark blue. "Midnight blue, like the sky," she would say, and the salesperson would answer, "Like navy blue?"

But she left; she walked away from the tropics where the stars burn like bright fires out of a sky so deep she glimpsed infinity.

"Aren't you tired?" she asks, drying her hands on the dish towel.

He is already walking toward the door. She puts down the towel and follows him outside. The intoxicating perfume of flowers, fruit, and earth rises to meet them. She inhales and her senses are awakened: smell, sight, touch, taste, the memory of pleasures past. This too she left behind.

"It wasn't because of me, was it?" Her father motions to two chairs, close to his fishpond. He will drop the politics, but his original question remains on his mind. "You didn't stay away because of me, did you?"

"Because of you?" She sits next to him.

"Because I moved you to the hill."

He surprises her, for they rarely speak of those days when she lived with them in the gated compound up the hill from the oil fields.

"When we moved to the hill, we had more than we ever had," she says cautiously. "We had a bigger house, a new car."

"I was always at work."

"But you always had breakfast with Mummy and me, and you always came home for dinner."

The family who prayed together, stayed together, her mother said. *The family who ate together, stayed together,* her father rejoined. He always found a way to return home for an hour to have dinner with them, even when he had appointments late at night. And there were many times he came home for lunch.

"I know you didn't have many friends on the hill," her father says, and crosses his legs. "But when you came back from graduate school we were living here, close to the city. You had friends in the city."

"School friends," she replies. "We had grown up and we had changed. They were planning babies. I was thinking of a career."

Is it Neil Lee Pak's innocent question as they were leaving the house that has stirred him so? she wonders. *Isn't Anna coming too?* Neil Lee Pak asked. *No,* her mother answered with a forcefulness that brought both men to an awkward silence.

"But later on, when things got better on the island, why didn't you return? There were jobs for you then."

"Tony," she says. "I was already dating Tony. We were planning to get married. Tony wouldn't live here. He didn't want to leave America."

Her father avoids her eyes. "Ah, that man didn't know the prize he had."

Prize? Did Tony know what a prize he had? Does her mother? Her mother did not want her by her side when they went to the doctor in the morning. But her father will not pry; he will not ask her about Tony. He has a respect for privacy. He will not ask her, either, what she and her mother talked about when her mother asked him to leave the room. He will not scratch the wound that has never completely healed between her mother and her. And perhaps this is what husbands must do. This is what the Bible instructs them to do. They must choose their wives first, above everyone else, even above their children.

The CD pauses between movements. Without the violins, a thick silence grows between them. She is the first to break it. She wants to change her father's mood. She wants him to think of other things, other times. *She* needs to think of other things, other times.

"Did your father like Vivaldi?"

"To listen to, not play. Father was good at the violin, but he was not that fast." He breaks into a loud chuckle. "Father used to say Vivaldi found one melody and he wrote seven hundred variations of it. Imagine! Seven hundred variations of the same theme. That was a clever priest!"

CHAPTER 16

"M usic is in the Sinclairs' blood," Mrs. Sinclair, John Sinclair's mother, informed Beatrice when Anna was born. Everyone in their family played a musical instrument, she said. Both she and her only daughter Alice, John's sister, were gifted pianists. They gave concerts in Town Hall and once Alice performed at Governor's House when a distant cousin of Queen Elizabeth was visiting the island.

The men played the violin, Anna's paternal grandfather, who was good but not fast, and Anna's father John, who was neither fast nor good. But John more than made up for his lackluster performance on the violin with his knowledge of classical music and his scholarship at school. The family forgave him, pinning their hopes instead on his children. He didn't have a boy. That was their second disappointment, but they nevertheless consoled themselves that his daughter, Anna, would fulfill their dream of having a Sinclair play in England's famous Albert Hall. So when Anna was five, Beatrice arranged for her to take piano lessons. The piano teacher was patient. Surely those stubby fingers would lengthen and their reach widen, and though they did, though by the time Anna was ten her hands in every way resembled her Aunt Alice's tapered spread, they failed to make music. Week after week the piano teacher tried, placing her faith in the power of genes to transmit talent, but after one particularly disastrous performance, she'd had enough. She drew down the lid over the piano keys and explained as gently as she could to Beatrice that she would not be returning. Her daughter did not have the talent. The Sinclair musical gene had apparently skipped a generation.

Beatrice was mortified. She was in an unspoken, unacknowledged competition with her husband's family, and the failure of her daughter was nothing less than a reflection of her own inadequacies. The Sinclairs fanned her guilt. Whenever Beatrice visited, Alice would play the piano and afterward John's mother would draw her hand melodramatically across her forehead and sigh, "The last of the line of accomplished Sinclair women. Oh Alice."

But Beatrice took comfort in her husband. He loved her. About that she had absolute confidence. If her hips were what attracted him at first, he soon became equally mesmerized by her deep-set eyes, high cheekbones, full upper lip, smooth brown skin, and firm, though tiny breasts. In the early years of their marriage, she would often catch him gazing at her with pure adoration in his eyes. When they went to parties, he danced only with her. Fishing and hunting took him away some weekends but he always came back more enthralled than before, wanting to make love to her every night, calling her from work and bringing her the sweets she loved: coconut ice cream and mangoes, especially Julie and Starch.

Of course, eating coconut ice cream and mangoes almost every day could have but one single effect on a woman's figure. And so it did with Beatrice. Her breasts grew larger, her hips wider, but John never seemed to mind. More of you to love, he said to her. And, indeed, though Beatrice got fatter, she did not lose her figure. Miraculously, her waistline kept its shape. She was voluptuous, not fat, her figure the classical hourglass that turned men's heads and made John proud he had such a wife.

The Sinclairs, however, were not impressed. They were

rail-thin, Albert, John's father, particularly so. His body cast a shadow no wider than a beam in their house. He was short and dark-skinned, with piercing black eyes and thick eyebrows planted on his prominent forehead like a dense bush at the edge of a smooth promontory. He got his skin color from his African mother, Ann Rose, and his long nose and thin lips from his Portuguese father who had married Ann Rose, though, in those days, such an arrangement was considered both unnecessary and unwise; unnecessary because a white man could easily bed any African woman he desired without need of sanction from either the law or the church; unwise because it threw into confusion the boundaries drawn between black and white, between the colonized and the colonizer. But the Portuguese man had not come to the island with the colonizers. His purpose was not to oppress; he himself had been oppressed by others. He had fled Madeira to escape the strangling strictures of Roman Catholicism. He would not oppress another. He would ask for Ann Rose's hand in marriage. She would have to choose him.

Ann Rose was a free woman, born after Emancipation to a mother who had been dragged from the west coast of Africa, along with forty million others, for the sole purpose of making Europeans rich by their back-breaking, brow-sweating, free labor on plantations that stretched across the Caribbean. There are some who say forty million is too low an estimate. There are some who say that in the end, counting the Atlantic, Arabian, and trans-Saharan routes, close to one hundred million Africans were affected. Many died in transport, others from diseases or indirectly from the social trauma left behind in Africa.

Given this history of suffering, Ann Rose would not dishonor her mother. She demanded respect, legitimacy of her relationship with the Portuguese man. And they had much in common. They both loved books, music, and art.

Ann Rose had been educated by the wife of her mother's former slave owner, who had committed herself to teaching her as a sort of penance, atonement for her brutal treatment of Ann Rose's mother, who had been forced to serve her. If not total reprieve from damnation, which she was terrified she deserved, she hoped to gain entry to Purgatory by improving the lot of one of the Africans. Giving Ann Rose the education she had given her sons was, to her mind, her ticket out of hell.

When Ann Rose's husband died just five short years after their marriage, she devoted herself to instilling in their two sons, Anthony, the older, and Albert, John's father, the same love for learning she shared with her husband. Before they entered primary school, she had taught her sons how to read, write, and do simple arithmetic. Later, both boys won scholarships to the prestigious Catholic secondary school established for the sons of the colonizers and the children of the French Creole planters. When he was alive, her husband distrusted Catholics, but Western religions did not matter to Ann Rose: one was the same as the other. The Catholic school was the best on the island; that was all that mattered to her.

Anthony immigrated to America and became a rich dentist in Harlem. Albert remained on the island. He married a French Creole, a white woman of indeterminate blood but whose ancestors no doubt had more than one encounter with the tar brush. He and this very fair-skinned woman had two children: John, who inherited his father's brown skin, and Alice, who was so light-skinned she passed for white, convincing the people of a small country village in England so effectively that not a single one raised a peep of protest when their mayor married her.

Ann Rose was still living when John married Beatrice. She told John she was glad she had lived long enough to see a Sinclair marry a dark-skinned woman.

Education and color gave the Sinclairs class, which did not necessarily mean they had money. They had some money, but only enough to acquire middle-class essentials: a house in a decent part of the island, a car when few had one, and the means to provide their children with the finest education the island had to offer.

Beatrice's brown-skinned family had neither the requisite color nor money. Beatrice's father, Joseph Collier, was a brilliant man but he was addicted to dice and squandered most of his weekly paycheck in obsessive dreams of a windfall. Forced to find employment to support the family, Beatrice's mother first found work in a bakery whose middle-class customers measured sophistication against the styles and habits of the English colonizers. When she began substituting mangoes and guavas for apples and peaches in the pies and tarts, they complained vociferously to the manager. If they wanted poor people food, they said, they would have gone to the poor people shop. Beatrice's mother would have been fired had not the chef at Governor's House rescued her. As it happened, he was in a pickle. The Governor's European guests were demanding exotic food, though nothing so exotic as to irritate the delicate linings of their stomachs. When the chef tasted the custard tarts Beatrice's mother had topped with succulent slices of Julie mango, he knew he had found a solution. He returned to the bakery and hired her on the spot.

Beatrice's mother could never count on her husband to take care of their daughter, so after school Beatrice joined her mother in the kitchen at Governor's House. It was there, peeping through a crack in the kitchen door, that Beatrice learned about fashion and etiquette and the English way of pronouncing words. Ultimately, the Sinclairs were forced to admit that what Beatrice lacked in education and in acceptable skin color, she more than made up for with what they assumed was instinctive good taste. She was reserved in dress, preferring muted colors, beiges, taupes, earth tones that balanced the occasional yellows and pinks she wore. She insisted on breathable fabric, linens, the finest cotton, and refused to succumb to polyester when synthetics became the rage. She was equally reserved in speech, rarely raising her voice and taking care to position her tongue between the teeth so that she did not fall into the habit so common among the citizens of the island, even, unfortunately, among the middle class, of pronouncing her *th*s as *d*s. She was always careful to say *that, they, there*, never *dat, dey, dere*.

Of course, Beatrice's conservative taste was cultivated rather than instinctive, as John cannily detected when he beat a rhythm to her stride down the pavement in the middle of the city. *Badoom, badoom, badoom.* She was not easily approachable, as many a man who made the mistake of associating her seductive figure with an openness to sexual adventure quickly discovered. Her hips swayed, but she carried her head high, and with a single withering glance could deflate the hopes of the most audacious of men. It was a quality that endeared her to John, who had followed her for blocks, unable to charm her into a single response until he fooled her into thinking a page had loosened from the sheaf of papers in the folder in her hand.

Had Beatrice been a shade lighter than the color of tamarind, her beauty, good taste, and reserve would have been enough to gain her entry to the island's social circles. In time, after she moved with John to the hill, she lost her fat and achieved a weight that would have been acceptable to her in-laws were they alive. In time, she had a daughter who was at university in America. In time, her daughter became a senior editor at a major publishing house in New York. Her daughter cannot play the piano, but she has inherited her father's taste in music. They listen to Bach, Beethoven, Schubert, Mozart, and Vivaldi. They are listening to Vivaldi now.

CHAPTER 17

Two weeks later, Beatrice has her second round of chemotherapy. Her husband, who has stayed with her, does not wait for the clinician's report. When the session ends, they leave immediately and he drives his wife home.

Lydia is in the kitchen when they arrive. John Sinclair blows the car horn, but she does not press the button on the kitchen wall that releases the lock on the electric gate quickly enough for him. He blows the horn again, three times more before Lydia finally reaches the button, presses it, and the gate grinds open.

Anna, alarmed by the many times her father has honked, fears the worst. She rushes out with Lydia to the driveway to meet him. The car is still rolling to a stop when she grasps the door handle. Her mother's head is thrown back on the car seat; her eyes are closed. Her father brakes and Anna opens the door. "Mummy, Mummy." She has to shake her mother before her eyes flutter open. "John," her mother murmurs. Anna reaches for her elbow. "John." Her mother raises a limp hand and waves Anna away. "Let me." Her father is already at his wife's side. Her mother braces herself against his outstretched arm and pulls herself up. She leans her full weight against his body and he tightens his grasp around her waist to prevent her from slipping. Arms around each other, they make their way along, three steps, stop, three steps, stop, until they reach the bedroom door. Anna opens the door for them and stands aside. Carefully, gently, her father guides his wife to their bed.

"This one was not as easy on her as the first one," her father says. He places a pillow under her mother's head. Her mother has shut her eyes again. Her breathing is shallow.

"Was she sick?"

"See how pale she is?" her father says.

"Did she throw up?"

"She's a strong woman. No, nothing like that. She didn't throw up."

"She looks so weak."

"She's tired," her father says. "She needs to sleep."

"Shall I leave?"

"Ugh." Both Anna and her father turn in unison toward her mother, surprised by the sound that came from lips that had seemed to lack the strength to open on their own. "No," her mother says clearly.

"What, Beatrice?" Her father leans over her.

"No. Don't leave," she says.

"I don't plan to leave. I am going to stay right here with you, Beatrice," her father says.

Her mother looks past him to where Anna is standing at the foot of the bed. "Don't leave. Stay with me." Her gaze lingers on Anna.

"Of course I'll stay, Beatrice," her father says.

Anna lowers her eyes.

"No. You go," her mother says. This time there can be no question to whom her words are addressed. She has turned her head toward her husband. "I mean you."

"Are you sure?" John Sinclair asks.

"Anna. I want Anna to stay." It has taken all her mother's strength to say this. Her face folds, the muscles around her mouth and eyes slacken.

"Anna?"

Her mother nods. She cannot, or will not, say more.

"I guess she wants me to leave," her father says.

"I don't think she means that," Anna replies.

Her father adjusts the blanket around his wife's neck, gazes lovingly at her, and then with effort turns away. "I'll have to change my clothes first," he says to Anna. He opens the door to his closet. "It'll just take me a minute."

"Daddy, I don't think Mummy—"

He does not allow her to finish. "Anna, I know my wife. She may be tired, but she knows what she wants. Anyhow, my fish are hungry. I need to feed them."

Thinking, mistakenly, her father is hurt by her mother's dismissal of him, Anna tries to reassure him. "Mummy needs you," she says.

Her father pulls out a pair of old khaki shorts from the closet. With his back to Anna, he responds matter-of-factly, "Of course I know your mother needs me."

Anna feels foolish. Like a little girl who has been chastised. She has made too much of her mother's demand. For demand it was. *You go. I want Anna to stay.*

"But for now," her father is saying, "it's you your mother needs. Give me a chance to change my clothes. I'll come and get you in your room when I'm done."

Outside her parents' bedroom, Anna nearly collides with Lydia, who is balancing a tray between her hands loaded with a steaming bowl, empty dishes, and a covered basket.

"I made soup and biscuits," Lydia says. "I was coming to ask if Mrs. Sinclair want some now."

Anna tells her that she does not think her mother's stomach can handle soup, but her father may appreciate some.

"I leave it for him then," Lydia says. "But you know Mr. Sinclair. He have his dinner at the same time only. I give him his tea now and leave the soup for him to have later."

Anna is touched by her solicitude. "You are too kind to my parents," she says. "You're too good to Mummy."

Lydia lowers her head. "Your mother good to me too, even though she don't show it."

Her father says her mother has forbidden Lydia to reveal what she has done for her granddaughter, so Anna thinks this is as far as Lydia will go, as much as she will say. But Lydia does not stop there. With her eyes still fixed on the tray, she tells Anna more. "From the time I was a girl and leave my mother house to go live with my son father, I never safe till I come to work for Mrs. Sinclair. My son, he fraid for me. He get a job in America but he fraid to leave me alone with his father. But his father fraid Mr. Sinclair." She shakes her head. "He fraid him bad. Mrs. Sinclair tell Mr. Sinclair he must get his big-shot friends in the police station to protect me. So my son father don't touch me after Mr. Sinclair talk to his big-shot friends. He don't follow me where I live. Now my son could go and make money in America." Her chin is trembling when she faces Anna again. "Mrs. Sinclair foolishness is a little ting for me to take, Miss Anna. Is a little, little ting."

In her room, waiting for her father, Anna's head reels. *Is a little, little ting for me to take.* If Lydia could dismiss her mother's actions as foolishness, why can't she? Why can't she find it in her heart to make peace with her mother?

Her friend Paula was right—Paula, her one true friend in New York, an immigrant like she is, from an island in the Caribbean. Paula was not fooled by her claims of spending more time on the island than usual because her parents are growing older, because time is not on their side nor on hers. She is on a mission, Paula said. She is going there this time because she wants, she needs, closure.

Anna will admit it now. She is uncertain of her mother's motive for asking her to stay with her in her room, but this is a chance to be alone with her, a chance for closure.

When her father comes to get her, she picks up the manuscript she is hoping to acquire for Equiano. The manuscript will distract her while her mother sleeps, she thinks, for in spite of her best efforts, she has not been able to stop the quivering growing more and more intense in her chest.

Her parents' bedroom is freezing. Her father has raised the air conditioner to its highest level and closed the blinds. The room is dark and Anna can barely make out the shape of her mother's body under the blanket. She is lying on her left side, on her own side of the bed. Her back is curled, her hips thrust outward. Involuntarily? By habit? For her husband's sake? Anna's draws in her breath. She has caught her mother in this position before, but only fleetingly. For in a blink of an eye her mother quickly uncurled her body and modestly brought her legs together.

Do they spoon? After they make love, does her mother put her backside against her father's stomach? Does she press her naked body against his private parts?

After they make love, does her father wrap his arms around her chest? Does he stroke her breasts? And if he does, if he did in those two years (two years at least, Dr. Ramdoolal said), did his fingers touch the hardened flesh, the seed the size of a pea he had allowed to grow to a lemon, to burst open and dribble blood?

For the sake of her privacy, her father said.

Anna's temples pulsate. She is angry, but not only with her father. She is angry with her father for what he did not do, but she is angry with Tony for what her father did do and Tony did not do. For Tony never wanted to spoon. He never wanted to stroke her breasts when they were done.

He was spent afterward, exhausted. He reached for his cigarettes, not for her.

Her mother stirs, turns her head, lengthens a leg, and pulls it up again. She is deep in sleep; she does not sense her daughter's presence. A piece of thread has unraveled from the hem of the blanket at her neck and flutters upward to the bottom of her nose. When she breathes in, the thread is still. When she breathes out, the thread quivers. Anna reaches over and removes it.

Soothing sounds envelop the room. The air conditioner hums, the blanket swishes softly when her mother moves. Anna sits on the armchair on her father's side of the bed. She leans her head against the soft backing of the chair. The room is dark. She does not turn on the bedside lamp. She needs this respite. Perhaps all her mother wants is company, a warm body in the room while she sleeps. Perhaps it was her husband's comfort she was thinking of, perhaps this was her sole motive for sending him away and asking her daughter to stay. Her husband has been with her when the needles were stuck in her arm. He needs a distraction. Let him feed his fish.

Anna's eyelids feel heavy; she is drowsy. She puts the manuscript she brought with her on the floor, near to her feet. There is a shawl hanging over the back of the armchair, next to her mother's side of the bed. She wraps it around her shoulders. She shuts her eyes. In seconds, she is asleep.

"For a moment there I thought you were my mother." Her mother's voice.

Anna's eyes shoot open. Her mother is sitting up on the bed, staring at her.

"The shawl," her mother says. "It was my mother's shawl. You look just like her. You are as beautiful as she was."

Anna rubs her eyes and readjusts the shawl on her shoulders. She cannot believe she has heard her mother correctly. A lump has formed in her throat that prevents her from speaking.

"With that shawl," her mother says, "you look just like my mother."

Anna is fully awake. Alert. Emotions, none she experiences with any clarity, none she can identify, rush through her body. Her face feels warm, her knees cold, as if drained of the blood that has risen to her face. She gets up and plumps the pillows behind her mother's head. "Here," she says. "Sit back on these."

"It's true." Her mother tries to catch her eyes, but Anna lowers her head and busily smoothens the creases on the pillow case.

"Sit back," she says again to her mother.

"You don't believe me?"

"You were dreaming," Anna says.

"I should have told you that a long time ago." Her mother rests her back against the pillows. "I should have told you how beautiful you are," she says softly.

When Anna was fifteen, the brother of one of her friends from school held her hand and said, "You are the prettiest of my sister's friends." She felt a surge of irrational happiness then. This is the feeling Anna finally recognizes in the confusion of emotions that swirl through her. Will they talk now? Will they have closure?

But the timbre of her mother's voice changes, the softness that was there evaporates. "I'm sure I didn't need to tell you that," she says. No emotion, a chastisement even.

The warm sensation that has just spread across Anna's face subsides. The irrational surge of happiness dissipates.

"Your friends. They must have told you so. Why don't you call them up? Call Teresa."

She has not spoken to Teresa in at least ten years. Teresa is married. Teresa has five children.

"I don't want you stuck in the house looking after a sick woman," her mother says. "Go out. Have fun."

With whom?

"I came to see you and Daddy," Anna mumbles. "I'm not stuck in the house."

"Reading, reading," her mother says. "That's all you do. Was that a new book you were reading yesterday?"

"A novel by Toni Morrison."

"Is she good?"

"She won the Nobel Prize in Literature."

"A woman?"

"The first American woman to win a Nobel Prize in literature."

"What a thing," her mother says. Her attention drifts. She looks across the room toward the window. "Your father always turns the air conditioner on too high," she grumbles. "Lower it for me, will you, Anna?"

But her father does not turn the air conditioner on too high. He turns it on to the temperature her mother wants.

The air conditioner protrudes from a rectangular hole cut out of the wall beneath the window. Anna walks over to it and turns it down.

"That's better," her mother says. She takes a pillow from her husband's side of the bed and adds it to the ones behind her back. "John is my best friend," she announces.

Anna clenches her hands. "You are lucky, Mummy," she says, and readies herself. The route will be a short one now from the friends she does not have to the husband who left her. First there will be a diversion.

Her mother sighs. "It takes time to build a true friendship, Anna."

"Time and things in common," Anna replies cautiously.

"You have things in common with your friends here."

"I got severed from my roots a long time ago," Anna says.

Her mother sighs again. "Call Teresa. I have her phone number."

"I'm happy being here with you and Daddy. And I have work to do."

Her mother peers over the bed. "Those papers on the floor?"

"It's a new book I'm editing."

"You must be important at Windsor."

"Not all that important. I'm merely an editor."

Her mother corrects her. "A *senior* editor."

"That only means more work for me," Anna says.

Her mother fiddles with the blanket covering her thighs and legs. "You work too hard. I worry about you. You say you don't have friends here. Do you have friends there, where you are in New York?"

"Of course."

Her mother considers this answer. "Of course," she repeats quietly. An echo. No conviction in her voice.

"You should sleep some more," Anna says.

"Yes. I think I'll do that."

"I'll fix the pillows." Anna removes them from the headboard. "You want one or two under your head?"

"One," her mother says.

Anna shifts the other two across the bed, away from her mother. "Here. Is that okay?"

Her mother slides down on the bed. They avoid brushing against each other.

"You're a good daughter, Anna, I just wish . . ."

And Anna thinks, here it comes: the end of the route, her mother's true purpose. The saccharine sweet tone, the compliments rarely given—a good daughter, as beautiful as her beautiful grandmother—all leading to her true objective. Her mother will draw her out now, she will force her to face her inadequacies, her failures. Her failure as a woman to fulfill the role her mother has successfully fulfilled. For isn't this the role society has prepared her for, expects of her: anodyne relationships of no substance, friendships whose purpose is to advance harmony in marriage? Children.

"What do you wish, Mummy?"

"I just wish . . ." Her mother inhales, exhales.

"What, Mummy?"

"I just wish you and Tony . . . Your father is such a comfort to me. I just wish you and Tony . . . You must be so lonely."

Anna does not respond, but it takes every ounce of restraint she has taught herself in the years in the Englishman's country, in the years she has chosen to live among people who make assumptions, who decide who she is, her likes and dislikes, the reaches of her heart, her intellectual capacity.

She steadies herself. "Sleep, Mummy," she says. "Sleep."

Once outside her mother's room Anna's legs buckle under her. She leans against the closed door and braces herself. She clamps her bottom lip between her teeth. She will not let the tears fall. *She cannot.*

You must be so lonely.

This is why her mother has asked her to stay, why she wanted her to remain in her room. But she has friends in New York. She has Paula. She is not lonely.

I wish you and Tony . . .

She and Tony are divorced. Tony has remarried. Even now Tony could be making love to the new woman he married. Why couldn't she have said that to her mother? Why couldn't she have said that Tony has moved on, found another to share his bed while she sleeps alone?

She does not want her mother's pity. Her mother's pity will take her down to a place too deep, too dark, to find the light again. Anonymity is what she sought when she chose New York, a chance to remake herself freed from the glare of judgmental eyes.

CHAPTER 18

E pluribus unum. Out of many, one. America's boast brazenly embossed on its coins. But in New York a blind man can find his way across the city by his nose, by the odors of food rising from the streets and through open windows. His ears can take him anywhere across the five boroughs. Even when the language spoken is English, he can tell the difference in the accents. He knows he is either uptown or downtown, in African American Harlem or Spanish Harlem, in Caribbean Brooklyn or in East Asian Queens. He knows when he enters the WASP enclave, or the territories carved out by Europeans.

"You think you are the United Nations?" Tony sneered when Anna claimed ancestors from around the globe. "In America, you are black. Don't go thinking other people see their relatives in you."

Tony is African American. If other bloods run through his veins, he pretends not to know. His Africanness comes before his Americanness, he said to Anna. And it did not matter when Anna pointed out that except for the two who had been dragged onto slave ships from Africa, he and all his relatives, his parents and grandparents and great-grandparents going back for more than four hundred years, had all been born and raised in America.

Was he the first African American she ever dated? he asked her.

No, she said. She had dated Americans. She did not think of him as the first American she ever dated.

"*African* American," Tony said. "I did not say American. Those two are not the same. You could get killed in America if you are foolish enough to believe they're the same."

The O.J. Simpson trial opened her eyes. Not that she hadn't noticed before.

People like being with people they know, people who have things in common with them, a white friend explained.

But she could not understand the bookstores, why even there American literature was separated: American literature on one side, African American literature on the other. Books are not people. Books do not choose to be with other books that have things in common with them. Then she got a job at Windsor and Tanya Foster clarified the nuances of niche marketing. Still, she finds it difficult to justify why a book that has nothing to do with cultural differences, a book on nuclear proliferation, for example, or on moral philosophy, ends up in the African American section because the writer is African American. Or why, when the scholar is African American, his exegesis on Milton is placed there.

To facilitate access, liberals say. Access, that perniciously deceptive "a" word. Does nuclear proliferation have a color? Is there one kind of moral philosophy for white people and another for black people? Does the color of one's skin determine one's ability to analyze literature?

Yet she is not without guilt. What hypocritical game was she attempting to play with her mother, deliberately withholding from her the fact that Toni Morrison is African American, pretending her color did not matter?

She said American. She could have said African American. She could have told her mother that Toni Morrison is the first American woman to be awarded a Nobel Prize in literature *and* she is African American. It might have made a difference to her mother, presented her with a different image to counter the ones on the nightly news.

Was it out of some misguided sense of moral superiority that she was silent about Morrison's racial identity? Did she hope to prove the unfairness of her mother's unquestioned acceptance of the negative images of African Americans beamed on international TV? But what about *her* acceptance? She has not told her mother about Equiano. She has not told her that the writers on her list at Equiano are writers of color. Is it embarrassment that makes her dissemble by omission so that her mother continues to believe she is a senior editor at Windsor?

Racism is a poison so insidious it finds its way through the tiniest slit in the soul and does its damage there even before one is aware. How to explain the black men, the political and cultural gurus, the intellectuals, who all but very few brought white women, their wives or mistresses, to the first congress of the newly independent nations celebrating the end of European colonization?

It should not matter. It should not matter. But for the black women who came to that first congress it mattered. Love is in the heart, they knew, but love is also in the will. One chooses with the heart; one acts with the will.

Her mother, at least, does not dissimulate; she is honest; she is forthright. She does not mince her words. She says she would rather risk surgery on her island, in a hospital that lacks sufficient equipment, than have it in America where there are doctors and equipment for Americans, doctors and equipment for African Americans.

"You'll learn," Tony said. "Stick to your kind. Stick to your own race. You'll find you'll be happier in America."

Your own race. Anna believes there is only one race, the human race.

Tony, of course, meant black people, and she is forced to admit that there is something of the truth in what he said, something of the truth in the ease of bonding with her own kind, with people from the Caribbean islands.

Her mother heard the lie in her answer. *Of course*. Of course she has friends in America. But the reality is that Paula is her only true friend. She has social acquaintances, people she meets at parties, at office functions, and there are the odd coworkers, but with none of them does she spend Easter Sunday, Thanksgiving, or Christmas. Only with Paula does she celebrate those special holidays. Their friendship is founded on their common roots. They belong to two-season landscapes where the rain falls incessantly for months on end, where dense green jungles sprout out of ordinary backyards and thick vines strangle the leaves of high-reaching trees. They belong to islands that gave birth to the myths of the soucouyant, douennes, La Diablesse—a place where a people stripped of their musical instruments invented new music from discarded oil drums. The names of their fruit tell their tales of displacement and colonial conquests: pomme cythere, pommerac, mammy sepote, gru-gru boeuf, tamarind, mango, doungs, chennette, guava. Mixed-up names: none the pure languages of the European colonizers, neither English, French, nor Spanish, none pure African, Indian, or Amerindian either.

Her mother's best friend is her husband. Her mother is her husband's best friend. Anna thinks it is their common roots that nourish them, people, places, events they can recall together, that temper resentment, that warn them instinctively of the dangers of transgressing boundaries.

Her father waits for her mother's approval to acknowledge the blood on the vest she wears to bed.

Her mother rips out her beloved orchid bed to build a fishpond she hopes will ease the grief consuming her husband's heart.

Roots allow her parents the generosity to forgive. Roots allow her mother to forgive an offense Anna had thought unforgivable: her father's betrayal that siphoned color from her mother's lips and planed the soft curves on her breasts and hips.

Anna had come home from New York for her annual visit, timed this year for her mother's birthday. She brought with her a diamond-studded bracelet her father had asked her to purchase, a gift for his wife. She'd had to quarrel with the jeweler to make him understand that the circumference of her mother's wrist was less than six inches. He had been in the jewelry business for more years than she had been on earth, the jeweler told her. He knew the circumference of a grown woman's wrist. But her mother's wrists were unusually tiny, and so Anna could be forgiven if at the airport, when her parents came to meet her, what she noticed first about her mother was that the measurement she had given the jeweler was accurate. And then, little by little, her eyes took in the rest: the scaffolding exposed on her mother's face, cheekbones so pronounced they hollowed her eyes, her dress clinging to the frame of a scarecrow.

"A new diet," her mother murmured. Anna did not believe her.

Inside the house her mother extended her arm for her husband to put on his gift to her. Anna saw the thick corded veins that snaked under her mother's skin. They veered in every direction, sluggish tributaries of a dry-season river.

"It's beautiful," her mother said, but there was no light in her eyes, no happiness in her voice.

"Let's see," he said.

She raised her arm and the bracelet slid down, almost halfway on her forearm. She lowered her arm and the bracelet fell off. The thud of diamonds and metal against the hardwood floor echoed with accusation. In the empty space where the sound dissolved, her mother stood frozen, her hand a fist in her mouth.

Her husband reached for her elbow. "Beatrice, come now."

Her mother flinched, the bones on her shoulders grazing her earlobes.

"Beatrice, don't."

She pushed him away. Her sobs rattled through her throat, a staccato not unlike the coughing of a consumptive, as she ran to her room.

Later that night, her mother quiet now, still in her room behind closed doors, her father explained. He had met a woman. He had fallen in love.

CHAPTER 19

In the morning her mother is her old self again. Her skin glows, her eyes are bright. She has come to breakfast in her favorite chocolate brown linen pants which she has paired with a cream-colored linen tunic, one with a Mandarin neckline that she has fastened at her throat. The sleeves on the tunic cover her arms. Nothing is exposed that will give the lie to the picture she presents of perfect health. There are no hints that under the front of the tunic a tumor grows.

Lydia is beaming when she greets her. "Miss Sinclair, you look so pretty. You look like a million dollars."

Her mother purses her lips. Lydia has crossed a boundary, one that separates employer from employee. The domestic helper in her employers' house must learn to be circumspect; even compliments can be considered an invasion of their privacy.

Anna is quick to intervene. "Lydia wanted to bring your breakfast to your room, Mummy."

"Well, you can see there is no need for Lydia to do that," her mother says stiffly.

"She made something special for you."

"Something special, Lydia?" Her mother arches her eyebrows.

"I make fry bake and buljoil," Lydia says.

"Fried bakes and buljoil?" This is her mother's favorite breakfast meal. Her lips relax. "Thank you, Lydia," she says.

Lydia grins. "Is a little ting."

John Sinclair is standing behind his wife. He does not approve. "Won't buljoil and bakes be too heavy for your stomach, Beatrice?"

Her mother takes the seat he pulls out for her. "Dr. Ramdoolal said that if I feel well, I should eat what I want. And I feel well." She opens her napkin.

"But so soon?"

With the deftness acquired through years of learning which matters are or are not serious enough for her husband to be willing to compromise, she diverts his attention. "Can't you find something better to wear, John?" she says, her eyes traveling across his clothes.

Her father is wearing the same clothes he changed into when they returned from Dr. Ramdoolal's office. They are the clothes he wears when he works outside in the backyard. He wipes his hands on the legs of these shorts; yesterday's sweat clings to the armpits of his knit shirt. "I'm not going out," he says.

"Still." Her mother clicks her tongue.

"I'll change if I need to go out."

Her mother shakes her head in frustration, but she has won. She will have her buljoil and bakes. Yet her father gets his way too. He sits back in his chair and loosens the belt at his waist.

"Must you always do that, John?" Her mother glares at him.

He pats his stomach. "For a breakfast of fried bakes and buljoil, yes."

Anna laughs and her laugh infects her mother. In spite of her best efforts, the muscles on the sides of her mother's mouth begin to twitch. The smile rises to her eyes. "Your father." She throws up her hands in mock exasperation. "What can I do?"

All is well, Anna thinks, relieved. The tumor can lie there insidious, waiting, but it is hidden; it is out of sight. For now, they will have breakfast. Fried bakes and buljoil. For now, all is normal. There are three long weeks before the next chemo session. For now, they can pretend.

Lydia brings the warm bakes in a basket and presents the buljoil on a silver-plated tray. The marinated saltfish is mixed with an appetizing medley of colors: translucent pieces of raw onion, chopped red tomatoes, yellow and red sweet peppers, and sprinkles of fresh green chives and parsley.

Anna's stomach has grown unaccustomed to this rich fare at breakfast. In New York, she has bagels and cream cheese, sometimes cereal and bananas for breakfast, nothing more complex. For the last two days she has managed to pick her way through sardines and herring, but the saltfish is too much. She will not be able to keep it down. Raw onions irritate her stomach. She reaches for the bakes. She will have one, with butter and cheese, but not the buljoil.

"Pass the buljoil to Anna, John," her mother says. "I'm sure Anna's not had buljoil in New York."

Anna crosses her hands. "Not for me," she says quickly.

"Not for you?" Her mother narrows her eyes.

"Too rich," Anna says.

"Too rich?"

"So early in the morning."

"Lydia went through a lot of trouble," her mother says. She takes the platter from her husband's hands.

"Lydia made the buljoil for you, Mummy." Her mother wants to trap her with guilt, but she will not let her.

"And because she thought you'd appreciate it too." Her mother passes the platter to her.

"I do, I do." Anna looks over to the kitchen and catches Lydia's eyes. "I do, Lydia." Lydia smiles.

"The least you could do is eat it," her mother says.

"I can't. Really, I can't."

Her mother puts down the platter

"But the bakes. I love the bakes," Anna says, slicing one of them in two.

Her mother spoons some buljoil on her plate and turns to her husband. "Did you notice, John, how she picks at everything? She doesn't like our food. Did you hear her last Sunday? She doesn't like callaloo. It's practically our national dish and she won't eat callaloo."

"I'd just prefer cheese this morning, that's all," Anna says.

"She means cream cheese, John."

"I can have the cheddar."

Her mother ignores her. "Do you know what cream cheese is, John? It's not real cheese. Not in my opinion."

Her father concentrates on the buljoil on his plate. He piles a sliver of saltfish with bits of tomato and onion delicately on the back of his fork.

"She's become American, John," her mother presses on. "She eats only American food."

Her father chews slowly. He does not say a word.

"I suppose saltfish is beneath her, now she lives in big New York."

Anna has had enough. "Don't speak about me in the third person, Mummy. I'm here. Speak to me."

Her mother faces her. "Then how is it that buljoil is too rich for you? You used to eat it when you lived here. You loved it."

"Raw onions make me sick," Anna says.

"That's it? Raw onions make you sick?"

"I can't eat it so early in the morning."

"You used to. John, didn't she used to?" Her mother challenges her father to take her side. He puts down his knife and fork. "Yes, Beatrice," he says indulgently. "She used to. But if she doesn't want to eat it now, you shouldn't force her."

Her mother stretches her hand across the table and pushes the dish of buljoil away from Anna. "I suppose Americans don't eat raw onions for breakfast," she mutters under her breath. "I suppose that's it."

A numbing pain shoots through the base of Anna's head, the muscles tightening into a ball. She cradles her neck in the palm of her hand. Her father glances at her sympathetically. "Beatrice, Beatrice," he pleads. "Let it go."

Her mother retreats. They finish their meal making small talk about the weather and the recent rash of robberies in the neighborhood.

After breakfast her mother goes to her garden. Singh is already there, pulling up weeds among the flowers. Through the open window in her bedroom Anna can hear them talking.

Singh says: "If bossman buy two clay pots, I put de two orchid plants de wife send for you in dem and I hang dem under de orange tree. It go be like you have orchids growing on your orange tree."

Her mother tells him that her husband's name is Mr. Sinclair, not bossman. He should call him Mr. Sinclair.

Singh pretends he has not heard her. "If bossman too busy, I get de clay pots for you," he says.

"Mr. Sinclair," her mother repeats. "His name is not bossman."

"I does call him dat from when I did start to work for you. I call him bossman. I call you madam. I doe change."

Her mother makes grunting sounds. Then she says, "Will you have the time to do that? To get the clay pots?"

"Anything for bossman," Singh says.

"How much do I owe you?"

"For what?"

"For the orchids you brought."

"Is a present from de wife and me," Singh says.

All is quiet outside. Anna waits for her mother's response. Seconds pass. A shift has occurred in their relationship. Singh is not the hired hand; he wants no money for the thing he has done; it is a gift he offers, from one human being to another.

Anna moves closer to the window. Her mother's voice is soft but clear. "They are beautiful. You are so kind to me, Singh. So kind, you and your wife."

"We was worried, you know, madam," Singh says. "Den Miss Anna say you seeing Dr. Ramdoolal. I feel better when she tell me dat."

Her mother returns to the house. She says she will take a nap before lunch, but at lunchtime she is still asleep. She sleeps past teatime. It is close to six before she emerges from her room. Her father is worried. She feels well, she says. Rested. She needed the sleep, but now she is starving.

While her husband sits next to her nibbling his evening sandwich, she eats everything Lydia had prepared for her lunch: stewed chicken, rice, fried plantains, steamed cabbage, carrots. Her plate is empty when she refolds her napkin. Afterward, they sit in the veranda. John Sinclair has put on a Bach CD, the Brandenburg concertos.

Anna washes the dishes. Her parents have not invited her to join them in the veranda, so when she has finished, she goes to the living room to work on the manuscript. Through the glass sliding doors she has a clear view of her parents. They do not appear to be saying much to each other. Her mother's head rests on the back of her chair; her hands are folded on her lap, her legs are spread apart, though only slightly. She seems at ease, perfectly relaxed.

When Anna looks up next, her father is standing over his fishpond, rubbing his chin. He says something to her mother, who nods. He looks down on the pond. Her mother says something to him. He turns away from the pond, bends down, and plucks out the weeds that have pushed their way through the cracks on the pebbled concrete border.

Her mother has asked him to do this, Anna thinks.

When her father is done he returns to the chair next to her mother.

The fifth concerto comes to an end. Her father rises again and goes to the kitchen. He passes the entrance to the living room, but he does not look inside. If he knows his daughter is in there, he has decided not to disturb her. But perhaps he does not know she is in the living room; perhaps his mind is elsewhere, with his wife who is waiting for him in the veranda.

The electric kettle whistles. Her father reappears. He is carrying a tray with two cups of tea. In the veranda, he and his wife sip their tea in silence. When the music comes to an end, her father gets up, returns to the study, and puts the CD on again.

It is almost ten when Anna finally gathers up the pile of manuscript pages on the cocktail table next to her chair and turns off the light in the living room. Her father, who has still given no sign that he knows she is in the living room, suddenly calls out, "Leave the light on, Anna. Your mother and I will stay out here a little while longer."

Common roots. They do not have to speak, sitting next to each other. A sigh, a frown, a clearing of the throat, a smile, the softening of the eye, legs crossed and uncrossed. Body language. That's all they need.

Late into the night it rains, a hard rain that pounds the roof of the house. It beats a rhythmic drum, loud and in-sistent. Anna bolts upright from a deep sleep. For a moment she does not know where she is. Gunfire? It is her first thought. She lives in Brooklyn, Fort Greene, not far from the park. Sometimes there are muggings, sometimes gunfire. But it is not gunfire she hears. The drumbeat is furious, behind it a waterfall, the deafening sound of rain sluicing down in gallons from the clouds. Her bedroom, the whole house, seems overpowered by this force of nature suddenly unleashed.

Be not afeard: the isle is full of noises, / Sounds and sweet airs that give delight and hurt not.

When she was a child, she was not afraid. She is afraid now. She presses her face against the window pane. Then she remembers a childhood rhyme. *June too soon, July stand by, August come it must, September remember, October all over.*

She is here, in June, too soon for the rainstorms that knock down trees, that blow off the roofs of houses. June, the end of the dry season, too early for the wet. In her parents' backyard, the flowers on the two mango trees have already dropped their petals. Green fruit cluster at the ends of branches, weighing them down. Yesterday, the grass was brown. Tomorrow, soaked by the rain, it will be green again.

Anna's mother continues to improve. No nausea, no headaches, no weakness in her limbs. Dr. Ramdoolal credits her recovery to all that good, natural food she ate as a child. He says the ground provisions and the vegetables they grow on the island without artificial fertilizers are no match for the packaged foods full of toxic chemicals sold in grocery shops today. But Anna knows her mother's improvement is temporary. There are two more chemo sessions to go; the third one, a week before she must return to her work at Equiano. She has not yet made up her mind what she will do, whether or not she will stay for the fourth session the doctor has scheduled. The manuscript she has brought with her has to be presented soon to the editorial board. Tanya Foster has not opposed her decisions so far, but there is much she will have to do to persuade Tanya to publish this one.

Her mother is in such a good mood that two days after the chemo sent her to bed for twelve hours straight, she announces she is ready to spend a day in the country.

"Come with us," her father suggests.

"Yes, Anna. You'd like it. It's beautiful on the north coast," her mother says.

Perhaps all her mother is doing is stating a fact—it *is* beautiful on the north coast of the island—but her words get under Anna's skin. She is not a foreigner, a tourist.

"I've seen the north coast," Anna says irritably.

"So you won't come with us? Beatrice!" Her father turns to his wife in dismay. "Tell her to come. She'll have a great time."

"It's just that you've been in America so long," her mother says, trying to reason with her.

"I've lived there for eighteen years, Mummy."

"More there than here," her mother says.

"It's still my country."

"Anna, Anna, you've become so sensitive. Of course this is still your country. Nobody's saying otherwise. Your father and I wanted to show it to you, that's all."

"Show it to me?"

"You know . . ." Her mother shrugs. "Just in case."

"Just in case what?"

"It's been a long time since you were there."

Why is she so thin-skinned? So sensitive, as her mother says. She wants to go. For all her protest about the indelible stamp of her early years on the island, for all the resentment she feels when her mother intimates she has become American, she is forced to admit to herself there is much she has forgotten, much she can no longer claim as hers.

She does not want to lose her moorings, she does not want to be set adrift on some Sargasso Sea like the emigrants who left the island before her, the ones lured by England's siren song, only to discover that once they cleared the rubble left in the wake of the war, once they had rebuilt the Mother Country, England no longer had need for them.

She wants to see more of the island, she needs to remember, to hold onto home, to sunlit backyards perfumed with the scent of ripe mangoes, to salt-filled rain, to skies washed clean blue, to flamingoes turning green trees in the mangrove to red, to fishermen pulling in seines in the silvery dawn. She needs to fix in her head waves breaking on the rocks below the narrow winding road to the north coast.

Her mother tries again. "I've asked Lydia to pack us lunch. Come with us, Anna. Please."

Remorseful, ashamed now of her childish reaction, Anna agrees to go.

Her mother is right. She has forgotten how beautiful the north coast is.

The sun is a dry-season sun that illuminates everything: fluffy white clouds that drift lackadaisically across a pristine blue sky, brown earth that sparkles when sunbeams gild metallic stones. They pass through small villages at the foot of the mountain, tiny houses clustered at the edge of the road once a dirt track for horses pulling carts and donkeys loaded with produce for the market. They see a donkey now, burlap bags bursting at the seams grazing its flanks. The man sitting astride it waves his machete. All the villagers wave, laughter and talk suspended when the Sinclairs pass by in their fancy car.

The higher up the narrow road to the north coast they go, the fewer houses they see, only flashes of galvanize and painted wood here and there between dense vegetation. Two days of heavy rain and sporadic showers have watered roots, and, like magic, trees have sprouted new leaves, vines new tendrils that loop across branches. On the sea side of the road, the land plunges down deep precipices. Below, the water is rough. Waves crash against giant black rocks, miniature islands broken off from the land, and pitch glittering white sprays of sea water up to the sky. Anna drinks in the air that rushes through the car window. Salt carried on the wind stings her nose. This is what she needs to remember, what she needs to lock in her heart for wintry days in New York.

"We're almost there!" Her father brings the car to a crawl. He can barely suppress his excitement.

"Yes, I can tell we are near now." Her mother strains her head through the window. The muscles on her neck rise and stiffen.

Do they have a specific destination? Until now Anna had not thought so.

"Where are we going?"

"You'll see," her mother says.

The road bends and the sea disappears. They are entering the mountain now. On both sides the forest grows thicker. Tall trees have spread their branches wide at the tops and their leaves form a canopy shading the sun, but beneath them, new trees have multiplied and bushes grow wild.

"In a couple of weeks, you'll need a machete if you have to stop to pee," her father says.

Anna braces herself for her mother's response to this crude remark, but her mother giggles. Like a schoolgirl, Anna thinks.

They drive a few yards further. "Stop! Stop!" Her mother grasps her father's arm. "I think this is the spot. I think it's here, John."

The steering wheel is on the right side of the car. Her mother is sitting on the left, on the passenger side. The rules here are still British. What her mother wants her father to see is on the right side of the road. She is practically on top of him when she points her finger toward the bushes.

"I'll have to cross the road," her father says.

"Yes. Park there. On the side, under that tree."

The road, though barely wide enough for one car, is a two-way road. Just a mile back, a car had come barreling toward them and her father had to swerve to avoid an accident.

"Be careful now." Her mother directs him across the road. "Yes, this is it. I'm positive."

Her father brakes. He squints, studying the bushes. "You're right," he says at last. "This is it. Your mother has good eyes, Anna."

Anna sees trees, big ones, smaller ones, bushes, tall grass, no special marker, no difference in the landscape from the cluster of trees they have just passed.

"Your mother and I used to catch birds here." Her father is beaming.

"*Mummy*?"

"Remember, Beatrice?"

But her mother is already out of the car. "It's still here. I see it. Come, John." She quickens her pace.

Her father hurries toward her. Anna tries to follow them but the sleeves of her blouse get caught in a knot of twigs. She stops to untangle herself and nettles cling to her pants. She bends to pluck them out. She clears one leg only to find the other leg of her pants crimped with more nettles. She reaches for a limb of a tree to steady herself and her fingers grasp the sharp ends of a branch. Everywhere she turns she is stuck, pricked, prodded. She stumbles over dried branches and loosened stones. They are far ahead of her. She cannot see them. She hears only their voices.

"Imagine that," her father says.

"Come." Her mother urges him on. "We're almost there."

The rain that fell has thickened the underbrush. Above, the sky strains through tiny spaces between leaves at the tops of giant trees, but below the green is dark. Threatening, it seems to Anna.

The forest is closing in on her. She can barely see more than two feet in front of her. Her heart is hammering. Her parents have stopped speaking. There are no human voices to guide her. All around her the leaves on the trees swish ominously. Fruit falling on the ground make sounds like the explosion of bullets. Birds fluttering their wings terrify her. A black, yellow-beaked crow caws. She stifles the urge to scream. *Be not afeard.* This is her island, her rain forest, but she cannot quiet her heart. It hammers still, beating loudly in her throat. Then, suddenly, in a parting of the trees, she sees them. They are standing a hair's breadth from each other, so close that when a breeze ruffles her mother's blouse, the edges brush against her father's shirt. They are looking intently at something. What? Anna cannot distinguish it from the browns and greens in the forest. She draws closer. Shapes become more distinct: branches, leaves, vines winding into a shed, or what was once a shed. There is no roof, no windows, no door. Four wood pillars jut up from the floor; the skeleton remains of a staircase lead to the entrance. Slats of wood once nailed to the frame are scattered on the ground. Vines twist through spaces where they have fallen off.

"We should have come back here before now," her father is saying.

"Yes," her mother replies. Regret weighs down the word.

Anna clears her throat. The noise she makes is slight but it startles them.

"Anna!" Her mother spins around. They stare at her, eyes stretched open wide as if they had forgotten she has come with them.

"Did I surprise you?"

"Of course not." Her mother quickly recovers her composure. "Your father and I were reminiscing."

"About this shed?" The absurdity of the question causes Anna to rephrase it. "Did it belong to someone you knew?"

"No. It was ours," her father says. "We built it."

"You?"

"*We* did, your mother and I."

"I used to come here sometimes with your father."

The picture refuses to form in Anna's head.

"When I was a young man I came here to catch birds," her father explains. "After your mother and I got married, she came with me."

"Mummy?"

"Well, if you can't stop them, you have to join them," her mother says gaily, far too gaily for the woman Anna thinks she knows.

"She wanted to come," her father says.

"I was curious," her mother retorts.

"She missed me," her father says.

"Oh, John, you say such silly things."

They are bantering like teenagers. Anna is certain her mother batted her eyes. Her father plucks her mother's blouse playfully. "Well, it's the truth. You missed me."

Anna cannot imagine her mother here, in this shed, in this dark forest. She cannot imagine her mother tramping through the bushes, dried twigs scraping her arms, nettles in her hair.

"I built the shed to protect your mother from the rain and the sun," her father says.

"I helped," her mother insists.

Above them the leaves rustle. Bright yellow plumes like tiny suns twinkle among the greens. Two birds. Semps. The violaceous euphonia, the sopranos of the forest. They fly one behind the other and vanish into the branches of another tree. Her father puts his finger on his lips. "Shh," he says. They are quiet, still as statues. Then one bird whistles. Her father pulls his lips forward and emits a long, melodious trill. The bird answers. Her father whistles again. Another bird joins in, and another. Anna can barely distinguish where her father enters and the birds respond.

"He was always good at this," her mother says. "He would put laglee on a tree branch and whistle until a bird came closer. The bird would think it's another bird. They would whistle to each other, back and forth, and finally the bird would fly to the branch and its feet would get glued to the laglee."

"I was young and foolish then," her father says and scrapes the ground with the tip of his shoes.

"Foolish?" Anna raises her eyebrows.

"The semps are almost all gone now. We were lucky to hear them just now."

"What did you do with them? The birds you caught?"

"Most of the time your father freed them," her mother says.

"Not before I showed them to you." Her father grins at her gratefully.

"And the ones you did not free?" Anna presses him.

"Only one. It wasn't a semp. But it was so beautiful. Remember, Beatrice?"

"Hmmm." Beatrice nods.

"I had never seen such pretty blue and yellow feathers. I kept it for a while in a cage and then I gave it to the zoo."

"Your father is sentimental," her mother says.

"I don't know why you say so, Beatrice. You were the one who made me give the bird to the zoo. Telling me the poor thing needed room to fly."

Her mother smiles shyly. "And the white lilies. Do you remember the white lilies we found, John?"

"Those were the good old days. Those lilies were huge. Big and bright white. We dug them up and took them back with us."

"The ones at home next to the mango tree?" Anna asks.

"We didn't take all." Her mother is quick to defend her husband again. "We left most of them in the forest."

"So they're still there?"

"I'm sure. They grow wild here. But I don't think we could find them now. We were lost that day we came upon them."

"We had to spend the night in the shed," her father says.

Her mother blushes.

"A whole night. Isn't that so, Beatrice?" Her father nudges her mother's arm.

But her mother is embarrassed by his talk about their night in the forest. "It's time to go," she announces abruptly. "We need to find a place where we can eat."

Her father does not give up so easily. "It was so dark that night we could barely see each other. Not that we needed to. Right, Beatrice?" He winks at her.

Her mother is not amused. "Don't forget I'm not well, John." It is all she needs to say to return him to the present he has momentarily suspended.

They walk back to the car, her father supporting her

mother by her elbow. They do not pause, they do not look back.

A few yards away from the car, they see a man peering through the window. He is tall and has to bend down low to look inside. He is scantily dressed: frayed dark shorts, a creamish-looking shirt that could have once been white. He is not wearing shoes. Even from where they are, Anna notices the muscles running down like rope along his chocolate brown arms and sturdy calves. He has a full head of tightly knotted hair sprinkled with gray. They do not see his face until Anna's father calls out to him.

"Hey! You there! What are you doing?"

The man straightens up and turns around. "Johnny!" His eyes are beads in their sockets. Bird's eyes. They dart from side to side. His nose is wide, his lips thick, his skin leathered and tough.

"Bertie!"

For a moment the shock of recognition causes both men to remain bolted to the ground.

"Johnny!"

"Bertie!"

Life comes to their feet and they hurry to each other. They grasp hands and pump their arms up and down, up and down, vigorously. Their eyes sparkle, their smiles radiate across their faces.

Anna stands next to her mother, watching.

"And de lady of de house? Dat's her, Johnny?" They have released each other and Bertie is looking past his old friend's shoulder.

"Come." Anna's father slaps Bertie on his back and walks with him toward his wife.

"You still beautiful as ever," Bertie says and makes an elaborate bow before Beatrice, raising his arm and swinging it across his waist. His arm catches the hem of his shirt and exposes a naked stomach, flat and hard.

"Same old Bertie," Beatrice says.

"And my daughter," John Sinclair says.

"Sweet mango don't fall far from de tree." Bertie makes the same bow before Anna.

"He was my hunting partner," John Sinclair explains to his daughter.

"Still hunting," Bertie says. He is looking steadily at Beatrice when he says this. His lips are smiling, but not his eyes.

"Isn't it time you settled down?" Beatrice says sharply.

"Will have time enough when dey trow dirt in my face."

The glare from his eyes is too strong for her mother. She turns away from him.

"Your fadder and me use to be boys together," Bertie says to Anna. "We use to hunt together, even when we get big. But Beatrice didn't like her Johnny to hunt."

"Same old Bertie," Beatrice says again.

Contempt is too strong a word, Anna thinks, to characterize her mother's attitude toward this man. She seems sympathetic even, though condescendingly so. But it is Bertie who has the upper hand here. If time has stood still for him, it has marched on for his friend. He looks younger than her father. It is not only his full head of hair that makes him look so, or the muscles in his arms and legs. Her father is almost bald, but his muscles are firm. There is something else about Bertie and Anna struggles to identify it. Next to him her father is the essence of refinement, a man remade through nurture. Bertie is a creature of nature, a man of the earth. *Salt of the earth.* This is the phrase she has been searching for. Her father wears shoes. Bertie's feet are unshod; his toes grab the dirt and keep him steady. Fallen branches, protruding twigs, nettles, none of these will harm him.

"Your fadder is a good man," Bertie says to Anna. "De bestest of all de best men."

Her father takes out his handkerchief and wipes the sweat dripping down the sides of his face. Anna is perspiring too. Her blouse is wet and clings to her skin.

"It's hot," her mother says. She fans her face with her hand. "I need to get out of the sun."

"Car have air condition?" Bertie asks. His face is dry. His shirt falls loosely over his body. It does not cling to his skin.

"My wife's not feeling well," John Sinclair says.

Beatrice frowns at her husband. It is the only signal he needs. He quickly revises his explanation to Bertie. "The heat," he says.

"Since when heat get to you, Beatrice?" Bertie comes closer to her. "You born and bred here."

"John!" Beatrice appeals to her husband for his intervention.

"Of course Beatrice was born and bred here. You know that, Bertie. Stop teasing her."

"Dis not England, you know, Beatrice."

"I need to get in the car." Beatrice puts her hand to her forehead and shades her eyes.

"The car is air-conditioned," John explains, but this is not enough to still Bertie's suspicions. His beady eyes inspect Beatrice. Her face is damp, the skin ashy. "You sick, Beatrice?"

"Beatrice just needs to cool off," John says.

"Dat's it?" Bertie's eyes do not leave Beatrice's face.

"Tired," she says.

"Tired?"

Beatrice nods. "I'm not as young as I used to be. Not like in the old days."

"You look de same to me, Beatrice," he says softly. "Always pretty. Still pretty."

Beatrice rewards him with a wan smile.

John Sinclair places a firm hand on his friend's shoulder. "Well, we must be going. I'm really glad to see you, Bertie, but we have to go."

Bertie's eyes linger a second more on Beatrice. They narrow and darken. "You eating right, Beatrice?" he asks.

"She's really tired," John says and tugs Bertie's shirt.

Bertie backs away. "When you come back, Johnny?"

"We'll catch up."

"When?

"Soon, Bertie, soon."

"We used to have some good old days," Bertie says.

Beatrice coughs.

"Anna!" John Sinclair catches her attention and inclines his head toward Bertie. "Anna, say goodbye to Bertie."

"You come by this way soon again, Johnny?" Bertie is clearly not ready to part from his friend.

"I promise."

"All we days count now, Johnny."

"I know. I know."

"We not getting any—"

"John!" Beatrice does not mask her impatience.

"Bertie, we can't stay. Beatrice . . ."

"I know, I know. She tired."

John Sinclair opens up his arms and spreads out the palms of his hands in surrender.

"Go, go," Bertie says.

Anna extends her hand. Bertie takes it and brings it to his lips. "You have de bestest fadder, pretty girl. When my boys was in school, is your fadder pay dey school fees."

In the car, Beatrice slumps down on her seat. She is angry with her husband. "You don't have to tell the whole world about my business," she says.

"I didn't tell the whole world. That was only Bertie and all I said was that you were tired."

"And not feeling well. You didn't have to tell him that. Did you see the way he looked at me? He knew."

"And if he knew, or he guessed, what does it matter, Beatrice?"

"I don't want pity," she says.

The air is tense between them. Her father has allowed Bertie to penetrate their privacy. He has exposed her mother to his pity.

They drive further down the mountain. Her father attempts an apology. "Don't worry, Beatrice. Bertie is an old friend."

Her mother grimaces. "Friend? What do you think he meant by telling me this was not England? Like I don't know this is not England."

"Bertie meant nothing by that, Beatrice."

"He just wants to blame me for everything. As if I was the one who stopped you from being friends with him."

"Bertie was just being Bertie. He was teasing you."

"Well, I didn't like it."

"He likes you. If you ask me, he's jealous of me for having you as my wife. Did you hear what he said? *Always pretty, still pretty.* You really can't think he has anything against you."

Beatrice clasps her lips together.

Her husband makes another attempt to placate her. "What about lunch? Don't forget we have a picnic hamper in the boot of the car, Beatrice. I could find a quiet spot for us to stop and eat."

No, her mother says. She has had enough for one day. She has pushed herself too hard. She wants to go back home. They are hardly off the mountain before her head rolls back on the headrest and she falls fast asleep.

In the quiet of the car Anna asks her father about Bertie. Is it true he paid the school fees for Bertie's children?

That was a long time ago, her father says. He keeps his eyes on the road.

But is it true?

Her father groans. "It'll take Bertie to remember that," he says.

Chapter 20

e bestest of all de best men. The bestest fadder. Didn't she herself give him a pen and pencil set inscribed with the words:

To the best Father in the World.
Love, Anna

Twenty-six years ago. She is fourteen. She is with her father. A little girl chimes: "You are the bestest godfather in the world." Behind her, a chorus of tiny voices. "Mr. Sinclair is the best godfather in the whole wide world."

John Sinclair is not the little girl's godfather. He is not the godfather of this gaggle of boys and girls.

They are at the gates of the Catholic orphanage. Her father has asked her to come here with him. They are carrying baskets heavy with ripe mangoes. It is the year of a strange fecundity. A hundred babies born in one week on an island of less than a million, forty abandoned at the orphanage. The nuns have their hands full with crying babies needing feeding and burping, needing diapers changed and washed. They have left the toddlers in the care of the older children, the ones now running toward Anna and her father.

That morning Anna helped her father pick the mangoes. Twice in this fecund year the mango trees have borne fruit. Mangoes lie rotting on the ground in their backyard, most of them without a blemish or the sign that they have been pecked by birds. For in the trees the birds sit drowsy-eyed, their bellies glutted with mango juice, ballast weighing them down.

Her father has parked the car in the street and they have walked to the orphanage. Two boys open the gates for them. The children who sing out the greeting eye the baskets of mangoes but do not ask for them.

Three brown-skinned nuns appear. They are local women accustomed to the sun, but the mid-afternoon heat is unbearable. Their faces, framed by long white veils that cut across their foreheads, are moist with sweat. One of the nuns signals to the boys to take the baskets. "We are so grateful to you, Mr. Sinclair," she says. "The children look out for you every day."

Every day?

The nun explains to Anna: "The children count on your father. When mangoes are in season, he brings the best for them every day."

"Goodbye, Godfather! Goodbye, the bestest godfather in the whole wide world!"

The children wave to them as they leave.

And yet he betrayed her mother. And yet this man, de bestest of all de best men, the bestest godfather in the whole wide world, the man who paid the school fees for the children of his impoverished friend, the man who brought mangoes for the children in the orphanage, who goes to the police station to demand protection for his domestic helper, who gives her money for her granddaughter, who, as far as Anna can tell, loves his wife, has always loved her, had confessed to her, his daughter, that he had met a woman. He had fallen in love. Her name, he said, is Thelma.

What had gone wrong? What had made him break the vow he had made to her mother before the priest and the law? He had sworn to cherish her, to love her, until death do we part.

He is a man who prides himself in his integrity, his honesty, his principles. Character is all, he tells his daughter. A man without character is no more than a talking animal. A man who lets his whims, his desires, his passions, his greed, dictate the decisions he makes in his life is one who, though born a human being, has never learned to be human.

"Your mother has changed," he said to Anna that night she returned home from New York for her mother's birthday and could not deny the scaffolding on her mother's face, could not pretend when the bracelet—a traitor's gift, she knows that now—rolled off her mother's hand.

He expected his daughter to empathize with him. For wasn't she a woman by then who knew the ways of the world, the fragility of the human heart? "Your mother is not the same woman I married," he said.

If his eyes were not so shadowed with pain, if the muscles in his face were not so taut and strained, Anna would have laughed at him. Even a schoolboy knows that people change, that the girl he met at the corner store is not exactly the same girl he is dating.

He expected her to feel sorry for him because she would understand that the heart needs what the heart wants. But surely he must have realized that she was no longer the fourteen-year-old who made no demands, who did not ask to see any more than what she saw on the surface. She was not that young, inexperienced girl who looked up at him in wide-eyed awe as the children in the orphanage chanted, "The bestest godfather in the whole wide world."

"Your mother was fun to be with. She used to laugh at my silliest jokes. You'd think I'd given her jewels when I brought her mangoes. I loved the way one bowl of ice cream was never enough to satisfy her. She would have to have two. Even more."

Anna lashed out at him. "And you cheated on her for this? For ice cream and mangoes? Because she didn't laugh at your jokes?"

"I fell in love," he said.

"In lust. That is what you mean."

"I was lonely. Your mother became a different person when we moved to the hill."

"*She* was lonely. People laughed at her. Your own family called her Boo Booloops."

"I loved her the way she was. But she began all that dieting, all that exercising. She lost her figure."

"You cannot be so shallow, Daddy. You cannot want me to believe you stopped loving Mummy because she lost her figure."

"All that seemed to matter to her was what those European women on the hill thought of her."

"She had to live with them. It was hard for her to live with their scorn."

"I tried to tell her that it didn't matter to me what they said or thought. But she stopped eating." He looked away. "She stopped doing more than that . . . She wasn't fun anymore."

"Fun? Is that what you called it?"

"Your mother and I . . ." He hesitated, waiting for a signal from her that he had said enough, that she understood, but Anna would not give him the reprieve. She wanted a full confession, an admission of his guilt. "It's been over a year now," he murmured.

A year because her mother suspected he had a lover. Women can tell, they know when their men have taken a lover. Suddenly, out of the blue, a kiss too passionate or not passionate enough, a change in the usual rhythm in bed.

"And does this woman do *that*? Is she fun?"

"I want to be happy. I deserve to be happy, Anna."

"Does it matter if your happiness costs Mummy her happiness?"

"We're all responsible for our own happiness, Anna. I'm not responsible for your mother's happiness."

"You promised her for better or worse."

"I can't be a good husband if I am unhappy."

"Is that the excuse you gave Mummy? A mid-life crisis! Is that what you told her? I thought you'd be more sensible than that."

"Sensible?"

"That, that . . ." Anna shook her head in frustration searching for the right word. "That pabulum excuse men claim when they reach forty."

"Reason has nothing to do with the fact that we die, Anna. Intelligence can't prevent our freefall into the grave. When you reach forty, you'll realize you've lived more than half your four score and ten. Talk to me then about pabulum excuses."

"So that's it? All this is about your fear of dying."

"Don't let anyone determine your happiness, Anna. Take control of your future. Do what you know will make you happy."

"You want me to understand that some tawdry affair is what makes you happy?"

"It's not a tawdry affair."

"Yes, I suppose in your estimation nothing you do can ever be tawdry."

"Anna, Anna," he pleaded. "Don't speak to your father this way."

But at that moment he was not her father. She had lost all respect for him as a father.

"We are talking about your wife, my mother. Can't you

see how much weight she has lost? She is skin and bones. Can't you see how much she is suffering?"

"I was suffering too."

"So what should Mummy do? Get a lover, like you did? It is you who has changed. You are not the same man I knew as my father."

"Anna, Anna." Furrows moved vertically in tiny waves across his cheeks, outward from his mouth. A grayish pallor spread over his brown skin.

He was begging for her understanding, but even now, when she is almost forty, the age when he claimed she would understand, feel empathy for him, she does not empathize. She forgives, but she cannot forget.

She does not remember choosing the words she said to him that night when in the darkness of the veranda he told her his tawdry story. She does not remember deliberately selecting this phrase over that, this order of sentences over that. She does not remember thinking at all, but she remembers what she said, her exact words to him. "I will tell you this," she said. "I will make this clear to you. If you leave my mother, you will not have a daughter. Make your choice now: your family, a wife who has been at your side for twenty-one years, a daughter who has respected and loved you for twenty years. Choose us or choose the woman you claim to have fallen in love with. You cannot have us both."

She does not know what made her say those words. As far as she was aware, she felt no special attachment to her mother. Then, in those days, her greater loyalty was to her father.

Four days passed and each night her father disappeared after dinner, the sound of his car accelerating up the road bringing tears to her mother's eyes. Each morning at breakfast her mother's eyes were black pools ringed with purple. Anna wanted to help. Her mother pushed her away. "This is between your father and me," she said, as she was to say again to her daughter years later on the first day of her chemo treatment.

Another day passed, and on the sixth day her mother came to the breakfast table dry-eyed. As usual her husband pulled out her chair for her. Not as usual, she did not sit down. "I want the keys to the car." She held out her hand. Her husband stared at her in disbelief.

"I want the keys, John," she repeated.

"But you don't drive."

"Anna drives."

She does not need Anna. When he comes home from work, he will take her wherever she wants to go, her husband said.

"Give me the keys, John." The muscles around her mother's lips were tight, her darkened eyes hard.

Her father tried again to reason with her. "And how will I get to work, Beatrice?"

"Walk," she said.

They faced each other, two warriors, their swords drawn. In the end her father surrendered. Mumbling something about unreasonable women who let their feelings take control of them, he slapped the keys on the table.

After he was gone, Anna waited for her mother's instructions.

"Give me a moment to get dressed," her mother said. "Then we'll go."

But go where?

"You'll see." It was all the information Anna could pry from her.

When her mother finally emerged from her room she seemed different. Her complexion was brighter, no doubt because of the makeup she had applied to her face—lipstick on her mouth, rouge on her cheeks, concealer under her eyes that masked the purple circles. But she had lost the calm self-assurance she displayed earlier that morning. She seemed nervous. In the car, she crossed and uncrossed her hands. From time to time, she bit her lower lip. When Anna reached to switch on the car radio, she clamped her hand over her wrist and stopped her. She needed to think, she said. She didn't want to be distracted.

But distracted from what? Where did she want to go? She would not give Anna an answer.

At the end of the highway, at the roundabout, the road split in two.

"Turn here." Her mother pointed to the left.

Anna did as she was told.

"Go ten blocks."

Anna did as she was directed.

"Turn here to the right."

Anna turned to the right.

"Go three traffic lights."

Anna counted one, two, then three traffic lights.

"Now to the left."

Anna drove to the left.

"Now to the right."

Anna drove to the right.

"Twenty-one, twenty-two, twenty-three." Her mother counted the houses. "Twenty-four, twenty-five, twenty-six." She was sitting on the edge of her seat, her head straining forward. "Stop!" She grasped Anna's shoulder. The car swerved. Her mother's head bounced back.

"This is it!" Her mother was at the edge of her seat again. "Twenty-six. Stop!"

They were in an old part of the city where the roads were narrow and the houses tiny, built close to each other.

All had peaked alcoves on the front trimmed with fanciful white fretwork in the style of tropical mansions of the Victorian era. Clusters of tall flowering plants—bougainvillea and hibiscus especially—bloomed over fences and along the short walkways that separated the houses.

Number twenty-six was a pretty blue one. Bougainvillea blossomed in a carnival of pinks and oranges.

Her mother got out of the car and unlatched the wrought iron gate on the fence that enclosed the house. She walked up the pathway to the front door, a woman on a mission, her head erect, her shoulders thrown back. She knocked on the door. There was no answer. She knocked again, three quick raps with her knuckles. The curtain at the window fluttered.

"Thelma!"

Anna sucked in her breath.

Her mother called out again. "Thelma!"

Anna's heart raced.

"If you don't want a scene in front of your neighbors, open the door, Thelma." Her mother tugged the black handbag hanging in the crook of her right arm and pulled the straps over her shoulder.

The curtain moved again and then went still. The door opened. A woman appeared, a full-figured woman of no particular distinction except for wide hips that strained against the tight fabric of her skirt, a woman with a figure like her mother's used to be.

They spoke in hushed tones. Her mother said something. The woman shook her head. Her mother said something again. The woman shrugged and turned away. Her mother raised her voice. "You're lying, Thelma."

Thelma put her finger to her lips.

"I know you're lying." Her mother drew her handbag close to her chest. A shield to protect her.

Thelma whispered something again.

"He's in there!" Her mother was shouting now. "Tell my husband to come home!"

Thelma backed into the doorway.

"Now, Thelma!" her mother said.

The door at the side of the house cracked open. Anna saw a foot, a hand, and then the whole body. *Her father!* He was dressed as he had been when he left that morning, in a gray suit, white shirt, and striped blue tie. He looked as he looked when he had left that morning: his face serious, his mouth determined, a man on his way to work.

Her father stepped through the doorway. Her mother turned her head when she heard his shoes crunch on the graveled pathway. Thelma whimpered.

At the gate, John Sinclair waited for his wife. He opened the car door and his wife slid inside. She barely glanced at him.

The rain that had threatened that morning poured down from the sky.

"My car will get a good cleaning," John Sinclair said to his wife.

"And so will your soul," his wife replied.

Always promising, her mother said, when for years her father promised to replace the rusty galvanize over the fishpond with the fancy wire netting she wanted. *Always promising. That's your father.* But he kept the promise he must have made to her mother that afternoon. At Mass the next Sunday he walked behind her on the Communion line. At the altar, he clasped his hands in prayer below his chin, he closed his eyes. *Lord, I am not worthy . . .* He thrust out his tongue.

The soul, every parishioner knows, must be free of sin to receive Communion. That Sunday her father made his contrition public for those who had suspicions.

CHAPTER 21

Every Wednesday at three, her mother's bridge friends come to play a game and drink tea. This Wednesday is no exception. Lydia sets up the card table and chairs in the veranda. On a separate table, close to a circle of cushioned wicker armchairs, Lydia puts out the meat pies and sweet pastries she baked that morning. She lays out the best china, the Wedgwood with the blue rim Beatrice's mother-in-law gave her when she married her son. It is part of a set that for two generations has stayed in the Sinclair family. Beatrice inherited six cups and saucers, six dessert plates, the teapot, and the matching sugar and creamer bowls. Lydia puts four cups and saucers on the table with the teapot, the sugar and creamer, and four dessert plates.

Her mother's bridge friends are punctual. They arrive together in a black antique Morris car that belongs to Mrs. Busby. All her mother's friends have their drivers' licenses but only Mrs. Busby actually drives. Mrs. Busby is a widow while the other women have husbands who drive them around.

All the women are about her mother's age. Like many of the people in their social circles, their skin is brown tinged with that pretty rich red undertone that comes from living in the tropics. Mrs. Busby is a thin wisp of a woman who never regained the weight she lost when her husband died. In contrast, the other women are quite plump. Mrs. Farrell is short and squat. She has twinkling eyes and rather thick lips that seem always spread in a smile. Mrs. Baden-Grant is tall and big-boned. It would be both unkind and unfair to call her fat. Her breasts rise high on her chest, but her hips are narrow for a woman her size. She has a long nose that flares slightly at the tip. Her lips are thin. Like the lips of her English mother, she says.

The women are attractively dressed. Mrs. Busby has on a flower-print cotton dress with a rounded white collar. Mrs. Farrell and Mrs. Baden-Grant are wearing slacks, Mrs. Farrell tan ones with a white linen shirt; Mrs. Baden-Grant, white slacks with a greenish print shirt. Anna's mother is also wearing white slacks, but her top is much prettier and more expensive than those of the other two women. It is a designer blouse Anna bought for her in New York, made out of breathable linen in a muted red and taupe paisley pattern. Anna's mother stands out among these women not only because she is clearly the most beautiful, but because she is also the most fashionably dressed. Anna can tell her mother enjoys this special status. She is deferential without being subservient, confident that the women already feel their disadvantage in her presence.

Lydia's timing is perfect. As soon as she hears the women's voices, she removes the teapot and the creamer from the table. By the time the women have sat down on the wicker armchairs, she has brought out a steaming pot of tea and the creamer filled with Carnation Evaporated Milk.

Anna comes out to the veranda to greet the women and Mrs. Sinclair instructs Lydia to bring another cup and saucer and a dessert plate for her daughter. Anna declines her mother's invitation to join them. She has to finish working on a manuscript, she says.

Mrs. Sinclair emits a high-pitched laugh. "Working, always working, my Anna," she says with exasperation, which the women know from past experience to be false.

She is not exasperated; she is in fact delighted to have the occasion to boast about her daughter.

"Still at Windsor?" Mrs. Baden-Grant asks, her nostrils flaring.

"Of course, Eunice," her mother answers before Anna can get a chance to slip in a word. "Of course she's still at Windsor. Working on a Windsor book," she says.

"Can you tell us who's the writer?"

"You won't recognize the name," Anna says. "It's a new author."

"Anna is an acquisition editor," Mrs. Sinclair declares. She explains that her daughter finds books for Windsor. Agents send books to her; Anna makes the decision on which ones the company will buy.

The women are duly impressed.

"What young women are doing today!" Mrs. Farrell says in awe. "In our day, Beatrice, the most we could aspire to was to be typists. Now your daughter is an acquisition editor. You must be proud to have a daughter doing something so important."

Anna's mother is gracious. "You say that as if you don't have a daughter doing something more important." She turns to her daughter. "Did you know that Mrs. Farrell's daughter is a judge, Anna?"

Mrs. Farrell expresses her gratitude for the compliment by elaborating on the one she had given before. "But to be an acquisition editor in New York for one of the largest publishers in the world! *That* is an accomplishment."

Anna does not have the heart to tell her this is not exactly the truth. She will not embarrass her mother. She will not deny her this momentary victory. She excuses herself and leaves the veranda. From the living room, she hears the bursts of laughter. Her mother laughs the loudest.

Her mother has not told the women she has cancer. To

talk of cancer is to stir memories of shame and defeat. To talk of cancer is to conjure pictures of rotting flesh, women reduced to stinking carcasses, raw meat leaking onto ulcerous sores. Nothing masks the stink of fungated cancer, not cologne, not perfume. Not all the roses in the whole wide world.

These women do not talk about cancer. They are afraid to talk about cancer. Cancer has no regard for class or good breeding. Cancer does not care if the blouse you are wearing was bought in New York, if the label is a designer's. It does not care if the china you have is Wedgwood, if your maid wears a uniform and knows how best to serve tea and pastries to your admiring friends. Cancer cannot be defeated, so cancer is best kept in secret. Cancer is best hidden from the view of Mrs. Sinclair's good company.

A week later, her mother is brushing her hair in the bathroom and when she lowers her hand she sees clumps of her dyed black hair wedged between the bristles of the hairbrush. She screams. Her husband is not at home. He has gone to the city for the monthly luncheon meeting of the Rotary Club. Anna is in the kitchen talking to Lydia. They almost trip over each other in their race to the bedroom.

Her mother is sitting on a stool before the mirror. She is in her underwear, a white cotton bra and panties that reach to her waist. Hair blankets her naked shoulder. She sees them through the mirror and spins around. Involuntarily her naked legs spread apart, exposing her crotch. In that split second her eyes shift rapidly from Anna to Lydia and the contours of her face change from terror to anger. She drops the hairbrush on the floor, grabs her robe, which is lying on the counter behind her, and pulls it up to her neck hastily covering her bra and panties.

"Lydia!" For Lydia is the object of her anger. "Knock!

How many times have I told you to knock? You can't come to my room without knocking."

Lydia tries to explain. "I think something bad happen to you, Mrs. Sinclair. I come to help. I sorry. I knock de next time."

Anna puts her arm around Lydia's shoulders and leads her out of the bedroom. When her mother gets so sick she cannot dress herself, will Lydia be permitted to enter her bedroom without knocking? For when she gets so sick and cannot wash herself, Lydia, or someone like Lydia, will have to see her nakedness.

Her mother is crying freely when she returns to the bathroom. "My hair, Anna. My hair. What am I going to do?"

Anna picks up the brush from the floor and untangles the hair from the bristles. "This was to be expected, Mummy," she says.

Her mother places her hands over her head. There is a bald spot in the middle where her hair has fallen out. "I'll look old. I'll look terrible." The words come out of her mouth in gasps between her tears.

In as calm a voice as she can muster, Anna reminds her of Dr. Ramdoolal's warning. "The doctor told us this would happen. Remember?"

But remembering the doctor's warning does not console her mother. "What am I going to do? How they will laugh at me!"

"Don't you see this means the chemo is working?" Anna says reasonably.

Her mother glares at her, eyes red-rimmed. "Working?"

"Killing the cancer cells," Anna says.

"Killing me. Destroying me." Her mother covers her face with her hands and bursts into a fresh round of tears.

This is her mother. Anna cannot watch her in this distress and do nothing, say nothing, to help her. "Cut it," Anna says. The idea enters her head partially formed and then blossoms. "Cut it all off. You'll look great with short hair."

Her mother drops her hands and regards Anna with puzzlement. "Cut off what little I have? That's what you want me to do? You want me to look worse than I already do?"

"You'll look beautiful. And fashionable."

"Fashionable?"

"Short hair is fashionable in the States."

Her mother reaches for a tissue and dries her eyes. "In the States," she says. "Short hair is not fashionable *here*."

It is not the reaction Anna has hoped for. Still, her mother's defiance is a good sign. Better than self-pity. "You'll be a funky old lady," Anna says.

Her mother wrinkles her nose.

"Nice funky," Anna adds quickly.

"You mean a white-haired old lady." Dye masked the visible strands of her mother's hair, but at the roots it is white.

"So you'll be a funky white-haired old lady. A silver fox."

"A silver fox?" Her mother crinkles her eyes.

Anna can tell she is not displeased by the image her words have conjured. She hastens to cement the picture for her mother before it drifts away from her mind's eye. "Daddy will get a new you," she says.

Her mother takes another tissue and blows her nose. "Your father may not want a new me."

"Daddy likes anything you do."

"Yes." Her mother is suddenly pensive. She folds her lower lip into her mouth. "Yes," she says again, dreamily.

"With your face, short hair will be perfect for you."

Her mother twists her jaw back and forth.

"It's true, Mummy."

Her mother releases her lip. "Your father is so good to me."

"He loves you," Anna says.

Abruptly, her mother stands up. The robe falls to the floor. She is exposed again: white bra and waist-high panties. Anna cannot see the lump under her arm, in her lymph nodes, but the tumor on her breast protrudes above the top of the bra. She shifts her eyes away from the protrusion.

"Let's do it now, Anna. Let's cut it now." She says this like a child unable to contain her excitement in anticipation of a gift she is yet to open. "Now. I don't want to wait a minute longer."

"Now?"

"Yes, now. *You* do it, Anna."

This is not what Anna is prepared to do. This is not what she has expected her mother to ask of her.

"I'll get the scissors." Her mother is moving toward the mahogany cabinets in the bathroom.

"I can't. I don't know how," Anna stammers.

Her mother is already rummaging through the top drawer. "Will this do?" She holds up a huge pair of scissors with bright orange handles.

Anna backs away. "I can take you to the hairdresser."

"No. I want to do it now." Her mother sits on the stool in front of the mirror. "I want to be a funky white-haired lady now. I don't want to go to the hairdresser. I want *you* to do it."

"*Me?*"

They do not touch in their house. Her mother waits on ceremony to dole out her kisses. A kiss for her birthday, a kiss for Christmas, a kiss for New Year's Day. Cheek against cheek. Never lips on cheek. How is she to cut her mother's hair without getting physically close to her, physically closer to her than she can remember?

"I don't think I would have the courage to let anyone else cut my hair the way it is now," her mother says. She points to the towel rack. "Put a towel around my shoulders, Anna."

Anna takes a towel from the rack and drapes it over her mother's shoulders. Her fingers graze her mother's skin. A touch, ever so lightly. She breathes in the citrusy scent of her mother's soap. Longing floods her being. Her knees feel weak.

"Here, take the scissors."

She takes the scissors from her mother's hand but her fingers become a vise. They tighten around the holes in the handle. They will not loosen. She raises her hand. It stiffens; it remains suspended in midair.

Her mother is watching her through the mirror. "What's taking you so long, Anna?"

What has taken them so long? To touch, to feel, skin against skin. A mother and a daughter.

"Just cut it, Anna."

An order. It snaps Anna into motion.

What boiling spoiling, the old people say. What ent boil yet ent spoil yet. What done boil done spoil.

"Do it, Anna."

Anna swallows the flow of longing, regret, recrimination, welling inside of her. The past cannot be recovered. *What done boil done spoil.* She snips, she trims. Hair rains down her mother's back, in some places it falls down in clumps.

After lunch, her father calls. The president of the Rotary Club has invited special guests from Canada to the luncheon meeting and he will be expected to entertain them. He should be home no later than teatime, he says.

Anna goes to the living room to deliver her father's message. She finds her mother sitting on a sofa, looking out the sliding glass doors, toward her orchid garden. Her gaze is distant, blank. There is a pile of magazines at her feet. If she intended to read them, she seems to have changed her mind. When Anna approaches her, she starts, her shoulders twitch. She swivels around. "Why did you come up on me so silently, Anna?"

But Anna had not come upon her silently. She had said her name, she had called out: "Mummy!"

She is worried, Anna thinks. She is afraid her husband may not like the way she looks now. "You don't have to worry, Mummy," Anna says. "You look great with short hair."

Her mother brushes her fingers lightly across her cheekbones. "Hair? I have no hair."

There is some hair left on the front of her head and at the sides, but even there it is thin, her bare scalp visible.

"So much white," her mother murmurs.

"It suits you," Anna says. "You shouldn't ever dye your hair again."

Most women her mother's age would look old with such scanty hair, but her mother does not. She has no wrinkles on her face, and her perfect bone structure—high cheekbones, smooth forehead, rounded jaw-line—sets off her deep-set eyes, her softly curved nose, her full top lip. That the hair remaining on her head is all white makes no difference. She is as beautiful as ever.

"Try saying that to yourself when you get to be my age," her mother says.

At her present age, Anna is already turning gray. Once a month her hairdresser dyes her gray strands brown. She doubts she will stop dyeing her hair when she reaches her mother's age. She doubts she will be as fortunate to look as youthful as her mother does at her age.

"Well, I hope I don't shock your father too much."

"You and Daddy have lived together almost all your lives. You can't shock Daddy now," Anna says.

"Oh, I suppose he'll be as shocked as I was when I looked into the mirror." Her mother reaches for one of the magazines at her feet. "But as you say, we've lived a lifetime together. He'll recover. As a matter of fact, he'll forget I had hair at all."

Has she misread her mother's mood? Anxiety, she thought, had put that blank gaze in her mother's eyes, but her mother's tone is flippant. He'll recover, she says. She does not seem at all nervous that her husband's reaction to her shorn, almost bald, head will be any more lasting than her own. He will love her no matter how she looks, she says. "I know your father."

"When I came in the room, you seemed miles away."

"I was thinking," her mother says.

"About you and Daddy?"

"I suppose, but mostly about you and Tony." Her mother opens the magazine. Her eyes are lowered on the page in front of her but it is obvious she is not reading.

"About Tony and me?"

"Why can't you find it in your heart to forgive Tony, Anna?" Her mother looks up at her.

This sudden shift from her mother's pain to hers momentarily unhinges Anna. She flops down on the armchair next to her and barely manages an answer. "Mummy, you know about Tony and me. You know we are done. Finished."

"I forgave your father," her mother says.

"I'm not you, Mummy."

"Do you think it was easy for me to forgive your father?"

"I don't know. I just know you forgave him."

"I didn't forget."

"You forgot enough to be able to live with him," Anna says.

"And you can't put your husband's indiscretion aside for the sake of your marriage?" Her mother has not taken her eyes away from her.

"It wasn't an indiscretion. Tony betrayed me."

"Is that what you think your father did? You think he betrayed me?"

"I don't know what happened between Daddy and you."

"Yes," her mother says. "You don't know. You think a small thing like hair can damage our marriage."

"You said—"

"I know what I said. I wasn't speaking about our marriage. I meant at our age change is hard to accept. We like things to be the way they were. I wasn't speaking about our commitment to each other."

Anna squirms under the sting of her mother's dismissal. "What Daddy did was not a simple indiscretion."

"Men will be men. They cheat on their wives."

"I can't accept that," Anna says.

"Adultery is not the worst sin. Cheating on you is not the worst thing a man can do. There's friendship, companionship, love." Her mother puts down the magazine. "You don't throw those things away."

"There's trust," Anna says.

"Trust?"

"Your belief in your husband. Your confidence in him."

"I believe in your father. I have confidence in him. I trust him."

Anna will not let her off that easily. "I'm not like the women here. I can't have a husband who has women on the side."

"So that is it? You think you're better than the women here?"

"That's not what I mean."

"What *do* you mean?"

"The women here take it for granted that their men will be unfaithful. They let the men get away with anything."

"*Anything*?" Her mother's eyes are flashing. "Is that what you think?"

"I'm not like that. I'm not like them."

"You are so American, Anna."

Her mother's words are daggers in Anna's heart. "Don't, Mummy," she says quietly, her voice lost in a sob that comes without warning, tightening her vocal cords. "Don't."

"Oh, Anna," her mother groans. She presses her fingers against her lips, genuine regret brimming her eyes. "I didn't mean . . . I'm sorry."

"You always want to cut me off," Anna says, fighting tears.

"You have American ways, but you'll always be a Caribbean girl, Anna. You know that. But . . ."

"But what?"

"Things have changed since you lived here."

"It's still the place where I was born, where I grew up. My memories are here."

"I know, I know," her mother says. "But the island is different now."

"You always do that. You always take every chance you get to tell me I don't belong."

"Anna, Anna," her mother coos, but she does not reach out to Anna. She does not attempt to touch her.

"You cut me off from my country. From you."

Somewhere in the back of Anna's head there is a voice reminding her that her mother is not well. This is not the time to agitate her. Her hair has fallen out. Soon she will be completely bald. But the voice is not strong enough to dull an ancient pain, still fresh, insistent, tensing the muscles in her stomach, making it impossible for her to be charitable, to be selfless. "You say I'm American because *you* don't want me here."

"I? How can you say such a thing, Anna? Of course I want you here."

"You've never asked me to come back."

"I've never asked you to come back because America can give you more than we can give you here. You have a big job in America. You are an acquisition editor. You work for the largest publishing house in the world. You wouldn't have a job like that if you stayed here."

"I work for Equiano," Anna murmurs.

Her mother wrinkles her forehead. "What?"

Anna raises her voice. "I work for Equiano."

"Equiano? What's Equiano?"

"Equiano is a small imprint of Windsor."

"A small imprint?"

"We publish books by people of color."

"People of color?"

"We are a specialty imprint. We publish only people of color."

"Not other people?"

"No. Not other people."

Her mother passes her hand across her forehead. She swallows down hard. "Equiano? Not Windsor?"

"No, I don't work for Windsor proper."

"A small publishing company?"

"An imprint of Windsor," Anna says again.

"I told my friends. I boasted to poor Mrs. Farrell."

"*You* told them. I didn't tell them," Anna says.

"And all the time you were lying to me? Letting me lie for you?"

"You wanted me to lie to you. I am important to you because of what you can boast to your friends about me. Not because of me. I am a trophy for you to put on your shelf, to dust off when you are entertaining your friends."

There, she has said it at last, words she has held in her heart for years. There! She waits for her mother's answer, but her mother slumps down on the sofa. Her shoulders collapse. "I'll take a nap now," she says.

She has won. So she has won. So she has taken advantage of her mother at her weakest point, when she is most vulnerable, when she is terrified that the disease blooming inside of her will kill her. Anna flushes with shame. "It's a new imprint, Mummy," she says, remorseful now. "Well-respected. We publish major writers. That man who won the Commonwealth Writers' Prize last year, we published him."

Her mother is not so easily cheered. She is tired, she says. Her husband will be home soon. She needs to rest so she will be ready to greet him. "Tell Lydia I'll have my tea when your father comes."

Anna tries again. "You did the right thing sending me away, Mummy. I would never have had the opportunities I have in America. By now, I could have been a frustrated housewife with a husband who drinks."

Her poor attempt at humor gets lost on her mother. "You are separated, Anna," she says flatly. "You still have a husband."

"*Had*, Mummy," Anna replies, doing her best to soften her tone. "Tony and I are divorced."

"Divorced?"

"Last year."

"Oh, Anna." Her mother's head falls back on the sofa. "Oh, Anna," she whispers.

"It's not that bad, Mummy. I'm happy."

"Did he blame you? Your father blamed me."

"Daddy was wrong."

"Men always blame the women. At least, in the end, your father said he was sorry."

"Tony never apologized."

"Oh, Anna," her mother says again. "Who will look after you when you're old like me? What would have happened to me if I had left your father? What will happen to you if you get ill like me?"

CHAPTER 22

So in the end it is her mother who wins. What indeed will happen to her when she gets as old as her? What will happen to her if at her mother's age she has cancer?

Her mother goes to her room to take a nap and Anna heads outside to the garden. Singh is crouched at the edge of a flowerbed, digging the earth with a metal trowel. Sweat drips from his forehead and courses down the sides of his face. His black T-shirt is soaked across his back and under his armpits. His bare legs glitter in the sunlight. The brown of his skin is the brown of the earth. His black rubber clogs barely mark the difference.

Salt of the earth. Singh belongs. No one says: You are so Indian, Singh. Or if they do, they do not mean: You are so Indian from India, Singh. They know, Singh knows, he is an Indian from the Caribbean. He is Caribbean. He is Indo-Caribbean, it has become fashionable to say.

The dry leaves crackle and crunch beneath her feet and Singh swings his head around in her direction. He waves. She waves back and moves on. She is in a dark place. She does not want to talk to Singh. She must build a wall, a fortress to protect herself from yielding to the downward slide into the bottomless pit of self-pity. For who will rescue her after she leaves, when she is no longer on her island but there, in New York, alone, in a country still alien to her in many ways?

Her mother has her husband. Her mother has her country. Her mother has friends she has known since childhood. Her mother has a child, a dutiful daughter.

In the city where she lives, in New York, Anna has looked into the eyes of immigrant mothers of American children and seen incomprehension registered there. They sit on park benches, these mothers, fingers nervously plucking the edges of their skirts, silently measuring their distance from their squealing children running and jumping merrily through the grass, their little faces bright with carefree joy. Flesh of their flesh, yet a chasm yawns between these mothers and their children. Born in America, the children belong to America. The hearts and souls of their mothers were forged in other lands.

What will happen to you if you get ill like me?

Singh shouts out her name and forces her to stop and acknowledge him again. "If you want, Miss Anna," he says, "you could sit on de bench under de mango tree. Dem ants ent go climb up de concrete."

Even Singh pities her. Singh knows she has no husband.

Yes, she says, she will sit awhile on the bench under the mango tree.

"Is me dat build it for de bossman," he says, reminding her, establishing his right to a place in her parents' home.

Her mother wanted a bench made out of wood, with a back and armrests. Singh convinced her to compromise. "Mango go fall on de bench, bird go poop on de bench, ants go climb de bench to eat de mango and de poop dat fall on de bench. Den de ants and termites go eat de wood on de bench," he said to her. So the frame and arms of the bench are made out of concrete, the slats on the seat out of wood. Singh has painted the concrete frame and arms white, the slats bright green. "To match de grass, as madam did tell me," Singh will say to anyone who admires his handiwork.

Dried bird droppings smear the slats and arms of the

bench. At the bottom there is an anthill and climbing up the trunk of the mango tree is a black trail leading to an enormous termite nest in the cup of a thick branch. But in over fifteen years, the wood on the bench has survived. Termites and ants approach the concrete frame and, finding no food there, turn back.

Anna has sat on this bench, under this mango tree, many times before. The sunlight here is filtered and yet if she looks up, she can see the sky twinkling through the leaves, today made radiant blue by a dazzling sun. In front of her the green lawn is punctured with blooming flowerbeds, Singh's pride and joy. But the lawn itself belongs to her father and the boys he employs to mow it. After he is done with his fish, feeding them or clearing the pond of frogs, her father scours the lawn for weeds. No matter how hot the day, he crouches down on the grass and plucks out every weed he finds.

Anna sits here now and recalls a past, Tony complaining: "Work, work, work. All you think of is work. You're too ambitious."

They met when they were both in graduate school taking classes at night, she for her Masters in English, he for an MBA. They got engaged when they graduated and married two years later. She was twenty-eight, he was thirty-two. He wanted to start his career right away. He said they had time enough to have children. He got a job trading stocks for a brokerage house, then the place collapsed and he was unemployed. For one year he floundered, moving from brokerage firm to brokerage firm. Finally, he gave up and went to work as an assistant to a manager in a department store. The pay was ten times less than what he formerly earned, a third less than what she was making at Windsor.

"Work, work, work," he said. "All you think of is work. That's why you can't make a baby," he declared.

She knew he spoke in self-defense, out of feelings of inadequacy. He was ashamed. Without her income, they could not meet their monthly mortgage payments. Without her income, he could not keep the Mercedes-Benz he had bought when he worked at the brokerage firm.

He wants a child, he told her. If she were any kind of a woman, she would give him a child.

And yet they could not afford a child. They could not afford weeks without her income while she stayed at home to care for a child; they could not afford the cost of child-care when she returned to work. Not if they wanted to keep their duplex, not if he wanted to keep his Benz. Young, talented, aggressive junior editors were nipping at her heels. She could not risk losing her place on the ladder to the top. There was the promise of Equiano, a Windsor imprint that would be hers to direct. At nights she fell asleep with manuscripts scattered on the bed, her reading glasses sliding down her nose.

Should she have blamed Tony when she found a phone number in his jacket pocket with Crystal's name next to it? Crystal did not read manuscripts into the night while Tony lay, ignored, on the other side of her bed.

She called; Crystal answered. Terrified of the truth, she dropped the phone.

What would her mother have done? Her mother marched up the front steps of the house where her husband's mistress lived. She demanded the return of her husband.

Was that what she should have done? Should she have said to Crystal: *The man you are screwing is my husband. If you don't give him up . . . ?*

There's the rub, the futility of an empty threat. *If you don't give him up . . .* Then what? Who in New York, in America, will take her side? She may get sympathy; she may get advice. Friends, colleagues who offer to help, will refer her to a therapist, but no one will chastise her husband, reprimand him, remind him of his fidelity to vows. What Tony did is not exceptional. One in three marriages in America ends in divorce. An affair is the most common of causes.

Her mother has tradition on her side. The community, the neighbors heap shame on the man who abandons his wife. A husband may have a mistress but even the mistress understands he can never leave his wife. Discretion is all that is demanded. A good husband guards the reputation of his wife in public. She is the one, the only. A good husband keeps his mistress out of sight.

Her mother pities her. *What would have happened to me if I had left your father?*

Her father is her mother's sole support. Her mother was always a housewife; her father was always the breadwinner.

But Anna never needed Tony to support her. Anna was never a housewife; Tony was never the sole breadwinner.

A breeze rushes across the top of the mango tree and the branches part. Sunlight streams through the gap between the leaves and lays bare the tiniest of cracks along the wood slats on the bench. Anna raises her hand and shades her eyes.

Men always blame the women, her mother said, but she will not accept blame for Tony's betrayal. She will not fall victim to the babblings of pseudo psychologists who fault black women with ambitions like hers for undermining the egos of black men. She will not yield to pseudo sociologists who claim the increase of women in colleges and the higher incomes they earn when they graduate are the cause of the absence of black men in colleges and the lower incomes they earn. In this sense, her mother is right: she is American; she will assert her right to pursue her own happiness. Tony had a choice; he chose himself, he chose his self-centered desires rather than their marriage.

She gets up and walks toward the house. The sun pours down on her. In an instant she is wrapped in a warm and glorious light.

CHAPTER 23

The next day, early in the afternoon, Dr. Ramdoolal calls. He has good news. Dr. Paul Bishop will be coming to the island. It's his parents' fiftieth wedding anniversary and the Bishops are planning a huge celebration.

"I'm sure your parents will be invited," he says. "They'll get to meet Dr. Bishop and he'll change your mother's mind. Has your mother said anything more about her surgery?"

"Not a word," Anna says.

"You already know what I think. Her chances are much better if she has the surgery in the States."

Anna does not need convincing. "Mummy is stubborn," she says.

"Her next chemo could be brutal. Chemo doesn't only attack the cancer cells; it destroys the good cells too, the ones she needs to fight off infection; platelets that keep her from bleeding to death."

Anna is silent. Her vacation ends in two weeks, one week after the session that could be brutal for her mother.

"There are drugs for this, of course. You'll have to bring her to my office. I'll start building up her blood count, and we'll have to monitor her. Has her hair fallen out?"

Anna finds her voice. "There's some still left," she says. "She has tufts on the sides and back. Wisps in the front."

Dr. Ramdoolal laughs. "Tufts and wisps! Tufts and wisps! That's funny. Tufts and wisps!" But soon he is the professional again. "For many women, this is the most dif-

ficult part. Besides the mastectomy, of course," he is quick
to add. "Have you thought of getting your mother a wig?"

"I don't know if Mummy will wear one," Anna says.

Dr. Ramdoolal sighs. "I suppose you won't be going
back to the States until this is all over?"

She cannot tell him she has made no such plans. She cannot say that there are writers depending on her return, one
writer in particular. They are speaking about her mother.
She is her mother's only child.

"Naturally," she says, as if it is natural, as if the laws
of nature demand it, demand that she abandon her work,
abandon her responsibilities to her writers, to the publishing company. *Abandon her life!*

Aujourd'hui, maman est morte. So begins Albert Camus's
tale of man executed for his indifference, for the unnatural
response of a son on learning of the death of his mother.

"This is a lucky coincidence," Dr. Ramdoolal is saying.

"Yes." She repeats his words. "A lucky coincidence."

"You being here and Dr. Bishop coming. Not the best
of circumstances, but given the situation, we couldn't hope
for better, could we?"

"Yes," she says again.

"Do you want me to speak to your mother now?"

"This minute?"

"Yes, ask her to come to the phone. I want to tell her
what a great opportunity she will have to speak to Dr. Bishop
directly."

Anna says her parents are not at home, they have gone
shopping.

"Shopping?"

"For groceries."

"Ah," Dr. Ramdoolal says approvingly. "Good. It's good
your father has gone with her. There will be days she will
not be able to go. It's good that he learns now."

But her father has always gone with her mother to the grocery. He does not need to learn now. In the early days he sat in the car and waited for her, leaping to her side the minute she made her grand entrance into the street, followed by a retinue of one, sometimes two, schoolboys she had engaged to push her cart loaded with groceries. Now her father is the schoolboy. Now he is the one who pushes the cart through the store a few steps behind her while she points to this or that item on the shelf. Like a well-behaved child, he obeys, he reaches, he plucks this or that from its place, he puts this or that in the cart for her.

Resentment like the rising tide once again floods her being. Why is she so resentful? Why is she so full of anger toward her mother for this, for this that her father of his free will chooses to do, that he wants to do for the wife he loves?

Does she wish Tony had done the same for her? *Just once!* Just once, that he had gone shopping with her, gone to the grocery store with her, to the clothing store? But shopping is woman's work and Tony did not do woman's work.

Her father does more. She could say to Dr. Ramdoolal that shopping for groceries is not all her father does for her mother. After the grocery, later in the week, he goes to the market for her. It is an open market, an enormous shed protected from the elements only by a corrugated galvanized roof. Farmers from the country, butchers and fishermen, all bring their produce there. In this place, there is not a hint of the sanitized order of the supermarket. Women sit on stools or crosslegged on the ground beside huge round baskets of ground provisions, vegetables, and fruit. Some cradle new babies in the sinks of their laps. Snotty-nosed toddlers clutch their mothers' skirts. The men sell the fish and meat in open stalls, their aprons bloodied with the entrails of carcasses. The unwashed and the poor slither by, hands outstretched, begging for alms. This is no place for Mr. Sinclair's wife. Mr. Sinclair has declared so himself. But he wants his fish fresh, his fruits and vegetables still smelling of the earth.

"Daddy knows about shopping for groceries. He knows the market," she says to Dr. Ramdoolal. "If the time comes, Daddy will be prepared."

At three thirty her parents arrive. Her father has timed their return precisely. Lydia's after-lunch siesta ends at three. At three, she is in the kitchen preparing pastries for their four o'clock tea and making the sandwiches and salads they will have for dinner later.

Lydia!" Her mother is at the kitchen door. "Lydia! How many times must I call you? Come, help Mr. Sinclair with the bags."

Her mother leans against the door, her hands clasped below her stomach. She is ill. She cannot be expected to help Mr. Sinclair lift the grocery bags out of the car. But even when she was not ill she could not be expected to help.

Lydia wipes off the dough that has adhered to her fingers and hurries out to the driveway. Beatrice enters the house and collapses on a chair at the breakfast table. She is wearing a straw hat. In the back, at the nape of her neck, hair protrudes, gray curls that are almost white now. But Anna knows that under her hat, at the top of her head, she is completely bald.

"Anna, bring me a glass of water, will you?" Her mother rubs the back of her neck. She is breathing hard.

Anna opens the refrigerator and takes out the jug of ice water. Her mother removes her hat. In the absence of hair, the structure of her mother's face is more pronounced and Anna is struck again by how beautiful she is, how stunning she must have been when she was young.

"Anna, you make me self-conscious," her mother admonishes her.

Anna blinks. She has been staring. Embarrassed, she busies herself looking through the cabinet for a water glass.

"Any glass will do," her mother says.

Anna fills a tall glass with ice water and hands it to her mother. "I told you you'd look more beautiful with short hair."

"Pssh!" her mother says. "My hair is not short. I'm bald."

"Then bald suits you," Anna says.

Her mother gulps down the water greedily. "I didn't realize how thirsty I was. It was hot and crowded in the supermarket. The manager needs to lower the temperature on the air conditioner."

"Couldn't Daddy get the groceries by himself?"

"If I could trust those girls."

"What girls?"

"The girls in the supermarket. They won't leave him alone."

"Daddy?"

"Switching their hips around him. Mr. Sinclair this, Mr. Sinclair that. We just got a new shipment of chocolates from Switzerland, Mr. Sinclair. You want to get those, Mr. Sinclair? If I let your father go in the supermarket without me, we'll pay twice as much for our groceries. The minute those girls see me, they scatter. Not another word about chocolates from Switzerland."

Could she be jealous? As ridiculous as that thought seems to Anna, she finds herself entertaining the possibility. "Daddy has eyes only for you," she says.

"Oh, it's not me I'm concerned about. Did you think I was worried about your father's affection for me? Not at all. I hate to see your father make a fool of himself. Those girls take him for an idiot. Your father is not an idiot. He's just too polite. He doesn't know how to tell them to go away. Scat! It's the manager who sends those girls to him."

Still, Anna thinks, she has not made a mistake.

"Switching their hips," her mother says again. "Your father is a married man!"

After all these years! Jealous, after all these years!

She was not jealous of Tony. She felt rejected, spurned, hurt, angry when he took a lover, but not jealous, not enough to fight for him, not enough to confront his mistress, to demand she stop the affair with her husband.

After all these years! Must one be in love to feel jealous? Was that what Tony wanted: accusations flung across the room like missiles? Tears? A confrontation with the other woman? *Tell my husband to come home! Now!*

They have their tea in the veranda. Lydia serves. She opens folding tables in front of the wicker armchairs where each of them is sitting. She brings the pot of tea and the cups and saucers and she leaves. After a few moments she returns with the pastries, tiny fruit pies she made in the afternoon. Beatrice's mood is much improved. She compliments Lydia on the fruit pies. Lydia smiles broadly.

It is a good time to tell her about Dr. Bishop, Anna thinks. She begins with Dr. Ramdoolal's telephone call.

The announcement unnerves her mother. "Dr. Ramdoolal called?" The cup in her hand rattles against the saucer. "Is something wrong?"

"Is it about your mother's condition?" Her father will not use the word *cancer* in her mother's presence. Her mother has given him this directive. He says *condition*, but the word comes out of his mouth tense, strained.

"Oh no," Anna says quickly. "Nothing like that. He had good news. Dr. Bishop will be coming here soon."

Her initial fears eased, her mother sips her tea and adjusts her body comfortably in her chair. "And why is that good news, Anna?"

"His parents' wedding anniversary is in two weeks. Dr. Ramdoolal says he's sure the Bishops have invited you."

"Yes," her father says. "We've received an invitation."

"Is he coming alone?" Beatrice glances at her daughter.

"Who?" Anna is momentarily put off by the oddity of the question.

"Dr. Bishop. Is he coming alone?"

"Why do you ask?"

"Does he have a wife?" her mother asks.

"What difference does it make?" Anna replies irritably.

"I like to have all the facts."

"He's divorced," John Sinclair explains. "I saw his father some time ago. He told me so."

"There, Anna," Beatrice says. "Now we have all the facts." She reaches for another of Lydia's fruit pies.

"And now you have that fact, are you going to their wedding anniversary party?" Anna asks.

"No. We're not going," Beatrice says emphatically.

"Not going?"

"Not with my hair like this. For everybody to laugh at me? No."

"Why would they laugh?"

"Oh, they wouldn't laugh in my face, but they will feel superior. They will know I am on my way out."

"In the first place, Mummy, you are not on your way out. In the second place, we are all on our way out."

"But I am getting there faster."

"*Sailing to Byzantium*," her father murmurs.

Her mother twists her head angrily toward him. "What are you talking about, John?"

"Nothing. Oh, nothing," he says and looks away from her.

"You know what I said is true. They'll all feel superior. *Poor Beatrice. Poor, poor Beatrice.*"

"You can wear a hat, Beatrice. You look beautiful in a hat," her father says.

"Or a wig," Anna adds.

"That may be an American fashion, but here, if you haven't noticed, Anna, it's too hot to wear a wig. Rivers will run down my face."

Anna flinches. "They make wigs now that it would be almost impossible to tell you are wearing one," she says, making a valiant effort to sound encouraging.

"And where will I get such a wig on this island?" her mother asks.

Anna does not respond. Her father comes to her rescue. "Beatrice, hats suit you. You have the face for hats."

"Well, I am not going," she says. "And that is that."

And that was that. They finish their tea with small talk. Afterward her mother retires to her room for a nap before dinner.

Later, Anna finds her father at the pond feeding his fish. He is humming. The tension that tightened the air earlier has evaporated. "*Figaro, Figaro,*" he sings. He's listening to a Mozart CD, *Opera Highlights,* that she had bought for him a year ago. "*Figaro, Figaro.*"

Anna fights a sudden impulse to cry. She has let him down. The musical gene the Sinclairs have carried for generations has withered and died in her; in spite of the years of piano lessons the seed did not take root. She approaches her father quietly. "Don't you wish I knew how to play?" she asks him.

He is stooped down on the concrete border of the fish-pond, balancing on his toes, scooping flotsam from the surface of the water with a green net attached to a long thin pole. "The piano? Play the piano?" He does not turn around.

Anna can tell by the lightness of his tone that he has not taken her question seriously. He continues to skim the net over the water. "*Figaro, Figaro*," he sings.

"Mummy was disappointed," she says. "Were you?"

He stops singing. "No, Anna, I was not disappointed." He stands up, stretches his hand over the water, and with the net reaches for the twigs that are scattered on the far end on the pond.

"*She* was."

Still gathering the twigs, he says, "Your mother was not disappointed in you, Anna."

"She's disappointed I'm divorced." Anna knows without asking that her mother has told her father this.

"Nonsense! Why do you say that?"

"You heard her? *Does he have a wife?*"

"She meant nothing by that."

"She's not even met that . . . that Dr. Bishop, and already she's lining him up as a potential husband."

"Your mother wants you to be happy. She belongs to a generation that believes that married women are happier than unmarried women."

"Do you believe that?"

He has gathered all the twigs and he pulls in the net. "I read somewhere," he says, carefully picking out the twigs from between the loops in the net, "that married women live longer. I guess it's because they have a companion."

"I have friends," she replies. "I have a fulfilling life. I love my work." *Friends* is a lie, but her life *is* fulfilling. She loves her work.

"I know. I know. But your mother worries. I worry. You need a companion when you get old, someone to talk to, who loves you. I don't know how I would have been able to bear old age if your mother were not with me."

He, too. *"Who will look after you when you're old like me?"* her *mother said.*

"We love you, but neither of us has many years left."

"Your father lived into his nineties."

"I may not be so lucky. And there is your mother. We didn't count on this. The cancer."

She does not fear death or growing old without a companion. But she fears death in a country where she has no roots. She fears dying there, growing old there, alone, without a companion. She has imagined returning. Which immigrant does not dream of returning to the place of her birth, to retire there, to settle down there after a lifetime of work? But if her mother dies and her father dies, who will be there on the island to receive her? Who will be there to attest, to prove that she once belonged, could belong again?

Mozart wafts between them. She does not like this talk of death. She reaches for safer ground. "Your parents and your sister were so talented."

"I suppose."

"I could tell Granny was disappointed that I didn't play the piano like Aunt Alice."

"You can't live your parents' dreams," he says. "I couldn't manage the violin. Your grandmother should have been more disappointed in me than in you, but she loved us both."

"Yes, but I must have been a disappointment to you and Mummy."

He looks up at her. "Anna, Anna," he says. "Your mother and I could not have asked for a better daughter."

She is ashamed of herself. She is far too old to be fishing for compliments and reassurances this way, but if she started this conversation without ulterior motive, she is conscious now of having one. Guilt has nagged her since Dr. Ramdoolal asked his question, posed rhetorically, with an assumption of her answer. Yet she has no plans to stay longer than the four weeks of her vacation.

"You are too kind," she says to her father.

He is walking away from her toward the orange tree. "No kinder than your mother," he replies as he places the net against the trunk of the orange tree.

It is not what she wants to hear. She wants justification, she wants exoneration for the decision she has not yet made, but is likely to make. She wants to assuage the guilt that is hounding her.

"I don't know how you can stand it," she says. "Mummy is so . . . so intransigent. Even when something is good for her, she'll say no."

Her father wipes his hands on the towel he hangs on one of the lower branches of the orange tree. It is an old towel, frayed at the ends and stained with clumps of dried fish food, or, rather, dog food. He has resisted her mother's attempts to wash it, or to hang it out of sight at the back of the house. Her mother may be intransigent, but he can be stubborn too. He needs everything to be in one place, he has told her mother. The towel should be next to the net, which is next to the orange tree. He scrapes off the dried dog food and declares the towel perfectly clean.

"It'll be good for her to go to the Bishops' party," Anna says. "No one would care if she has on a wig."

Her father puts the towel back on the tree. "She's afraid, Anna. That was fear speaking."

"What about you? Weren't you friends with Mr. Bishop?" She is standing close to him. "Why should *you* be stuck in the house? Why should she prevent *you* from going to the party?"

"She isn't preventing me," he says.

"If she won't go, you won't go."

"That's right," he says. He bends down to pick up an orange. There are several that have fallen from the tree. He gives her the one in his hand and bends down to pick up the others. "Lydia can make orange juice with these for breakfast."

"Why do you *always* agree with her?" She is aware that her voice has risen to a pitch close to a child's whine.

"Your mother is not a fool, Anna. She knows what Dr. Ramdoolal is up to. The Bishops' son from the States will be at the party."

"But isn't that the point? Isn't that what you want? Mummy needs to have her surgery in the States. You know that."

"It's your mother's life." He has two oranges in one hand and two in the other. "I can knock down some more from the tree," he says. "Would you want me to?"

"I don't want to talk about oranges," she responds tersely. "I want to talk about Mummy. Why won't you face the fact that she can die if she does not have the surgery?"

"But she intends to have the surgery," he says calmly.

"You know what I mean. I mean in the States."

"Your mother has a right to make the decisions that affect her life."

"But what if her decisions affect your life?"

"My decisions have affected her life," he says. He begins to walk toward the kitchen.

"How can you be so . . . ?"

"Understanding? Because your mother and I understand each other. She is frightened now, but in the end she'll make the right decision."

"I doubt it," Anna says.

"I know your mother."

She wishes he is right. She is not unaware that her wish is motivated by selfish reasons, but she convinces herself that her reasons are not so selfish as to exclude consideration of her mother's welfare. If her mother goes to the States she will get the surgery she needs, and Anna, on the other hand, will be able to continue her life uninterrupted. She will return to work. She will be able to meet her deadlines.

"You are too good, Daddy," she says.

"Good?" He stops and squints at her.

"To Mummy. You're a saint."

He looks steadily into her eyes. "You know better than that, Anna. You, above anyone else. You should know I am not a saint."

Two women pass by the house on their way to the bus stop, ten blocks away, at the main road. They are holding umbrellas open over their heads for shade from the stinging rays of the sun. Mortified by her father's forthrightness, his unwillingness to let her get away with her juvenile, fairy-tale illusions of a perfect father, a faithful husband, Anna turns toward the two women.

Her father follows her eyes. "Come," he says. "Let's go for a walk."

There is only an hour of daylight left in spite of the blinding light. Already the ibis are on their way from the continent, heading for the mangrove swamp on the island. Already their scarlet-feathered bodies are cutting a bloodied trail across the brilliant blue sky.

"Isn't it too late?" she asks.

"We'll be back before dark."

"What about the dogs? I'm afraid of the dogs."

At this hour, the dogs that roam the streets are restless, sniffing empty pails for remnants the garbage men have left behind. For the strays, this is their last chance for a meal.

They must find some hovel, some corner, perhaps under a tree, where they can spend the night. Most of the dogs have metal tags around their necks. In the day, their owners let them out and they patrol the streets, trotting back and forth, up and down, the nails on their paws clicking against the hard asphalt, their dog tags tinkling merrily. But let no one be fooled by this playful jingle of dog tags. These are vicious animals, ready to pounce on anyone who gets too close to their masters' gates.

Anna resists the temptation to say to her father that in the States the owners of these dogs would be fined, if not imprisoned. She was almost bitten once. The dog's jaws were clamped around her leg, its saliva dribbling down her shin bone. It was about to sink in its teeth when, from a nearby house, its owner shouted its name. There were apologies, but no apparent remorse. The owner pleaded for compassion. "They're closed up all night in a little space in the yard. Is hard to begrudge them a little freedom."

Locals on the island are not like the English who live there. They do not allow their dogs to sleep in their beds; they do not kiss their dogs on the mouth, but their affection for them runs no less deep.

"I have a stick for the dogs." So says her father, the hunter, the man who used to love nothing more than to spend his weekends in the forest with a pack of yapping dogs. "I don't have to touch them. I raise my stick and they back away."

"And Mummy?" Her mother will not remain in the house alone. The electric gate, the bolts on her door, are not enough to make her feel safe from the drug lords and their minions.

"I'll ask Lydia to stay with her until we come back," her father says. "Lydia won't mind."

* * *

There are no dogs on their street, but as soon as they turn the corner, Anna sees four, one on one side of the street, three on the other. None of them look particularly vicious, but her memory of the time she was attacked causes her to stiffen.

"Don't show fear," her father warns. "They smell fear. They'll attack you if you let them know you're afraid. You have to show them you're the stronger one. It's the law of the jungle."

There is no pavement along the sides of the streets. The sidewalks, if they can be called that, are extensions of the gardens and manicured lawns behind the iron gates that enclose the houses. They are dotted with clumps of flowering trees and graceful palms that make walking on them almost an act of defacement, but difficult as well. One has to make one's way around flowerbeds and plants and the occasional bundle of branches that need to be cut down frequently from fast-growing trees in backyards. The neighborhood is stylish, yet the streets are narrow and covered with potholes. Open gutters are strewn with refuse.

Does America do this better, insisting on the improvement of communal spaces? America has a reputation for capitalistic greed, for selfishness. Here, the locals pride themselves on the neighborly concern they have for each other. Yet in this stylish neighborhood, the contrast is stark: well-tended lawns on one side of the iron gates where the prosperous live, deteriorating asphalt and garbage on the other side where the workers must travel.

She is critical of the people on the island who allow their dogs to roam the streets unleashed. The narrow roads, the potholes, the garbage raise her ire, and yet her mother has not once expressed outrage, or if she is outraged she has chosen to hold her tongue.

Is this what she needs to learn: tolerance for those who

do not share her views? *Go with the flow.* It is a slogan she has seen on billboards on the island. Should she go with the flow and say nothing to her father about the importance of leashing dogs, clearing sidewalks, and repairing roads? Has America so seeped into her bones that she cannot go with the flow without great effort?

Her father motions her to walk on the road. The sidewalk can be treacherous, he says. The dogs eye them. They trot forward but keep their distance. When Anna and her father slow down, the dogs move ahead, but a few yards further they stop, turn, cock their heads to one side, and wait for them.

"Why don't they just go away?" Anna asks.

"Maybe they like our company," her father says.

"Maybe they smell the hunter in you."

"Or they see the stick in my hand."

They must sidestep dead frogs, flattened by cars and dried stiff in the sun. Their front and back legs, splayed out on the road, are fused into the hot asphalt.

Her father nods his head toward a sun-dried frog. "Looking for water. Too bad the canals are dry."

At the end of the road is a small park, a memorial for a previous resident, a rich merchant, perhaps. There are three benches, one of them under a royal palm tree, the bottom half of its trunk a distinctive red. Red berries are clustered at the base of its fronds.

"Let's sit here," her father suggests.

The dogs have followed them. Two of them chase each other playfully around one of the benches. The other two settle down on the ground at the entrance of the park.

"They like us," her father says. "We'll be safe here. They'll protect us."

"The island was never like this before I left. We could feel safe anywhere."

"Oil and drugs," her father says and he gives her an opening. His purpose may have been to cool the tension that had flared up between them, but the walk they have taken has not lessened Anna's anxiety. Must she stay on the island until her mother has had her last session of chemotherapy?

"You know, Daddy," she begins, "I often wondered if the Europeans would not have left if they knew the oil was going to return."

"In the first place, the oil never went anywhere, so you can't exactly say it returned. The Europeans had poor equipment. When the Americans came they brought harder drills. They were able to reach untapped beds."

"So the Europeans would have stayed if they knew there was more?"

"No one had a crystal ball. The oil was there and then it was not. Who knew it would be there in such quantities? Who knew the island would be oil rich today?"

"I remember the pumps. You remember, Daddy? When we first drove to the hill, we saw them. None of them were working. Remember?"

Her father fiddles with a button on his shirt. Anna senses his discomfort but gives no ground. She is focused on her purpose now. If her father could compromise what he ought to have done for what he needed to do, why can't she? She needs to return to New York. The manuscript she wants to defend is not chick lit or urban lit, the types of books Windsor has assigned to Equiano, convinced that these are the only novels by black writers that are marketable. It is a serious literary work that demands her serious attention.

"I think when the company offered you that job," she says to her father, "they believed the oil was drying up."

"Is that what you think?"

"Well, don't you?"

"They didn't fool me."

"You took the job."

"Wasn't life better for you when I took the job?"

They had more money, she had more things, but she cannot say life was better for her on the hill.

"Weren't they sort of using you?" she asks.

"Maybe. I suppose I knew they never would have offered me a management job if they didn't think the oil was drying up."

"Then why did you take it?"

He shifts his gaze to the dogs. "In life," he says, "we always have to decide what matters most."

"And your job mattered more?"

"More than what?"

"Exposing them." She dares to remind him of the reports in the newspapers when the European oilmen left. *Traitor*, one headline read, referring to her father who retired at the same time, five years before his retirement age. *Independence was coming and the British knew it*, a reporter wrote. *They skimmed what they could from the oil wells, stuffed their pockets with our money, and ran. John Sinclair colluded with them. The British weren't stupid. They hired a black man to do their dirty work. Sinclair has no conscience. He took their blood money.*

"You can't have it all," her father says.

"Then sometimes the ends justify the means? Is that what you're saying?"

"Depends on the means. If the means you use hurt people, then I say no. That, to me, is the worst sin a man can commit: deliberately hurting someone for the sole purpose of benefiting himself."

"If a man hurts someone but he does not do it to benefit himself, is that okay?"

"We humans are flawed creatures. I don't think we ever do anything for purely altruistic motives."

"What were yours?"

"I was able to get better severance pay for the oil field workers," he says.

"And keep your job."

"Yes. Keep my job. I liked the money I was making, but I think—I suppose I need to believe—I made life better for the workers."

Tammy Mohun, the South African Indian, cried in her office. "I am so ashamed," she said. "But how else would black South Africans have got their groceries? Who else would have sold them milk and bread?" If Tammy Mohun's family got rich selling groceries to black South Africans, why should they be made to feel ashamed? Weren't they doing a service for black South Africans?

"In the end," her father says, "it turned out I made the right decision. I was in the right place at the right time."

So in the end, would it be the right decision for her to return to New York to be in the right place at the right time and help a deserving writer? She has stayed at Equiano because she believes, because she had hopes that one day she will be able to persuade Tanya Foster to allow her to publish literary novels. One day she will convince her that the risk of poor returns from a literary novel will be more than offset by the profits the company makes from the growing demand for chick lit and urban lit.

"In my job," she says, "I am also in a position of helping others, writers who would normally not get published."

"Your mother told me about Equiano."

She is not surprised. "I need to go back to New York in two weeks," she says.

"Need?" His eyebrows contract.

"If I'm not there, chances are that my writer will be turned down."

"Are you sure of that?"

"Aren't you sure that if you weren't there, the oil field workers wouldn't have got a decent severance pay?"

The two dogs lying at the entrance to the park sit up on their hind legs. Their ears perk up. Surely they have not sensed her insolence, for insolent she was to a father who has always been kind to her. Yet dogs have keen ears. Dogs that are sympathetic to her father have keener ears.

"Are you asking me if I was necessary?"

She does not answer him.

"Well, I'll tell you. I believed I was necessary. I took the job the Englishman offered me because I believed I would be in the best position to help the workers. And, in fact, when the strike came, I was in the best position to get the best severance pay for the workers. In the end, Anna, what matters is your integrity, what you think of yourself, not what others say about you. I went to bed at night knowing I had done my best. I had hurt no one."

Two of the dogs get up and trot away.

"Time for them to go home," her father murmurs. They sit silently side by side, father and daughter, their eyes turned in the direction of the dogs. When the dogs are no longer in view, John Sinclair says to his daughter, "Can't you stay longer? At least until your mother has her last chemo session? That's not too long to wait, is it?"

"It would be irresponsible of me," Anna says firmly.

"Your mother needs you."

"She has you."

Her father slaps his hand lightly on his thigh. "Ha!" he says. "You are just like your mother. Just as ambitious."

His remark offends her. Her mother's ambitions run no further than acquiring the latest style in dress and shoes. Her goals are no more than to impress her friends with the furniture in her house, the flowers in her garden, the dinners and tea parties she gives. No more than to dust off the trophy on her shelf, a daughter who she can claim works for the largest publishing company in America. No, her ambitions cannot be compared to her mother's.

"Mummy has domestic ambitions," she says. "I have more than domestic ambitions."

The sun is descending. In minutes it will sink below the horizon. There are no lights in the park, few along the street. Soon darkness will fall and enshroud them.

The two dogs that remain, the ones near the bench, have stopped playing. One lifts its leg and urinates. There is a dead frog on the asphalt pathway. They sniff it and scamper away.

Her father stands up. "It's time for us to go back."

Anna will not let his comment about her ambitions remain unchallenged. "You can't compare us in this way," she says.

"Come. It's late." He is already walking toward the exit, out of the park, and leaves her no choice but to get up and follow him.

"You have to explain yourself," she says.

He is walking briskly ahead of her, swinging the stick he brought for the dogs vigorously back and forth against his side. She has to struggle to catch up with him. Her lungs work hard to pump air in and out of her body. Indignation, more than exhaustion, makes her fight for breath.

"Mummy was a secretary. She filed papers, typed, and made tea for her boss."

"The head of the Treasury Department," he says. His eyes are focused on the road ahead.

"What?" She quickens her pace behind him.

"That was her boss. The head of the Treasury Department."

"She was still a secretary." She is breathing hard. For each step he takes, she has to take two.

"And you think that was all she was?" He stops and she reaches him. He is more than twice her age but he hasn't broken a sweat. Perspiration is running down her back.

"What else?" She presses her hand against her chest hoping to slow the rapid beating of her heart.

"How do you know she didn't want more?" He faces her. "Have you ever asked her?"

She avoids his eyes. "I have never heard her voice any ambition to work outside of the house."

"Ha!" he says. "Ha!" Abruptly, he resumes his pace, this time not so fast that she cannot match his stride.

"What? Do you know something more?" Anna is next to him, shoulder to shoulder. "Tell me," she says when he does not reply.

"Your mother was not an ordinary secretary. She was an executive secretary. *Executive*." He stabs his stick on the asphalt road. "Nothing left the Treasurer's desk unless she had checked it. She was meticulous."

Anna knows this quality in her mother. Her instructions to Lydia are always precise: one-eighth of a teaspoon of nutmeg, a quarter cup of sugar. She will not allow estimates. No guessing in her kitchen. She provides the measuring spoons and the measuring cups. She has scales to weigh ingredients. Singh knows better than to rearrange the potted plants in her garden. Her mother will inspect the garden after he has gone. Yes, her mother is meticulous. She does not doubt that the head of the Treasury valued this quality in her. But her father says more.

"Oh, she was not good at maths, but she could find the smallest error in grammar or spelling on a report. The Treasurer depended on her to check his sentences. That's what your mother did, Anna. She was an editor before you were an editor."

A car approaches and several more behind it. Her father

stretches his leg over the open gutter and extends his hand to her. She grabs it and he helps her onto the grassy sidewalk. Forever the gentleman, she thinks. Forever making up stories that paint a perfect picture of his wife.

"I know you love Mummy," she says when she is safely on the grassy sidewalk.

"So you don't believe me?" He has not missed the condescension in her voice. "Is that it?"

He is her father. She cannot say she does not believe him. "You've known Mummy before I was born," she says.

"It was frustrating for her."

She waits.

"It wasn't easy for a woman in the colonial days. Not easy for a man, either, but harder for a woman. When a woman got married she had to leave her job. The assumption was that she wouldn't need the money since she now had someone to take care of her. Your mother's boss had to sack her, but he kept her in an acting position and she was able to work a little longer. She was *that* important to him. All that ended, of course, when she got pregnant and began to show."

Anna resists the implication of this history he is drawing for her. "Mummy must have been glad to stop working."

"No," he says, "it was hard for her."

He leaves her no choice but to say out loud what he has implied. "I must have been inconvenient then."

"Oh, Anna," he says. "Why must you jump to negative conclusions about your mother?"

But he knows why. She does not have to tell him. He knows he can depend on her silence. He can depend on her silence now.

"She stopped because of me," he says. "Not you. I wanted her to stop. She stopped because she loved me. But you, you inherited her editing talent."

* * *

Her mother is in the veranda when they get back. She is speaking to someone on the cordless phone. She has changed from the tailored pants and linen shirt she wore to the supermarket and is now in something more casual, a shapeless flower-print dress that falls loosely from her shoulders. Her hair is brushed back and the bald space on her scalp is clearly visible. "John won't mind picking it up," they hear her say. "No. I'm sure of it."

They walk toward her. "What is it that John won't mind picking up?" her father asks in that pretend irritated tone he sometimes uses with her mother. Nothing on his face gives the slightest hint of anger.

"Oh, you're back." Her mother glances swiftly at him and then returns to her call. "Good," she says. "Yes, yes, I am sure he'll be glad to."

John Sinclair makes snorting noises. His wife puts her finger to her lips and warns him with her eyes to be quiet, and she quickly ends her conversation on the phone.

"Did you have a good walk?" She directs the question to Anna.

"Daddy kept the dogs from jumping on me."

"Those dogs know your father. They'll never bother you if you're with him. Did they follow you? They follow him, you know. They know his smell."

"What did you get me into, Beatrice?" The corners of her father's lips twitch in the beginnings of a smile.

"We have to make lunch for the priest tomorrow," her mother says.

"But I took lunch for the priest on Monday."

"Claire Matthews is not feeling well, so you have to pick up the food carrier from the rectory this evening."

Once a week her mother prepares lunch for the parish priest. There are seven ladies in all who do this; each takes a day in the week. The night before her turn, each of the ladies picks up the empty food carrier from the rectory and brings it back filled with food the next day. But in the case of Anna's mother, her husband does the picking up and the dropping off for her.

"Can't we have dinner first?" he asks.

"Lydia has been waiting."

Lydia is standing at the entrance of the kitchen, her face impassive. She has taken off her workday clothes. She has on a neatly pressed white blouse and a dark-colored skirt. She is wearing shoes not slippers. Her handbag, the latest style in America, a gift from her son in New York, is slung over her shoulders.

"I don't know why you and Anna had to run off so late in the afternoon. It's dark already," her mother says.

John Sinclair slaps his hand to his forehead. He is immediately apologetic. "How could I have forgotten? I'm so sorry, Lydia."

"Your father's memory is not the same," Beatrice says to her daughter.

"I'll take you to the bus stop right away, Lydia," John Sinclair says.

"So then you might as well continue on to the rectory, John. I'll call Father Jim and let him know you're coming."

When they leave, her mother takes the phone with her into the house. She does not return it to its cradle. "Your father may call," she explains.

"But he just left."

"He always forgets something or thinks he's forgotten something. Watch if he doesn't call to ask about the basket. Of course, he has to bring the basket. Where else would I put the carrier? He knows I always put the carrier in the basket, but still he calls."

Her patronizing tone irritates Anna. She thinks her

mother exaggerates her father's diminishing memory to remind him of his dependence on her, to remind him he needs her. That there can be no more Thelmas.

And why shouldn't she? Why shouldn't her mother arm herself against home-wrecking Thelmas, against firm-fleshed girls sent by grocery managers to seduce her husband, to tease him into purchasing chocolates from Switzerland he does not want?

"You don't know your father," her mother says.

A declaration of ownership. A challenge. Her husband is her exclusive domain; she alone has access to his mind and heart.

Why does this bother her? Could she be envious of the security her mother enjoys with a husband who loves her, will do anything for her? Does she wish she had someone—a lover, a husband—who felt the same way about her? *A mother*?

"Daddy tells me your old boss at the Treasury didn't want to let you go," Anna says. Ill will lurks beneath her words.

Her mother is momentarily startled. "He told you about my old boss?"

"Daddy said that you used to edit his reports for him."

"He said that?"

"That's what he said."

They are in the TV room. Her mother sits down on the couch and puts the phone on the low table in front of her. "It'll take your father to say something like that," she says.

"Well, did you?" Anna sits on a chair adjacent to the couch.

"I suppose you could say that's what I did."

"He said you checked his reports for grammar and spelling."

"Oh, I did more than that."

"He said your boss never sent out reports before you had a chance to review them."

"I suppose you could say I was a sort of editor. Yes, I suppose you could say I was an editor before you were an editor."

Anna notes the acknowledgment. She has referred to her as an editor. It seems she has overcome her disappointment, resigned herself to the fact that her daughter is an editor at Equiano, not, as she would have wished, at Windsor. Regardless, it must please her that her daughter is an editor in New York, the world's capital of the publishing industry.

"You inherited my talent, Anna. Yes, that's right. You didn't become an editor by chance, you know. Editing was in your blood."

Inherited from her? *I am an editor!* Anna wants to shout to her. Writers depend on me to help them shape their ideas, create their stories. You were a secretary, correcting grammar and spelling for your boss.

Her mother adjusts the folds of her dress on her lap. "The Treasurer used to have me rewrite even his personal letters. He used to say I could fix any bad sentence and make it sound like poetry."

Like poetry?

"I was good at it," her mother says with unaffected authority.

"You never said . . ."

"Anything?" Her mother shrugs. "You know I love to read. But you never want me to talk to you about what I read."

Each time she returns to the island Anna brings books for her mother. Usually they are books she has edited, but she has noticed that even before she leaves for New York, her mother has read them all. So she has begun to bring her other books, all kinds, ones from the New York Times best sellers list. They never talk to each other about these books she brings. Anna talks to her friend Paula about them. She especially loves to talk about the books she acquired, the books she edited, the writers she found. But she and her mother never discuss books.

"Why didn't you ever tell me about what you did when you were working at the Treasury?"

"That was my life. This is your life."

"You and Daddy, you keep so much away from me. From each other."

"Not from each other."

"You didn't tell him about your breast," Anna says spitefully.

"I didn't need to tell him," her mother responds.

Outside the dark grows deeper. The moon is yet a crescent low in the sky. Through the glass sliding doors, Anna can glimpse the outlines of trees, silvery in the dull moonlight. She wishes her father would call, say that he has forgotten something, ask about the basket. She wishes that this time he would prove her mother right.

Why don't they discuss the books she brings her mother? The answer comes unbidden: good fiction takes one through the corridors of the human heart. She is afraid to travel through the corridors of the human heart with her mother. She has never brought her Morrison.

"Come." Her mother stands up. The skirt of her dress unfolds and falls below her knees. "I want to show you something. Come."

Grateful, relieved to break through the dark cloud that has descended over her, Anna bounds out of her chair. "Where to?"

"Where I am standing. I want you to come over here."

"Over there?"

"Yes. Come nearer to me."

Anna takes two steps forward.

"You need to come closer."

Anna comes closer.

"Closer."

"What is it, Mummy? What do you want to show me?"

"I want you to look at my face."

Anna looks at her mother's face.

"Don't you see? Gone. All gone." Her mother burst into giggles.

Anna does not know what to do, what to think.

Her mother swipes her hand across her chin. "Here. Feel, Anna."

Does she want her to touch her skin?

"Do it, Anna."

Anna extends a finger. Her mother's breath brushes her lips.

"Touch it, Anna."

Anna withdraws her hand. Her heart is pounding in her chest.

"Touch it, Anna."

Anna lifts her hand and draws her finger across her mother's chin. The skin is smooth. Silky smooth.

Her mother giggles again. "I don't have to shave," she says. "Every little bit of it, gone. Every tiny stubble!" Her mother is laughing so hard, tears roll down her cheeks. "The chemo!" She can hardly get the words out of her mouth. "The chemo has destroyed the follicles!"

Her mother is still laughing when her husband returns.

CHAPTER 24

The immigrant survives by forgetting. The immigrant erases from her consciousness the past that is too painful for her to bear. The immigrant fantasizes. The past the immigrant chooses to remember is the past of an imagined home where the sea is always turquoise, the sand is always white, the grass is always green, the sky is always blue, the sun is always golden. In memories the immigrant has stored, home is always waiting in the brilliant colors of her remembered youth, in the greens, golds, blues, and whites she has left behind. There are no dark days in the immigrant's fantasies, no black skies, no stormy waters. Only in dreams do dark memories return. And this night a dark memory plays and replays in Anna's dream. She tosses and turns, but the memory persists. She is in elementary school, in Standard Two. They have not yet moved to the hill. Every day her father picks her up in his car and they go together to have lunch with her mother at home. This day her father has asked her to do something for him. It is a little thing. He should not have to ask. But they both know that if he does not ask, and if she does not agree, it will not be done.

What her father wants her to do is to kiss her mother when they arrive at home. Isn't this what all children do when they greet their mother? It isn't what they do at her home and her father knows this well. But he insists. "Kiss her." Her mother recoils. "What's this? What's this, John?" She points an accusing finger at her husband.

Anna wakes up shivering, her teeth chattering. She shuts off the air conditioner, opens the windows, and inhales, filling her lungs with air damp with morning dew pearled on the leaves of the trees outside her room. Dawn is breaking. The sun still lies below the horizon, but a pink streak ripples across the sky staining the clouds above it purple. Soon the sun will rise. Soon the memory will fade. Soon, *What's this? What's this, John?* will be buried along with the other images she cannot allow herself to remember.

Feathers flutter in the trees, birds quarrel, fruit fall, the garbage man's truck trundles by. Morning noises. The world is normal again. Then, oddly, a peculiar quiet. An angel passing, old people on the island say. And after the quiet, the sound of tapping on her bedroom door. *Tap, tap.* One more time, a pause, and then again.

"Anna?"

It's her mother.

Anna tiptoes to her bed and slides under the covers.

"Anna, are you awake?"

She shuts her eyes; she covers her ears with her hands.

"Anna, are you up?"

The voice does not go away.

"I thought I heard you moving around in your room, Anna."

Her mother stores clothes in the closets in the room where she stays when she visits. Perhaps her mother is here for her clothes and for no other reason.

Tap, tap.

Anna squeezes her eyes so tightly they hurt. She presses her hands against her ears.

Tap, tap.

She is being childish. Her mother will not go away. She opens her eyes and releases her ears. She removes the pillow from under her head and places it against the headboard. She sits up and readies herself. "Come in," she says. "The door is not locked."

Her mother enters the room and approaches the bed; her steps are tentative. "I don't want to disturb you if you're still resting," she says. But her mother has already disturbed her. "If you want to sleep some more . . ."

Anna fixes the hem of the sheet around her thighs and legs. "No, I've had enough sleep."

How long will it take for her to get the clothes she has come for and leave? Anna wonders.

"May I sit down?" Her mother is standing at the foot of the bed.

Not, *can*. Not, *Can I sit down?* She is asking permission.

"Of course, of course," Anna says. What else can she say? There are no chairs in the room. If her mother sits, she will have to sit on the bed next to her.

Her mother is in her nightgown, a thin blue silky garment that falls to her knees. She clutches the opening at the neck, drawing the fabric in a bunch to her throat. The rest of the silky garment gathers around her hips, and Anna can see she is not wearing panties. When her mother lowers her body on the bed, the mattress sinks slightly under the pressure of her weight. Anna feels its undulation in her most private parts.

Mother and daughter. She has come from her mother's womb. She has slid down her vagina.

A chuckle rumbles up her mother's throat. Anna waits. "That was funny, wasn't it?" her mother says. "What I showed you yesterday?"

Anna does not believe her mother has come here, this early in the morning, in her nightgown, to sit on her bed and say this.

"Not even a stubble on my chin."

But the hair that sprouted on her mother's chin had not

mattered to her husband. Her husband had not cared that she shaved. He placed his razor next to hers and sympathized.

Tony cared. Tony was embarrassed when she plucked out the strands that grew on her chin.

"It was good to laugh. I haven't had much to laugh about since this." Her mother touches the lump on her breast.

Should she seize the opportunity now to say to her: *You'll have more days to laugh if you go to the States, if you let Dr. Bishop do the surgery?* Is that why her mother is here? To be persuaded to go to the Bishops' anniversary party? Should she tell her now that she needs to speak to the Bishops' son, the doctor?

"You and Daddy should go out more often. Have fun," Anna says.

Her mother is not so easily fooled. It takes her an instant to guess Anna's intention. "No!" she says firmly. "I don't want to talk about Dr. Bishop. I've made up my mind. Your father and I are not going to the party."

A muscle twitches across the back of Anna's neck. She lowers her head and massages it.

"Don't turn away from me, Anna." Her mother touches her arm, but lightly and briefly.

Anna lifts her head.

"I have something to tell you. Something I've been wanting to tell you for a very long time."

Instinctively Anna's back stiffens, her body building its habitual armor to protect itself. She leans back against the headboard.

"It's about my father."

Her mother's father is dead. He was dead long before Anna was born. As the sons and daughters of dead parents often do, her mother romanticizes him. Her father was handsome, her father was kind, her father was a good man. This is what her mother chooses to believe.

"He adored my mother," her mother says.

A lie.

"And she adored him too."

Another lie.

"My father would have given her the world, but my mother was too proud to take anything from him."

Her father was a gambler. When he died, his wife was left with the burden of his gambling debts.

"The world," her mother says. "If she had let him give it to her. Money, clothes. Whatever she wanted."

"Mummy. You don't have to . . ." Anna raises her hand to stop her.

"You don't believe me?"

"It does not matter," Anna says softly. "It does not matter."

"She wouldn't take what he wanted to give her. Pride made her not take it." With one hand her mother plucks the skirt of her nightgown at her knees; the other hand is still at her throat.

"He was a gambler, Mummy. He had nothing to give her."

"There's much you don't know, Anna." The knuckles on her mother's fingers protrude, sharp and pale.

"I know what he did. I know he threw away everything he had on the gambling table."

"You are so judgmental, Anna. So judgmental." Her mother stretches out her fingers and claws the fabric of her nightgown, gathering it tightly around her throat.

"Your mother didn't deserve such a husband, or you such a father," Anna says.

"He made my mother an honest woman. He married her. *That* counted for a lot in my day."

"Counted?" Anna's jaw drops.

"You don't know what that meant. Being married. Marriage was important in my day. It's still important for a woman."

"You mean important for me?" Anna kicks away the sheet from her legs and gets out of the bed.

"Oh, Anna, I was not thinking of you at all."

"Why are you so ashamed of me for being unmarried?" Anna spits out the words at her. "Women live alone. They are quite happy living alone. I am happy living alone." She turns her back and walks across the room toward the window.

"You always misunderstand me, Anna. I thought last night, last night when we laughed . . ."

They laughed, but nothing has changed. She wants more. She wants a daughter who is an editor at Windsor, a daughter who is married to a successful man. She cannot boast to her friends about a daughter who is divorced, a daughter who is an editor of a small publishing imprint for writers of color.

"Why don't you give up, Mummy?" Anna leans against the windowsill and faces her. "I am almost forty. I have no children. I have no husband. I have no trophy career to offer you."

"Anna, Anna. That's not it at all. That's not why I am here. I want to explain . . . You need to know."

"What do I need to know, Mummy?"

"Why we haven't . . . you know. Why we haven't . . ."

She cannot say it. She cannot say: Why we haven't embraced. Why it's so hard for me to kiss my daughter.

"You don't have to explain," Anna says. She thrusts her head out of the open window.

"It's about my father. I came to tell you about my father. So you'd understand about me." Her mother pauses, swallows down hard. "My mother was pregnant with me by another man when your grandfather married her."

Anna swivels around.

"Didn't you ever wonder why my skin is so much lighter than your grandmother's?"

Blood drains down Anna's neck. Her knees buckle, the tips of her fingers are suddenly icy cold. "I hardly remember my grandmother," she murmurs.

"You've seen the photographs. You know what she looked like. Didn't you wonder? She had those cheekbones like you have. The Carib Amerindian blood in her. African and Carib she was, but her skin was dark. Didn't you notice how dark she was?"

"Grandpa . . ." Anna begins, but she needs more air.

"You've seen his photographs too. His skin was the color of tar. Black like tar. Didn't you notice his nose? Is my nose as flat as his? And his hair? Is the texture of your hair like his?"

She had noticed his tar black skin, his hair, his nose. She had indeed wondered: would two such dark-skinned parents give birth to a daughter with butterscotch brown skin like her mother's? She had stifled the question whenever it rose. "I don't remember," she whispers now.

"You *won't* remember. You remember he was a gambler. I remember he married my mother. I forgave him everything for marrying my mother." Beatrice releases her hold on the top of her nightgown bunched at her neck. Her shoulders droop. "My father, my real father, the biological one, was a white man. English."

A typical Caribbean story. The words sear like acid across Anna's brain. She does not voice them.

"From England," her mother says.

Why should she be surprised? Why should her mother's story be any different from the stories of so many other women on the island? Anna does not need her mother to tell her more. The air outside the window clears her head. She knows this story; it is common enough. It is the story of Englishmen who dropped their seeds on the island and went back home to their Englishwomen. Which is worse, Anna wonders: a grandfather who was a gambler, or a grandfather who discarded her grandmother after he sated himself?

"He loved my mother."

"Loved her?" Anna will not believe that.

"It happens. It happened many times. It still happens on this island. Men and women love each other; it doesn't matter their skin color."

"He abandoned your mother." If she wants to speak the truth, Anna thinks, let it be the whole truth.

"He couldn't stay with my mother."

"Couldn't or wouldn't?"

"He was married," her mother says.

"Hah! An adulterer!" Anna exclaims bitterly.

"He wanted to take care of her."

"He wanted a wife and a mistress," Anna says.

"He was willing to provide for her."

"But not willing to divorce his wife and marry her. Not that."

"We didn't do such things in my mother's time."

"Yes, an Englishman would not do such things as marry a black woman when he could have her as his mistress."

"You are wrong, Anna. He wanted to take care of me too. Then the colonial office sent him back to England."

"How convenient!"

"His wife had reported him to the colonial office," her mother says.

"And he tucked in his tail and went back home."

"You don't understand, Anna. He had no choice. He would have lost his job."

"So he preferred to let my grandmother pay the price."

"She didn't want him to lose his job."

"But he was willing to leave her to fend for herself."

"She wouldn't accept money from him. And then your grandfather, the one you called Grandpa, offered to marry my mother."

"They paid him?"

Her mother groans. "Your grandfather was not a bad man, Anna. No one paid him. He knew my mother from their school days. He had loved her since then. He wanted to help her. But she never loved him." Tears well in the canals below her eyes; they do not fall down. "No matter what he did, she could not bring herself to love him. He reminded her of what she lost, what she really wanted. She resented me too. She loved me, but she loved only that part of me that was a part of my father and her."

Anna has no memory of seeing her mother cry. The tears, though they remain at the edges of her mother's eyes, make her uneasy. She wishes they would go away. "Don't," she says.

"One day your grandpa came home drunk and tried to kiss my mother. Or I think that was what he tried to do. I was in my bedroom, but I heard them. She must have pushed him away. She always pushed him away whenever he got too close to her. She would flinch when he touched her."

You flinched when I touched you. You recoiled when Daddy made me kiss you.

"He must have been so drunk that day he lost his usual self-control. He began yelling at her. *When will you stop loving him and love me? I am here. I'm your husband, but you don't see me.* It was terrible. Afterward, my mother came to my room. She was weeping. She said that if she could love my father, she would love him. But we don't choose who we love, she said. She blamed Cupid. Funny, isn't it? She claimed that when she met my biological father some mythical god of love had sunk his arrow so deep in her heart she could never pull it out."

"And you believe that," Anna says quietly.

"About Cupid?" Her mother swipes the back of her arm across her eyes. The tears that did not come down, that seemed as if they were refusing to come down, get squeezed between her arm and the canals of her eyes. A bubble forms in each eye, bursts, and drips to the top of her cheeks. Her cheeks are damp when she faces Anna.

"I remember how I could not resist your father though I was angry with him for following me in the street that day. So silly. Following me everywhere until I had to stop. I don't know what it was: his sheepish look, that foolish hat he was wearing. I don't know. I can't tell. He came to my house every day and I couldn't say no. Did I have a choice? Did Cupid shoot his arrow in my heart? Like my mother, I couldn't pull that arrow out."

Anna draws in her bottom lip over her teeth and clamps her mouth shut. Her teeth sink into her flesh. She presses down harder, focusing on the pain, anything to silence the voice that wants to ask: *If you can love him, why is it so hard for you to love me?*

"With children it's the same," her mother says.

Anna's heart leaps in her chest. Her head swirls.

"It's not an arrow; it's the umbilical cord. I blamed you last night. I said you wouldn't talk to me about the books you brought home for me to read, but it was I who stopped you. I made it impossible for you to talk to me. I always make it impossible for you to talk to me." Her mother's voice breaks and the brick wall around Anna's heart totters.

"I learned well from my mother. I learned not to show my feelings for my own daughter." Her mother rubs her nose against her shoulder and sniffles.

A bird sitting on a tree branch in the garden outside the bedroom window stretches out its wings and leaps. Anna follows its flight.

"Not that I should blame her. She could not have survived if she had allowed herself to show her real feelings."

And what about me? How did I survive when my mother did not show affection for me?

Her mother trails fingers from one hand over the back of the other. Perhaps her thoughts are the same; perhaps she too wonders how her daughter survived. "In my day," she says, "mothers did not do that; they did not hug and kiss their children. The queen . . ."

Anna's brain will not allow her to wait for the rest. *The queen was not my mother!* she wants to yell. *You are. And you couldn't stand the touch of my lips on your cheeks.* But she is reasonable. She says: "We are not a colony of England anymore, Mummy."

"My mother was born in a colony of England. Her mother's mother and her mother. I was born in a colony of England. That was all I've known except for these past few years."

"Not a few. More than twenty, Mummy."

"Yesterday. It seems like yesterday to me. The queen didn't . . ." She pauses and looks up expectantly at Anna, but Anna does not interrupt her again. "The queen did not hug and kiss Charles and Anne. Yet what did it matter what the queen did?" Her mother flicks her hand in the air. "It mattered to us. She didn't care, but we cared. If she did not hug and kiss her children, we didn't hug and kiss our children. We learned restraint from her."

"Restraint?" Anna almost chokes on the word.

"We were good colonial subjects. We imitated the queen."

"She was protecting her progeny."

"I don't know what you mean."

"Lust," Anna says.

"Lust?"

"They weren't as lucky as we are. They didn't have birth control. So no hugging or kissing your relatives. Not even your children. It was one way to prevent pregnancy, to keep bad thoughts out of the minds of relatives."

"Oh," her mother says, Anna's meaning sinking in. "Still, I should not have . . ."

Anna holds her breath.

"I should not have . . . I should not . . ." Her mother looks away.

She cannot say the words. Years of restraint have calcified any impulse she may have now to say more.

In spite of herself, Anna feels sympathy for her. "It's okay, Mummy," she says. "It's okay."

Her mother's relief is visible when she turns around. The dullness in her eyes has vanished, her cheeks have softened, her lips loosened in the beginning of a smile. "But we laughed last night, didn't we, Anna?" There is a child's desperate hopefulness in her voice.

"Yes," Anna says. "We laughed."

Then her mother surprises her. She gets up and walks toward her. She reaches for her hand and squeezes it. "You cannot imagine, Anna," she says—it's the mother speaking now, not the desperate child—"You cannot imagine how many times I have wanted to tell you how much I love you."

At last. Cupid's arrow. The umbilical cord that binds the mother to the child, the child to the mother.

But they do not speak this way again. All day they pretend as though nothing has changed between them. Her mother goes about her usual chores. She gives her usual instructions to Lydia about the meals for the day. She makes her usual inspection of the house. She passes her fingers across the furniture to check for dust, she sniffs the air in the bathrooms. Later in the morning she has Singh unearth a row of red impatiens and replant them in a shady part of the garden. She does not rebuke him when he mumbles under his breath, "Last month you did tell me to plant dem somewhere else."

She is tired after lunch. She naps, has tea at four, dinner at the usual time, listens to Bach with her husband, and turns in to bed at eight. It begins to seem to Anna as if their early-morning talk had been part of her dream the night before, the better part, the part with the ending the little girl had always yearned for. Then, late at night, as she is walking toward her bedroom, the door to her mother's room cracks open.

"Do you know what I pray for?" Her mother is standing in the darkened narrow opening. The whites of her eyes seem whiter in the dark, larger on a face buttressed by bones that fan out to the smooth hard shell of her almost bald head. Through the nightgown she is wearing, Anna can see the outlines of her breasts and the dark triangle beneath her belly. Her mother scans the floor. "I pray every night that my child will come back to me."

She does not say *my daughter*. She does not name the child. She does not say *Anna*. She says *my child*.

Anna opens her mouth to speak, though she doesn't know what words will come. Then her mother closes the door. She does not wait for her response.

Anna wants to be more understanding. She wants to be forgiving. Her mother belongs to other times, to times before a world war deflated England's dreams of Empire, when, still puffed up with its victories in its colonies, England trained its colonial subjects to serve the Mother Country.

Then the kings and queens of England were the models to be emulated; kings and queens who did not hug and kiss their children, at least not in public.

An old man's prayer reverberates in Anna's ears.

Change ah we heart, O Lord. Change ah we heart.
Change ah we heart like mongoose kinna change he skin under
rock bottom.

CHAPTER 25

Her father has already opened the gate for Singh when she wakes up the next morning. From her bedroom she hears her mother fussing with Singh in the garden. "I don't care what you say, Singh. The plants need watering. The beds are dry."

"Madam, I tell you it go rain today." Singh's voice is syrupy. It is clear he intends to stand his ground.

"You're a hardhead, Singh."

Anna peeps through the window. She cannot see her mother's face, only her back. Her mother is in her house-coat, a bright pink cotton shift edged with white piping. Her blue nightgown flutters beneath it. In her hand is the garden hose.

Singh is facing her mother. Anna is struck once again by the color of his hair, how black it is, how thick. How it shines! How starkly it contrasts to the thin wisps and tuffs on her mother's head, to the bald spot in the middle!

Her mother hides her hair from her bridge friends, but not from Singh. Singh has been with her for forty years; she does not need to hide her bald head from him. Singh understands illness, the failure of the body, the inevitability of death.

"If you just wait an hour, madam," Singh pleads with her, "you go see how it go pour."

Anna looks up in the sky. To the west, dark clouds have gathered, but to the east, where the sun has just risen, the sky is a brilliant blue.

"You see de clouds over dere?" Singh points to the west. He is standing in front of the flower bed, his head cocked, his weight shifted to one side of his body. The expression on his face is one of pure forbearance, but of affection too. His eyes twinkle and his lips slant upward.

"I'm turning on the water, Singh," her mother announces. Her hand is on the nozzle of the hose. "If you don't move, you'll get wet."

Singh remains standing where he is. "Madam, I'm telling you it go rain." He shakes his head. His hair, slicked back with coconut oil, does not budge.

"I'm warning you . . ." Her mother marches to the faucet at the edge of the garden. "I'm warning you, Singh."

"I ent moving, madam." Singh's feet are planted firmly on the dry ground.

"I'm turning it on, Singh."

"I ent moving, madam."

Anna thrusts her head further out of the window. She cannot believe her mother will make good on this threat.

"Have it your way, Singh."

Water fans out from the hose, long translucent sprays that catch the sun and sparkle with rainbow colors. Singh, true to his word, does not move. Water splashes on his T-shirt and shorts. It wets his bare arms and legs.

"So that's what you want, eh, Singh? You didn't take your shower this morning. Is that it?"

Singh's laughter rumbles up his throat. Her mother is laughing too, a girlish peal that rings across the garden and drifts through the window.

"Is me or de flowerbed you want to wet dis morning, madam?" Singh hops from one foot to the other. Her mother continues to spray him with the hose.

"Okay, madam! Okay, madam!" Singh scampers across the grass toward the back of the house, his makeshift clogs slapping against his bare feet. Incredibly, her mother runs behind him, still wetting him down. Their laughter is that of children in the playground. It ripples through the air.

An overwhelming wave of sadness washes Anna. She slumps down to the floor. *How comfortable they seem with each other! How easily their quarrel dissolved into play!*

Long after she can no longer hear their voices, Anna wrestles with questions this all too brief scene has triggered in her: Will she be always on the outside? Will they, the ones who stayed, the ones who did not emigrate, always be on the inside, even Singh and Lydia?

She has made the effort but her mother remains an enigma to her, a bundle of contradictions, her relationship with Singh, Lydia, and her husband too difficult for her to comprehend. For how can she comprehend this woman who is ever observant of her social status, ever insistent on demanding acknowledgment of her class superiority, and yet protects her helper from abuse, and yet gives money to the poor, and yet pranced through the rain forest to help her husband build a shed so he could catch birds with la-glee, and yet is now skipping through the grass, squealing joyfully after her gardener?

As if this isn't enough, as if it isn't enough that her mother's laughter continues to ring in her ears, mocking her, later in the day Anna is confronted again with fresh evidence that there is much she does not know, much she does not understand. That in spite of forty years, though not all of them spent in her parents' house, she may have misjudged her mother.

The rain Singh promised arrives after lunch. It falls out of the sky in bucketfuls, in intermittent torrents of water that explode on the concrete and carve out miniature craters in the dirt. It comes suddenly and forcefully and then, just as abruptly, it ends. The sun blazes forth, its rays stinging, radiating heat. But the air is heavy with moisture and the sun is not strong enough to evaporate trails of water weighing down branches on the trees, clinging between the shoots of grass pooling in crevices. Anna is stretched out on an armchair in the veranda, the book she has been reading turned over on her lap where it has slid from her hands. Her body feels bloated, surely an illusion of the oppressive heat. She can barely breathe. Her parents are in their room, sensibly taking a nap. She thinks of doing the same. She lifts herself up and makes her way to the sliding glass doors at the entrance of the dining room. The television is on in the den. She hears voices, American voices. A soap opera. Perhaps her mother is not taking a nap. She approaches the den. It is Lydia who is there. She is sitting on the floor, her legs extended to one side, her body stretched out on the other, her head propped up on the palm of her hand, her arm anchored to the carpet. She is a figure in a painting, the woman lying supine. The mistress of the house.

Anna clears her throat and Lydia spins around, pulls down her skirt, and sits up. "Miss Anna, is something you want?"

An offer of service; there is no guilt in her tone. Anna may have caught her by surprise, but it is the suddenness of her arrival that causes Lydia to change her position on the floor, not fear of rebuke.

"Is *As the World Turns*," Lydia says when Anna asks about the program she is watching. "Madam and I does talk about it."

"Talk about it?"

"She does look at it in her room and I does see it here."

Anna finds this hard to believe. "But I never saw you in here before," she protests.

"Well, I know you visiting and I think you must want to use the den, so I don't come. But then I see you in the veranda. And it hot in my room . . ."

* * *

They talk. Lydia watches the soaps in the den and afterward they talk. What else do they do? What else do they
talk about when she is not visiting? Her mother claims she
learned restraint. Restraint is not natural to her—this is the
implication. But she is restrained with her daughter, un-
restrained with Lydia. Where else do she and Lydia have
their little chats? Is Lydia permitted not only to sprawl on
the floor of the den but also to sprawl on the floor of the
sanctuary of her mother's bedroom?

Her mother cracks open her bedroom door. Her eyes
are misty when she utters her soulful prayer: I *pray every night
that my child will come back to me*. But she does not wait for her
daughter's answer. She leaves. She closes the door.

CHAPTER 26

Anna sits on the garden bench in the shade of the mango tree. At her feet is the stack of manuscript pages she has finished editing. She is making notes for the presentation she intends to deliver at the meeting of the editorial board. She is planning a vigorous argument for the acquisition of this novel and a decent advance for the writer, something in the range of advances offered to literary novelists at Windsor. The last literary novel she presented from Equiano was approved reluctantly, but with such a meager advance and no budget for promotion that the writer refused the offer and took his novel elsewhere.

It is just past one in the afternoon and the sun is high in the sky. Every sensible person has sought shelter from the stinging sunrays, but in the foreground her father is stooped down low on the lawn plucking out weeds from between the blades of grass. He clears one area and then moves to another, each time piling up a small mound of weeds that quickly wilts in the torpid heat. He gets up, stretches, and then stoops down again. It would tire her to get up and down like that and she is far younger. He has made twelve tiny mounds before he stands up and claps his hands together. Flecks of dried grass flutter down to the ground.

"Finished?" Anna calls out to him.

"This area. I have more to go."

"Why don't you let the boys who cut the lawn do this for you?"

"Too lazy. They tell me they have pulled out all the weeds, but after they've gone I see weeds all over the place."

"Then get other boys to cut the grass."

"Easier said than done. I had a hard time getting the boys I have. Young people aren't interested in doing physical work these days. They have better alternatives."

He means the drug trade. He means that young people can make a hundred times more money being mules for the drug trade than they could in a month of cutting grass in the burning sun. He wants to remind her that drugs have made them prisoners in their old age, locked behind iron bars in their own house.

"What about Singh?" she asks.

"Singh belongs to your mother. I don't interfere with Singh."

He is standing close to her now. Sweat glistens on his balding head. "You should wear a hat," she says.

He passes his hand over his head. Sweat rolls down his neck. "What for?"

"To protect you from the UV rays."

"The UV rays had more than eighty years to do something to me. My skin is too thick for the UV rays."

"Still, you should cover your head when the sun is this strong."

He sits on the bench next to her and casts his eyes over the bundle at her feet. "Not done with the manuscript?"

"I'm making notes."

"For your boss in New York?"

"Yes. I have to make a presentation to the editorial board as soon as I get there."

"And there's no changing your mind?" he says softly.

Pain shoots through her heart. He is begging her. A father should not have to beg his daughter.

"She is terrified, you know," he says.

He has quoted Yeats to her mother. *Sailing to Byzantium*, he said. She thinks now of Eliot.

And I have seen the eternal Footman hold my coat, and snicker,
And in short, I was afraid.

"She needs you, Anna."

Much is different since her mother reached for her hand, squeezed it: *You cannot imagine, Anna, how many times I have wanted to tell you much I love you.* She could have kissed her mother then, she could have hugged her, but they kept their usual distance.

Her mother's father was not her mother's biological father and her grandmother did not love him. Wasn't that too much for her mother to bear? And he was a gambler and a drunk, the man who claimed to be her father. Wouldn't her mother have had to learn restraint to survive those years?

Why can't she, Anna, be more forgiving? Is it the habit of resentment, engrained over the years, that stiffens the muscles in her arms though she longs to be touched by and to touch her mother? Always a vise closes on her heart, always it leaves her no room to choose.

She is an adult, not a helpless child needing her mother's care. Why can't she unlearn what she unwillingly learned?

The Child is father of the Man, Wordsworth reminds her.

"Just until the last chemo session," her father pleads.

She cannot deny him.

Change ah we heart, O Lord. Change ah we heart.

Later that afternoon Anna calls Windsor. Her boss is sympathetic. She will temporarily assign Anna's books to another editor, she says.

Her easy acquiescence troubles Anna. Every ambitious editor has her sights set on New York. Is there someone younger and brighter waiting in the wings to take her job? Will her position as head of Equiano still be there for her when she returns? Anna does not ask her boss these questions directly. She asks whether there are any problems brewing at Equiano. Anything she needs to know.

Her boss laughs. On the contrary, she says, sales are picking up. Urban lit is taking off. We can't publish enough of it. There's a huge pool of young black readers out there who are just waiting to lap it up. Urban lit, chick lit, they fly off the shelves. We even have a new category, she says. Ghetto lit! She laughs so loudly Anna has to remove the receiver from her ear.

This is not what Anna wants to hear. These are not the books she wants Equiano to publish.

"And people used to say there wasn't a market for books by black writers," her boss gloats. "Look at what is happening now."

People. Her boss means white people. Her boss means the marketplace of black readers. Her boss believes that books by black writers have no relevance to *people's* lives.

This is the essence of racism, Anna thinks, this refusal of people to see themselves in the lives of others whose skin color is different than theirs.

Fiction best achieves the universal through the specific. It is by telling stories that are plausible, about characters who are believable, that the writer eases us into exploring the many facets of the human condition. So what if the specific characters are people of color? What if the worlds they inhabit are the worlds inhabited by other people of color? Are there universals for white people and different universals for people of color?

She grew up reading Enid Blyton. She sought adventures vicariously with the pink-cheeked English children in Blyton's mystery novels. As an adult she found herself in the heroines of Austen's novels. Shakespeare, Blake, Keats, Wordsworth, all spoke to her. It didn't matter that they were English. But her boss at Windsor seems to think that the reverse is not possible, that white readers cannot find themselves in the lives of black characters.

They refuse, Anna thinks. They *refuse* to find themselves in black characters. To see the commonalities we share as human beings is to bring down the wall that separates us, that has brought considerable financial profit to many, that has allowed many to delude themselves with notions of their superiority.

And yet why did it take her so long to admit to her mother that she is an editor at Equiano, not Windsor? How many times has she asked herself this question, none of her answers sufficient to quell a recurrent gnawing at her conscience? It is not, she knows, because the writers at Equiano are black. In the beginning they were Asian and Latino as well, all writers of color, but much has since changed. Asians and Latinos now fill mainstream Windsor's niche for exotica, Africans not far behind, now that movie stars are trumpeting Africa's cause. No, what has caused her to withhold from her mother her new position at Windsor's latest imprint is the kind of books Equiano serves up without apology, with pride indeed, as the literature of black writers—and the fact that in spite of this, she continues to work for them.

She tries. She names the writer whose novel she wants to publish. She is a fine writer, she says to her boss, a woman who uses the magic of language to open up a world in which her characters struggle to reconcile their private desires with their public responsibilities. Her novel tells a human story, but it is a story about people with black skin who live in communities of other people with black skin.

"I'm not sure a novel like that would earn its advance," her boss says.

"Does that mean you're not going to consider publishing it?"

"Yes, of course I will publish it. I trust your judgment, but I must warn you there won't be much of an advance and not much for publicity."

It is a death sentence. No book sells itself. Anna makes that point, and her boss listens patiently but she has already made up her mind.

"It's the best I can offer," she says.

This is the reason why she must return to New York. She needs to be there to fight for her writer. If the book does not sell, her boss will not publish the writer's next novel. But she must choose what matters most. She wants, *needs*, to be with her mother.

"I'll fax my notes," she says.

"Take all the time you need," her boss replies.

Her parents do not go to the Bishops' fiftieth wedding anniversary party. The next day, Paul Bishop calls. Lydia answers the phone. He'll be coming by in an hour, Paul Bishop says. He does not ask to speak to Mr. or Mrs. Sinclair. He simply asks Lydia to deliver his message.

Beatrice is surprised he has bothered to telephone, it being the acceptable custom for visitors to arrive without warning. It is a source of pride to the people on the island, evidence of their hospitality, that at a drop of a hat they can have a meal ready to offer the unexpected visitor. Anna remembers more than one time when she had to give up the slices of chicken breast she preferred for a thigh or leg because someone arrived at lunchtime. But Paul Bishop lives in America where such idiosyncratic (inconsiderate to some) behavior is not tolerated. He telephoned—though giving the Sinclairs merely an hour's advance warning—and he times his arrival between breakfast and lunch so as not to inconvenience the kitchen.

Nonetheless, Beatrice Sinclair panics. She issues orders: to Lydia to take the pastels from the freezer and begin steaming them immediately; to her husband to set out drinks on the bar; to Anna to find the chocolates she brought from America. She rushes out to the garden and instructs Singh to cut bunches of red ginger lilies and pink anthuriums and have Lydia arrange them in a vase on the cocktail table in the veranda, and then she disappears into her room. When she reemerges, she is wearing one of her best cotton flowered dresses, belted at the waist. Her head is wrapped in a blue silk scarf that matches the blue flowers on her dress. There is not much hair left at the base of her head and parts of her bare scalp are visible, but she has recovered a bit from her chemo session and her complexion is bright. Her face is not drawn; her eyes are not dull.

Anna brings out the chocolates. Her mother takes them from her and scans her outfit. Wanting to please her, Anna has put on white linen slacks and a pale yellow sleeveless shirt. The colors highlight her freshly tanned skin. "Good," Beatrice says approvingly. "You look nice, Anna. Just right."

John Sinclair, however, has not changed his clothes. He has on the same khaki shorts and dirty T-shirt he wore the day before.

Beatrice Sinclair admonishes him: "You wanted a towel, John. I gave you a towel. Why don't you use it instead of wiping your hands on your shirt?"

He frets with her. "What would you prefer me to do? Dress up like you or set up the bar?"

In the midst of this exchange the bell at the gate rings. Beatrice, flustered, sends Lydia to find a clean shirt for Mr.

Sinclair. "Quick sharp!" She claps her hand. The bell rings again and she runs to the electric buzzer in the kitchen. She presses it and the gate opens. "Anna, you go to meet Paul Bishop," she says.

Ordinarily Beatrice Sinclair would consider it improper for her daughter to greet a visitor in the driveway, but her husband is standing in the kitchen half naked and Lydia has gone to the bedroom for his shirt. This is not a time to insist on such social proprieties, not when a visitor of the stature of Dr. Paul Bishop could be standing in the driveway not knowing through which door he should enter the house.

Anna likes Paul Bishop right away. She finds him handsome, though not in a conventional way. When he comes out of the car, she discovers he is no more than an inch or two taller than she. And he is not well proportioned. He has a slight paunch that protrudes under his white-collared Polo shirt. It begins at his waist and hangs over the belt that holds up his tan slacks. He is as close to fifty as she is to forty, she surmises. There are sprinklings of gray on his closely cropped hair and on his thick eyebrows, but he has *presence*. This is the word that comes to Anna's mind. When he stretches his arm out to shake her hand, his entire being seems to come alive. His jet black eyes dance; his widening smile sends ripples across his cheeks; sunlight bounces off his smooth, plum-dark skin.

"Anna, do you remember meeting me?" Even his voice, she finds, has presence. It is a deep baritone that is immensely pleasing to her. "Of course you won't," he says when she doesn't respond. "You were a little thing, about four or five,"

"You couldn't have been much older," Anna replies.

"A boy always remembers a pretty girl. Your father brought you with him one day when he came to see my father. You were so pretty."

It embarrasses Anna that at this moment she should be grateful to her mother for making it known to her that Paul Bishop does not have a wife. She is glad too that for her mother's sake she is wearing one of her favorite outfits.

"All little girls at four or five are pretty," she says self-deprecatingly, and is conscious right away that she has opened herself to inviting a compliment.

Paul Bishop obliges. "And you have remained so, I can see."

Her parents are standing in the veranda, waiting. John Sinclair is now wearing a crisply ironed cotton plaid shirt and clean brown pants. On the cocktail table is the floral arrangement Lydia has made with the red ginger lilies and the pink anthuriums. Next to it is a white orchid in a clay pot. Beatrice Sinclair had asked Singh to cut the red ginger lilies and the pink anthuriums for the vase in the veranda. She did not ask him for the orchid.

Paul Bishop notices it immediately. He greets the Sinclairs and points to the orchid. "It's so unusual."

"Singh must have put it there." Beatrice Sinclair is clearly pleased.

"Singh?"

"Mummy's gardener," Anna tells him. "He knows how much Mummy loves orchids. He gave her this one."

"It's stunning." Paul Bishop touches a leaf. "He must really like you, Mrs. Bishop. You hardly see an orchid like this one."

"Singh's been with me for a long time," Beatrice says.

Did Singh anticipate Paul Bishop's response? Did he and Lydia cook up this plan together to have her mother warm up to him? Lydia has overheard their conversations. She knows this man is a surgeon in America.

Paul Bishop admits he's a gardener himself. An amateur, not an expert like you, Mrs. Sinclair, he says. Beatrice beams. I imagine you can't do much in the winter, Beatrice offers sympathetically. That's what I miss in New Jersey, Paul Bishop says. Spring, summer, and then it's over. Would you like to see the garden? I would like nothing more, Paul Bishop says. Beatrice gives him a tour. John Sinclair accompanies them; Anna stays behind.

Lydia is waiting with a tray laden with pastels wrapped in smoked banana leaves, slices of cold ham, plates, and cutlery when they return. She is standing at the doorway. Beatrice Sinclair motions to her to come forward. She is in a good mood. Paul Bishop is full of praise for her garden. The colors! The variety! The symmetry!

"Sit, sit." Beatrice invites Paul Bishop to take one of the wicker chairs. He sits, they all sit. Then John Sinclair spoils the festivities.

"We are so sorry," he begins. "So sorry we couldn't come to your parents' anniversary celebration. Beatrice . . ." He casts his eyes over to his wife. She is no longer smiling. "I . . . We . . ." He struggles to find the right words that will erase the frown growing on his wife's brow. "We don't get around much these days."

"I expect so," Paul Bishop says. "There is no need to apologize. I'm leaving tomorrow and I wanted to get the chance to see you before I left." He leans over to Beatrice. "How are you, Mrs. Sinclair?"

Paul Bishop's question makes Beatrice uncomfortable. She covers up her discomfort by turning her attention to Lydia. "Come, come, Lydia," she says irritably. "Don't stand there. Offer the doctor a pastel."

Paul Bishop shakes his head and raises his hands in a gesture of surrender. "All this good food! I love pastels, but I've gained five pounds since I arrived on the island." He rubs his stomach.

"You don't have to have it if you've just eaten," Anna says.

Her mother glances at her sharply. Anna clamps her mouth shut. She does not say another word.

"Lydia made these," Beatrice says. "I think they are the best she's ever made. Try one, Dr. Bishop." She puts a pastel on a plate.

"How can I refuse?" Paul Bishop smiles at Lydia who grins back at him.

"Here. Let Anna remove the banana leaves from your pastel." Beatrice points the plate in her daughter's direction.

Anna draws back her hand as if she has been stung.

Paul Bishop is gallant. "Oh, no, Mrs. Sinclair," he says, and takes the plate from Beatrice. "That won't be necessary. I can do this."

Beatrice is not to be outdone. "Anna helped Lydia make these. Didn't you, Anna?"

With as much sternness and finality as she can muster, Anna says to her mother, "I helped Lydia wrap them. That's all I did and you know that very well, Mummy."

Beatrice purses her lips. Her eyebrows converge.

John Sinclair wants to clear the air. "And what will you drink, Dr. Bishop?"

"I'm not fussy."

"Rum punch?"

"A little too early for me for alcohol."

"Lime juice with some Angostura?" Beatrice chimes in.

"Yes. That would be good. I miss having lime juice and Angostura."

"We've mixed it already." Beatrice sends Lydia to the bar for the pitcher and glasses.

Paul Bishop turns to John Sinclair. His father has never forgotten how John Sinclair helped the oil field workers, he says. "I wouldn't be where I am today if you had not helped him."

"According to Dr. Ramdoolal you are one of the best surgeons in America," John Sinclair says graciously.

Paul Bishop laughs. "Dr. Ramdoolal is a Caribbean patriot."

"Perhaps so, but he wouldn't lie for the sake of patriotism."

"Well, I can say I do surgery at one of the best hospitals in America. Oncology is my specialty."

"A cancer doctor!" But John Sinclair knows that already.

Beatrice Sinclair sits up in her chair. "I suppose Dr. Ramdoolal asked you to check up on me." Her eyes challenge Dr. Bishop to deny it.

Anna notices that her mother's scarf is slipping off her forehead, exposing her scanty hairline. A few stray hairs, resistant to the chemo, peek out from the sides.

"Yes," Paul Bishop says simply.

"And I suppose he's sent you to try to convince me to have surgery in America."

"I think that would be best," Paul Bishop responds.

Lydia has returned from the bar with the pitcher and glasses. She serves Paul Bishop first and then Mr. and Mrs. Sinclair and Anna, but she does not leave. She stands in front of Beatrice Sinclair, blocking Paul Bishop's line of vision to her employer. "Excuse me, Mrs. Sinclair," she says. "Is there anything else you want me to get you from the kitchen?" She brushes her hand over her forehead and slides it to the back her head. She looks steadily at her employer. After a moment, Lydia repeats the movement of her hand and inclines her head. Finally Beatrice understands. She mouths *Thank you* to Lydia. Her fingers are trembling as she adjusts the scarf on her head.

When Lydia goes, Paul Bishop returns to the subject of Mrs. Sinclair's surgery. He agrees with Dr. Ramdoolal, he says. Mrs. Sinclair should have her surgery in the States. "I will do it for you," he says.

Beatrice shakes her head.

"You can trust me. My father trusted your husband. I will do my best for you."

"Mummy thinks that black people don't get treated fairly in America," Anna says.

Paul Bishop puts his glass down on the cocktail table near to him and moves his chair closer to Beatrice. It makes a scraping sound against the terrazzo floor. "Is that what you are afraid of, Mrs. Sinclair?" He is speaking softly, gently.

"I see it on TV. I see what is happening there," Beatrice says.

"It's not the whole picture, Mrs. Sinclair. Look at me. I am the head of the surgery unit in my hospital. Most of the doctors under me are white. They don't treat me as a black doctor. They treat me as a doctor."

"Mummy is afraid," Anna says.

"Your tumor was bleeding, Mrs. Sinclair. If your cancerous breast is not removed, the cancer will spread and kill you."

Beatrice looks up at him in alarm. "Kill me?"

"The chemo is making the tumor smaller. When it gets small enough, you can come to my hospital, Mrs. Sinclair. I will remove it."

"Listen to Dr. Bishop, Beatrice," John Sinclair urges his wife.

"You have age as an advantage, Mrs. Sinclair. Cancer like yours feeds on estrogen. Luckily, at your age you don't have much estrogen left in your body to feed the cancer. I've seen women with worse tumors than yours. After they have had surgery, they continued to live for years. I have one patient who is ninety. I can tell you it won't be breast cancer that takes her away from here."

"Hear that, Beatrice?" John Sinclair pats his wife's knee. "Live to be ninety!"

"And afterward?" Beatrice asks, fear widening her eyes.

"There are prosthetic bras, Mrs. Sinclair," Paul Bishop says patiently.

"Then I'll have one breast. Is that so? One breast? I'll be deformed." She swings her body toward her husband. "Deformed, John."

"No one can tell when a woman is wearing a prosthetic," Paul Bishop says.

"John." Beatrice's eyes are glued to her husband's. He is her mate for life, the companion at her side through the best and worst of her days. "John." She wants his advice, his support, his approval.

He reaches for her hand. "I want you with me, Beatrice."

"And it won't matter to you? It won't matter that I am deformed?"

He folds her hand between both of his. "You are beautiful to me, Beatrice. You always will be."

"With one breast?"

"I won't know what to do if you are not with me."

"I won't look the same."

John Sinclair shifts his body closer to his wife. Their daughter and the doctor who is offering to do the surgery are in the room but they seem unaware of their presence. Shoulders almost touching, breath upon breath, he whispers to his wife, "We'll take showers together, Beatrice."

Anna is stunned.

"Go," her father says. "For my sake. For our sake, Beatrice. Have the surgery in the States."

Her mother leans closer to her husband. She breathes in deeply. She nods her head.

Anna turns away. *Privacy matters*, her father said, but privacy does not seem to matter to them now. What matters to them now is intimacy. In front of her, in front of a stranger, her father has talked of sex with his wife. They will be naked together. They will take showers together, he says.

Paul Bishop stands up; he is ready to leave. He hands John Sinclair his card. Have Dr. Ramdoolal call me, he says.

Anna walks Paul Bishop to his car. Her parents have already gone to their room when she returns.

CHAPTER 27

*It's very clear, our love is here to stay
Not for a year, but ever and a day*

Music pulls Anna out of a deep sleep. She stretches out her legs, turns her head on her pillow, unable, in the immediate return to consciousness, to sort out whether the music she hears is part of a dream or whether the sounds and words are real, taking place in real time.

*The radio and the telephone and the movies that we know
May just be passing fancies and in time may go*

Nat King Cole. Her brain registers the voice and the words. Her eyes shoot open. Nat King Cole, and not in a dream, but here, outside her bedroom door. She looks over to the clock on her bedside table. Two o'clock. The room is dark. In the garden, beyond the heavily draped windows, nothing moves, nothing makes a sound. The birds are sleeping. The frogs have settled down. No lizards scamper between the blades of grass.

But oh, my dear . . .

Violins soar. Two o'clock, the hour when her mother, no longer able to contain the terror that squeezes breath from her body, makes jelly of her limbs and a drum of her heart, places trembling fingers on the edge of the blanket she shares with her husband, and cautiously, so as not to awaken him, so as not to inconvenience him, lifts up the blanket and slides one leg and then the other across the mattress and onto the carpeted floor. Tiptoeing, she feels her way in the dark to the bathroom. There, she stretches her hand to the back of the linen closet, searching for the box of matches and the two candles she has hidden under the towels. In a drawer, she has tucked a flat-shaped saucer between the folds of her underwear. She takes it out and puts it on the dressing room table. She places the candles on the saucer, one next to the other. Her fingers shaking, she strikes a match and lights the wicks of the candles, blackened from use over many nights like this one. The room glows, but she has closed the bathroom door so the light will not awaken her husband.

There is a stool in the bathroom under the dressing room table. She pulls it out and sits in front of her dressing table. Shadows flicker on the wall. Though she does her best to avoid the mirror, her eyes, perversely, are drawn to it and she sees what she does not want to see or want to believe she sees: the bloodied vest, the lump protruding under the thin fabric. She prays. Ten rosaries if she must, ten rosaries if she can, before dawn streams through the diaphanous curtains that hang over the bathroom window. Ten rosaries so the Blessed Mother will intercede for her with her Son. Ten rosaries so the Blessed Mother will have pity on her. Her husband will be still asleep when she crawls back to bed. The mattress will shift under the weight of her body but he will not wake up. Or he will pretend not to wake up.

. . . our love is here to stay
Together we're going a long, long way

Two o'clock. Nat King Cole on the CD player. The music

streams out of the den. Is this where her mother has gone this time, now that she has consented, now that she has agreed to travel to the States for surgery? Now that she has accepted that the lump in her breast will not disappear? Now that prayers have not changed that reality?

This is the song her father played when he began courting her mother again, when the passion for the other woman that had flared up in him like a bush fire extinguished itself in the embers left behind.

Anna slips out of her bed. Quietly, she turns the knob on the bedroom door. She does not make a sound. Her slippered feet slide silently across the tiled corridor, down the three steps into the breakfast room, through the breakfast room and into the den.

But her mother is not in the den where the CD player turns the disk, Nat King Cole singing:

They're only made of clay
But our love is here to stay.

An open passageway separates the den from the drawing room. Anna hides behind the wall and peeps through the side of the passageway. Two bodies are glued together as one. Moonlight streaming from the uncurtained window at the top of the stone wall at the far end of the drawing room encircles the bodies in an aura of blue. The man, her father, is holding the woman, her mother, close to his chest, folded in his arms. He presses her head into the well of his shoulder. Light bounces off her mother's bare scalp, the skin stretched taut across hard bone. Her head glitters; it shines.

Her father draws her mother closer to his heart. They move, though they hardly move. Feet do not move; bodies move, torsos sway to the rhythm of King Cole.

Anna is a voyeur, an intruder. She has invaded their privacy; she has trespassed on their intimacy. Chastened, she creeps back to her room.

Paul Bishop telephones the next morning. He is worried he has offended her mother, pushed her too hard. "I sometimes sound more like a doctor than a doctor who is also a man. All that stuff I said about prosthetic bras."

"You were trying to help," Anna reassures him.

"I must have scared her when I told her the cancer would spread if she didn't have her breast removed."

"You helped Mummy come to a decision."

"I should know better. A breast is not just a body part. My patients tell me that every day."

"Daddy is there for her."

"He's a good man, your father."

"He knows what a good woman my mother is too."

The line goes still. Anna thinks it is the usual inter-ruption of telephone service on the island. Still, she tries. She says, "Hello, hello," into the phone. The third time she speaks, Paul Bishop coughs. "Are you okay? I thought it was the phone line."

"Just my throat. It itches sometimes. I'm fine."

Anna takes a deep breath. "I want to thank you for what you did for my mother, Dr. Bishop. Taking the time to come to see her."

"Paul," he says.

"I don't think she would have agreed—"

"Paul," he repeats. "Call me Paul."

"I don't think she would have agreed to go to the States if you had not persuaded her, Paul."

"I can't take all the credit. My father insisted. He and Mr. Sinclair go back a long way."

"But to come the day before you're going to leave, that was most kind."

"I've decided to stay a couple days longer."

"You're not leaving tomorrow?"

"I thought I would spend more time with my parents."

"How nice," Anna says calmly, but she is aware of a sudden quickening of her pulse. "I'm sure that would make them happy."

"I was thinking too that we should get to know each other better. It's been a long time. I was just ten or eleven. You were a little girl."

"Four or five. That's what you said."

The line goes still again. Paul Bishop coughs again. "I miss being on the island. I miss the sea, the land, the rain, the sun. I even miss the suffocating humidity at midday." There is a quiet longing in his voice, a nostalgia Anna recognizes. She nods. Paul Bishop cannot see her nod, he cannot see the empathy filling her eyes. Two emigrants, two immigrants, neither one fully at home on the island of their birth, neither fully at home in America where they live.

"Yes, I know," she says.

"I didn't realize how much. I miss the people. I miss not having to explain myself to people who don't share my background."

"Yes," she says again, nodding again.

"Over there, in America, I'm Caribbean-American, but that hyphen always bothers me. It's a bridge, but somehow I think there is a gap on either end of the hyphen. Sometimes I think if I am not careful, I can fall between those spaces and drown."

Exactly, exactly how she feels.

"Would you like to have dinner tonight? Talk about our hyphens and the gaps in between?"

Her pulse races again. "Yes. I'm free tonight. Tonight would be fine."

"Hyphens and gaps." He laughs, a dry laugh. "What a thing!"

And when Anna puts down the phone, she finds herself thinking that perhaps her mother knows more about life and about what her daughter needs than she has given her credit for.

Later that morning, her mother apologizes. She made a fool of herself, she said. It was so old-fashioned of her to ask her grownup daughter to open the pastel for Paul Bishop. As if the function of women is to serve men! Can Anna forgive her? And Anna thinks: perhaps her mother loves her more than she had thought possible. Perhaps this is so.

Acknowledgments

I am grateful to Patricia Ramdeen Anderson and Norman Loftis, who read early drafts of this novel and were unstinting in their encouragement and invaluable for their critical advice. My friend and colleague Linda Susan Jackson cast her poetic eye over the manuscript and asked incisive questions. I am grateful as well to my agent Carolyn French, whose literary instincts I trust completely. Johnny Temple at Akashic Books is in a class by himself: a courageous and intelligent editor who works tirelessly for his writers. My gratitude to my sister Mary Nunez for her love and support. My son, Jason Harrell, continues to be a bright light in my life.

Also available from Akashic Books

TRINIDAD NOIR
edited by Lisa Allen-Agostini & Jeanne Mason
348 pages, trade paperback original, $15.95

Brand-new stories by: Elizabeth Nunez, Robert Antoni, Lawrence Scott, Oonya Kempadoo, Ramabai Espinet, Shani Mootoo, Kevin Baldeosingh, elisha efua bartels, Tiphanie Yanique, and others.

"For sheer volume, few—anywhere—can beat [V.S.] Naipaul's prodigious output. But on style, the writers in the Trinidadian canon can meet him eye to eye . . . Trinidad is no one-trick pony, literarily speaking."
—Coeditor Lisa Allen-Agostini in the *New York Times*

IRON BALLOONS: HIT FICTION FROM JAMAICA'S CALABASH WRITER'S WORKSHOP
edited by Colin Channer
250 pages, trade paperback original, $14.95

Brand-new stories by: Elizabeth Nunez, Marlon James, Colin Channer, Kwame Dawes, Kaylie Jones, Alwin Bully, Sharon Leach, and others.

"The ability to eloquently delineate a particular experience—Caribbean life—accounts in large part for the significance and success of *Iron Balloons* . . . The anthology offers some of today's most prominent Caribbean writers, including Kwame Dawes, Elizabeth Nunez, and Channer himself, as well as such newcomers as Marlon James and Sharon Leach."
—*Toronto Star* (Canada)

RUINS
a novel by Achy Obejas
208 pages, trade paperback original, $15.95

"Compassionate and intriguing . . . Obejas plays out [the book's] conflicts in measured, simple prose . . . to illuminate a setting filled with heartbreak, confusion, and decay."
—*Los Angeles Times*

"*Ruins* is a beautifully written novel, a moving testament to the human spirit of an unlikely hero who remains unbroken even as the world collapses around him . . . A fine literary achievement, it's Achy Obejas at her best."
—*El Paso Times*

THE DUPPY
a novel by Anthony C. Winkler
176 pages, trade paperback, $13.95

"Winkler has a fine ear for patois and dialogue, and a love of language that makes bawdy jokes crackle." —*New Yorker*

"Every country (if she's lucky) gets the Mark Twain she deserves, and Winkler is ours, bristling with savage Jamaican wit, heart-stopping compassion, and jaw-dropping humor all at once."
—Marlon James, author of *John Crow's Devil*

THE AGE OF DREAMING
a novel by Nina Revoyr
332 pages, trade paperback original, $15.95
*Selected by the *Advocate* as one of the Best Books of 2008; finalist for the *Los Angeles Times* Book Prize

"*The Age of Dreaming* elegantly entwines an ersatz version of film star Sessue Hayakawa's life with the unsolved murder of 1920s film director William Desmond Taylor. The result hums with the excitement of Hollywood's pioneer era . . . Reminiscent of Paul Auster's *The Book of Illusions* . . . [with] a surprising, genuinely moving conclusion."
—*San Francisco Chronicle*

SONG FOR NIGHT
a novella by Chris Abani
170 pages, trade paperback original, $12.95
*Winner of a PEN/Beyond Margins Award and a *New York Times* Editors' Choice

"A devastating portrait of a boy holding onto the shreds of his innocence during a war that deliberately, remorselessly works to yank it away . . . *Song for Night* has the feel of a prose poem, with its primary focus on imagery and its spare, musical language. The lyrical intensity of the writing perfectly suits the material."
—*Los Angeles Times*